*continued . . .*

"This book's intelligent mixture of painful, pleasurable, serious, skeptical, and unexpected moments in a relationship where neither hero nor heroine can merge with the local norm, recalls the best kinds of magical realism. . . . Amusing details about the difficulties of living legal for vampires—and of being centuries old in the tradition-revering South. . . . One of the best vampire novels I've read in quite a while."
—*Locus*

"The goofy charm of Harris's world, with its humor and occasional terror, is what makes *Dead Until Dark* so delightful."
—*The Denver Post*

"Hilarious and introspective. . . . With the sure touch of a master, Harris mines the mundane to make her unnatural creatures that much more unsettling. . . . [She] creates a small Louisiana town peopled by quirky, vivid characters readers will want to revisit again and again."
—*Crescent Blues*

"An absorbing mix of romance, mystery, and the supernatural. Harris weaves humor with an edginess that makes for taut reading. Best of all, she's created a uniquely down-to-earth heroine in Sookie and an otherworldly charmer in Sookie's beau, Bill. Perhaps you'll never meet a more unlikely couple, but you won't forget them either."
—*Romantic Times*

# CLUB DEAD

## Charlaine Harris

**ACE BOOKS, NEW YORK**

**THE BERKLEY PUBLISHING GROUP**
**Published by the Penguin Group**
**Penguin Group (USA) Inc.**
**375 Hudson Street, New York, New York 10014, USA**
Penguin Group (Canada), 10 Alcorn Avenue, Toronto, Ontario M4V 3B2, Canada
(a division of Pearson Penguin Canada Inc.)
Penguin Books Ltd., 80 Strand, London WC2R 0RL, England
Penguin Group Ireland, 25 St. Stephen's Green, Dublin 2, Ireland (a division of Penguin Books Ltd.)
Penguin Group (Australia), 250 Camberwell Road, Camberwell, Victoria 3124, Australia
(a division of Pearson Australia Group Pty. Ltd.)
Penguin Books India Pvt. Ltd., 11 Community Centre, Panchsheel Park, New Delhi—110 017, India
Penguin Group (NZ), Cnr. Airborne and Rosedale Roads, Albany, Auckland 1310, New Zealand
(a division of Pearson New Zealand Ltd.)
Penguin Books (South Africa) (Pty.) Ltd., 24 Sturdee Avenue, Rosebank, Johannesburg 2196, South
Africa

Penguin Books Ltd., Registered Offices: 80 Strand, London WC2R 0RL, England

This is a work of fiction. Names, characters, places, and incidents either are the product of the author's
imagination or are used fictitiously, and any resemblance to actual persons, living or dead, business
establishments, events, or locales is entirely coincidental.

CLUB DEAD

An Ace Book / published by arrangement with the author

PRINTING HISTORY
Ace mass market edition / May 2003

ISBN: 0-441-01051-2

ACE
Ace Books are published by The Berkley Publishing Group,
a division of Penguin Group (USA) Inc.,
375 Hudson Street, New York, New York 10014.
ACE and the "A" design are trademarks belonging to Penguin Group (USA) Inc.

PRINTED IN THE UNITED STATES OF AMERICA

15  14  13  12  11  10  9  8  7

This book is dedicated to my middle child,
Timothy Schulz, who told me flatly
he wanted a book all to himself.

# ACKNOWLEDGMENTS

My thanks to Lisa Weissenbuehler, Kerie L. Nickel, Marie La Salle, and the incomparable Doris Ann Norris for their input on car trunks, great and small. My further thanks to Janet Davis, Irene, and Sonya Stocklin, also cybercitizens of DorothyL, for their information on bars, bourree (a card game), and the parish governments of Louisiana. Joan Coffey was most gracious with supplying information about Jackson. The wonderful and obliging Jane Lee drove me patiently around Jackson for many hours, entering thoroughly into the spirit of finding the perfect location for a vampire bar.

# Chapter One

BILL WAS HUNCHED over the computer when I let myself in his house. This was an all-too-familiar scenario in the past month or two. He'd torn himself away from his work when I came home, until the past couple of weeks. Now it was the keyboard that attracted him.

"Hello, sweetheart," he said absently, his gaze riveted to the screen. An empty bottle of type O TrueBlood was on the desk beside the keyboard. At least he'd remembered to eat.

Bill, not a jeans-and-tee kind of guy, was wearing khakis and a plaid shirt in muted blue and green. His skin was glowing, and his thick dark hair smelled like Herbal Essence. He was enough to give any woman a hormonal surge. I kissed his neck, and he didn't react. I licked his ear. Nothing.

I'd been on my feet for six hours straight at Merlotte's Bar, and every time some customer had under-tipped, or some fool had patted my fanny, I'd reminded myself that in a short while I'd be with my boyfriend, having incredible sex and basking in his attention.

That didn't appear to be happening.

I inhaled slowly and steadily and glared at Bill's back. It was a wonderful back, with broad shoulders, and I had planned on seeing it bare with my nails dug into it. I had counted on that very strongly. I exhaled, slowly and steadily.

"Be with you in a minute," Bill said. On the screen, there was a snapshot of a distinguished man with silver hair and a dark tan. He looked sort of Anthony Quinn–type sexy, and he looked powerful. Under the picture was a name, and under that was some text. "Born 1756 in Sicily," it began. Just as I opened my mouth to comment that vampires *did* appear in photographs despite the legend, Bill twisted around and realized I was reading.

He hit a button and the screen went blank.

I stared at him, not quite believing what had just happened.

"Sookie," he said, attempting a smile. His fangs were retracted, so he was totally not in the mood in which I'd hoped to find him; he wasn't thinking of me carnally. Like all vampires, his fangs are only fully extended when he's in the mood for the sexy kind of lust, or the feeding-and-killing kind of lust. (Sometimes, those lusts all get kind of snarled up, and you get your dead fang-bangers. But that element of danger is what attracts most fang-bangers, if you ask me.) Though I've been accused of being one of those pathetic creatures that hang around vampires in the hope of attracting their attention, there's only one vampire I'm involved with (at least voluntarily) and it was the one sitting right in front of me. The one who was keeping secrets from me. The one who wasn't nearly glad enough to see me.

"Bill," I said coldly. Something was Up, with a capital *U*. And it wasn't Bill's libido. (Libido had just been on my Word-A-Day calendar.)

"You didn't see what you just saw," he said steadily.

His dark brown eyes regarded me without blinking.

"Uh-huh," I said, maybe sounding just a little sarcastic. "What are you up to?"

"I have a secret assignment."

I didn't know whether to laugh or stalk away in a snit. So I just raised my eyebrows and waited for more. Bill was the investigator for Area 5, a vampire division of Louisiana. Eric, the head of Area 5, had never given Bill an "assignment" that was secret from me before. In fact, I was usually an integral part of the investigation team, however unwilling I might be.

"Eric must not know. None of the Area 5 vampires can know."

My heart sank. "So—if you're not doing a job for Eric, who are you working for?" I knelt because my feet were so tired, and I leaned against Bill's knees.

"The queen of Louisiana," he said, almost in a whisper.

Because he looked so solemn, I tried to keep a straight face, but it was no use. I began to laugh, little giggles that I couldn't suppress.

"You're serious?" I asked, knowing he must be. Bill was almost always a serious kind of fellow. I buried my face on his thigh so he couldn't see my amusement. I rolled my eyes up for a quick look at his face. He was looking pretty pissed.

"I am as serious as the grave," Bill said, and he sounded so steely, I made a major effort to change my attitude.

"Okay, let me get this straight," I said in a reasonably level tone. I sat back on the floor, cross-legged, and rested my hands on my knees. "You work for Eric, who is the boss of Area 5, but there is also a queen? Of Louisiana?"

Bill nodded.

"So the state is divided up into Areas? And she's

Eric's superior, since he runs a business in Shreveport, which is in Area 5."

Again with the nod. I put my hand over my face and shook my head. "So, where does she live, Baton Rouge?" The state capital seemed the obvious place.

"No, no. New Orleans, of course."

Of *course*. Vampire central. You could hardly throw a rock in the Big Easy without hitting one of the undead, according to the papers (though only a real fool would do so). The tourist trade in New Orleans was booming, but it was not exactly the same crowd as before, the hard-drinking, rollicking crowd who'd filled the city to party hearty. The newer tourists were the ones who wanted to rub elbows with the undead; patronize a vampire bar, visit a vampire prostitute, watch a vampire sex show.

This was what I'd heard; I hadn't been to New Orleans since I was little. My mother and father had taken my brother, Jason, and me. That would have been before I was seven, because that's when they died.

Mama and Daddy died nearly twenty years before vampires had appeared on network television to announce the fact that they were actually present among us, an announcement that had followed on the Japanese development of synthetic blood that actually maintained a vampire's life without the necessity of drinking from humans.

The United States vampire community had let the Japanese vampire clans come forth first. Then, simultaneously, in most of the nations of the world that had television—and who doesn't these days?—the announcement had been made in hundreds of different languages, by hundreds of carefully picked personable vampires.

That night, two and half years ago, we regular old

live people learned that we had always lived with monsters among us.

"But"—the burden of this announcement had been—"now we can come forward and join with you in harmony. You are in no danger from us anymore. We don't need to drink from you to live."

As you can imagine, this was a night of high ratings and tremendous uproar. Reaction varied sharply, depending on the nation.

The vampires in the predominantly Islamic nations had fared the worst. You don't even want to know what happened to the undead spokesman in Syria, though perhaps the female vamp in Afghanistan died an even more horrible—and final—death. (What were they thinking, selecting a female for that particular job? Vampires could be so smart, but they sometimes didn't seem quite in touch with the present world.)

Some nations—France, Italy, and Germany were the most notable—refused to accept vampires as equal citizens. Many—like Bosnia, Argentina, and most of the African nations—denied any status to the vampires, and declared them fair game for any bounty hunter. But America, England, Mexico, Canada, Japan, Switzerland, and the Scandinavian countries adopted a more tolerant attitude.

It was hard to determine if this reaction was what the vampires had expected or not. Since they were still struggling to maintain a foothold in the stream of the living, the vampires remained very secretive about their organization and government, and what Bill was telling me now was the most I'd ever heard on the subject.

"So, the Louisiana queen of the vampires has you working on a secret project," I said, trying to sound neutral. "And this is why you have lived at your computer every waking hour for the past few weeks."

"Yes," Bill said. He picked up the bottle of TrueBlood

and tipped it up, but there were only a couple of drops left. He went down the hall into the small kitchen area (when he'd remodeled his old family home, he'd pretty much left out the kitchen, since he didn't need one) and extracted another bottle from the refrigerator. I was tracking him by sound as he opened the bottle and popped it into the microwave. The microwave went off, and he reentered, shaking the bottle with his thumb over the top so there wouldn't be any hot spots.

"So, how much more time do you have to spend on this project?" I asked—reasonably, I thought.

"As long as it takes," he said, less reasonably. Actually, Bill sounded downright irritable.

Hmmm. Could our honeymoon be over? Of course I mean figurative honeymoon, since Bill's a vampire and we can't be legally married, practically anywhere in the world.

Not that he's asked me.

"Well, if you're so absorbed in your project, I'll just stay away until it's over," I said slowly.

"That might be best," Bill said, after a perceptible pause, and I felt like he'd socked me in the stomach. In a flash, I was on my feet and pulling my coat back over my cold-weather waitress outfit—black slacks, white boat-neck long-sleeved tee with "Merlotte's" embroidered over the left breast. I turned my back to Bill to hide my face.

I was trying not to cry, so I didn't look at him even after I felt Bill's hand touch my shoulder.

"I have to tell you something," Bill said in his cold, smooth voice. I stopped in the middle of pulling on my gloves, but I didn't think I could stand to see him. He could tell my backside.

"If anything happens to me," he continued (and here's where I should have begun worrying), "you must look in the hiding place I built at your house. My computer should be in it, and some disks. Don't tell anyone. If the computer isn't in the hiding place, come over to my house and see if it's here. Come in the daytime, and come armed. Get the computer and any disks you can find, and hide them in my hidey-hole, as you call it."

I nodded. He could see that from the back. I didn't trust my voice.

"If I'm not back, or if you don't get word from me, in say . . . eight weeks—yes, eight weeks, then tell Eric everything I said to you today. And place yourself under his protection."

I didn't speak. I was too miserable to be furious, but it wouldn't be long before I reached meltdown. I acknowledged his words with a jerk of my head. I could feel my ponytail switch against my neck.

"I am going to . . . Seattle soon," Bill said. I could feel his cool lips touch the place my ponytail had brushed.

He was lying.

"When I come back, we'll talk."

Somehow, that didn't sound like an entrancing prospect. Somehow, that sounded ominous.

Again I inclined my head, not risking speech because I was actually crying now. I would rather have died than let him see the tears.

And that was how I left him, that cold December night.


THE NEXT DAY, on my way to work, I took an unwise detour. I was in that kind of mood where I was rolling in how awful everything was. Despite a nearly sleepless night, something inside me told me I could probably make my mood a little worse if I drove along Magnolia Creek Road: so sure enough, that's what I did.

The old Bellefleur mansion, Belle Rive, was a beehive of activity, even on a cold and ugly day. There were vans from the pest control company, a kitchen design firm, and a siding contractor parked at the kitchen entrance to the antebellum home. Life was just humming for Caroline Holliday Bellefleur, the ancient lady who had ruled Belle Rive and (at least in part) Bon Temps for the past eighty years. I wondered how Portia, a lawyer, and Andy, a detective, were enjoying all the changes at Belle Rive. They had lived with their grandmother (as I had lived with mine) for all their adult lives. At the very least, they had to be enjoying her pleasure in the mansion's renovation.

My own grandmother had been murdered a few months ago.

The Bellefleurs hadn't had anything to do with it, of course. And there was no reason Portia and Andy would share the pleasure of this new affluence with me. In fact, they both avoided me like the plague. They owed me, and they couldn't stand it. They just didn't know how *much* they owed me.

The Bellefleurs had received a mysterious legacy from a relative who had "died mysteriously over in Europe somewhere," I'd heard Andy tell a fellow cop while they were drinking at Merlotte's. When she dropped off some raffle tickets for Gethsemane Baptist Church's Ladies' Quilt, Maxine Fortenberry told me Miss Caroline had combed every family record she could unearth to identify their benefactor, and she was still mystified at the family's good fortune.

She didn't seem to have any qualms about spending the money, though.

Even Terry Bellefleur, Portia and Andy's cousin, had a new pickup sitting in the packed dirt yard of his double-wide. I liked Terry, a scarred Viet Nam vet who didn't have a lot of friends, and I didn't grudge him a new set of wheels.

But I thought about the carburetor I'd just been forced

to replace in my old car. I'd paid for the work in full, though I'd considered asking Jim Downey if I could just pay half and get the rest together over the next two months. But Jim had a wife and three kids. Just this morning I'd been thinking of asking my boss, Sam Merlotte, if he could add to my hours at the bar. Especially with Bill gone to "Seattle," I could just about live at Merlotte's, if Sam could use me. I sure needed the money.

I tried real hard not to be bitter as I drove away from Belle Rive. I went south out of town and then turned left onto Hummingbird Road on my way to Merlotte's. I tried to pretend that all was well; that on his return from Seattle—or wherever—Bill would be a passionate lover again, and Bill would treasure me and make me feel valuable once more. I would again have that feeling of belonging with someone, instead of being alone.

Of course, I had my brother, Jason. Though as far as intimacy and companionship goes, I had to admit that he hardly counted.

But the pain in my middle was the unmistakable pain of rejection. I knew the feeling so well, it was like a second skin.

I sure hated to crawl back inside it.

# Chapter Two

I TESTED THE doorknob to make sure I'd locked it, turned around, and out of the corner of my eye glimpsed a figure sitting in the swing on my front porch. I stifled a shriek as he rose. Then I recognized him.

I was wearing a heavy coat, but he was in a tank top; that didn't surprise me, really.

"El—" Uh-oh, close call. "Bubba, how are you?" I was trying to sound casual, carefree. I failed, but Bubba wasn't the sharpest tool in the shed. The vampires admitted that bringing him over, when he'd been so very close to death and so saturated with drugs, had been a big mistake. The night he'd been brought in, one of the morgue attendants happened to be one of the undead, and also happened to be a huge fan. With a hastily constructed and elaborate plot involving a murder or two, the attendant had "brought him over"—made Bubba a vampire. But the process doesn't always go right, you know. Since then, he's been passed around like idiot royalty. Louisiana had been hosting him for the past year.

"Miss Sookie, how you doin'?" His accent was still

thick and his face still handsome, in a jowly kind of way. The dark hair tumbled over his forehead in a carefully careless style. The heavy sideburns were brushed. Some undead fan had groomed him for the evening.

"I'm just fine, thank you," I said politely, grinning from ear to ear. I do that when I'm nervous. "I was just fixing to go to work," I added, wondering if it was possible I would be able to simply get in my car and drive away. I thought not.

"Well, Miss Sookie, I been sent to guard you tonight."

"You have? By who?"

"By Eric," he said proudly. "I was the only one in the office when he got a phone call. He tole me to get my ass over here."

"What's the danger?" I peered around the clearing in the woods in which my old house stood. Bubba's news made me very nervous.

"I don't know, Miss Sookie. Eric, he tole me to watch you tonight till one of them from Fangtasia gets here—Eric, or Chow, or Miss Pam, or even Clancy. So if you go to work, I go with you. And I take care of anyone who bothers you."

There was no point in questioning Bubba further, putting strain on that fragile brain. He'd just get upset, and you didn't want to see that happen. That was why you had to remember not to call him by his former name . . . though every now and then he would sing, and that was a moment to remember.

"You can't come in the bar," I said bluntly. That would be a disaster. The clientele of Merlotte's is used to the occasional vampire, sure, but I couldn't warn *everyone* not to say his name. Eric must have been desperate; the vampire community kept mistakes like Bubba out of sight, though from time to time he'd take it in his head to wander off on his own. Then you got a "sighting," and the tabloids went crazy.

"Maybe you could sit in my car while I work?" The cold wouldn't affect Bubba.

"I got to be closer than that," he said, and he sounded immovable.

"Okay, then, how about my boss's office? It's right off the bar, and you can hear me if I yell."

Bubba still didn't look satisfied, but finally, he nodded. I let out a breath I didn't realize I'd been holding. It would be easiest for me to stay home, call in sick. However, not only did Sam expect me to show up, but also, I needed the paycheck.

The car felt a little small with Bubba in the front seat beside me. As we bumped off my property, through the woods and out to the parish road, I made a mental note to get the gravel company to come dump some more gravel on my long, meandering driveway. Then I canceled that order, also mentally. I couldn't afford that right now. It'd have to wait until spring. Or summer.

We turned right to drive the few miles to Merlotte's, the bar where I work as a waitress when I'm not doing Heap Big Secret Stuff for the vampires. It occurred to me when we were about halfway there that I hadn't seen a car Bubba could've used to drive to my house. Maybe he'd flown? Some vamps could. Though Bubba was the least talented vampire I'd met, maybe he had a flair for it.

A year ago I would've asked him, but not now. I'm used to hanging around with the undead now. Not that I'm a vampire. I'm a telepath. My life was hell on wheels until I met a man whose mind I couldn't read. Unfortunately, I couldn't read his mind because he was dead. But Bill and I had been together for several months now, and until recently, our relationship had been real good. And the other vampires need me, so I'm safe—to a certain extent. Mostly. Sometimes.

Merlotte's didn't look too busy, judging from the half-empty parking lot. Sam had bought the bar about five years ago. It had been failing—maybe because it had been cut out of the forest, which loomed all around the parking lot. Or maybe the former owner just hadn't found the right combination of drinks, food, and service.

Somehow, after he renamed the place and renovated it, Sam had turned balance sheets around. He made a nice living off it now. But tonight was a Monday night, not a big drinking night in our neck of the woods, which happened to be in northern Louisiana. I pulled around to the employee parking lot, which was right in front of Sam Merlotte's trailer, which itself is behind and at right angles to the employee entrance to the bar. I hopped out of the driver's seat, trotted through the storeroom, and peeked through the glass pane in the door to check the short hall with its doors to the rest rooms and Sam's office. Empty. Good. And when I knocked on Sam's door, he was behind his desk, which was even better.

Sam is not a big man, but he's very strong. He's a strawberry blond with blue eyes, and he's maybe three years older than my twenty-six. I've worked for him for about that many years. I'm fond of Sam, and he's starred in some of my favorite fantasies; but since he dated a beautiful but homicidal creature a couple of months before, my enthusiasm has somewhat faded. He's for sure my friend, though.

" 'Scuse me, Sam," I said, smiling like an idiot.

"What's up?" He closed the catalog of bar supplies he'd been studying.

"I need to stash someone in here for a little while."

Sam didn't look altogether happy. "Who? Has Bill gotten back?"

"No, he's still traveling." My smile got even brighter. "But, um, they sent another vampire to sort of guard me? And I need to stow him in here while I work, if that's okay with you."

"Why do you need to be guarded? And why can't he just sit out in the bar? We have plenty of TrueBlood." TrueBlood was definitely proving to be the front-runner among competing blood replacements. "Next best to the drink of life," its first ad had read, and vampires had responded to the ad campaign.

I heard the tiniest of sounds behind me, and I sighed. Bubba had gotten impatient.

"Now, I asked you—" I began, starting to turn, but never got further. A hand grasped my shoulder and whirled me around. I was facing a man I'd never seen before. He was cocking his fist to punch me in the head.

Though the vampire blood I had ingested a few months ago (to save my life, let me point out) has mostly worn off—I barely glow in the dark at all now—I'm still quicker than most people. I dropped and rolled into the man's legs, which made him stagger, which made it easier for Bubba to grab him and crush his throat.

I scrambled to my feet and Sam rushed out of his office. We stared at each other, Bubba, and the dead man.

Well, now we were really in a pickle.

"I've kilt him," Bubba said proudly. "I saved you, Miss Sookie."

Having the Man from Memphis appear in your bar, realizing he's become a vampire, and watching him kill a would-be assailant—well, that was a lot to absorb in a couple of minutes, even for Sam, though he himself was more than he appeared.

"Well, so you have," Sam said to Bubba in a soothing voice. "Do you know who he was?"

I had never seen a dead man—outside of visitation at the local funeral home—until I'd started dating Bill (who of course was technically dead, but I mean human dead people).

It seems I run across them now quite often. Lucky I'm not too squeamish.

This particular dead man had been in his forties, and every year of that had been hard. He had tattoos all over his arms, mostly of the poor quality you get in jail, and he was missing some crucial teeth. He was dressed in what I thought of as biker clothes: greasy blue jeans and a leather vest, with an obscene T-shirt underneath.

"What's on the back of the vest?" Sam asked, as if that would have significance for him.

Bubba obligingly squatted and rolled the man to his side. The way the man's hand flopped at the end of his arm made me feel pretty queasy. But I forced myself to look at the vest. The back was decorated with a wolf's head insignia. The wolf was in profile, and seemed to be howling. The head was silhouetted against a white circle, which I decided was supposed to be the moon. Sam looked even more worried when he saw the insignia. "Werewolf," he said tersely. That explained a lot.

The weather was too chilly for a man wearing only a vest, if he wasn't a vampire. Weres ran a little hotter than regular people, but mostly they were careful to wear coats in cold weather, since Were society was still secret from the human race (except for lucky, lucky me, and probably a few hundred others). I wondered if the dead man had left a coat out in the bar hanging on the hooks by the main entrance; in which case, he'd been back here hiding in the men's room, waiting for me to appear. Or maybe he'd come through the back door right after me. Maybe his coat was in his vehicle.

"You see him come in?" I asked Bubba. I was maybe just a little light-headed.

"Yes, ma'am. He must have been waiting in the big parking lot for you. He drove around the corner, got out of his car, and went in the back just a minute after you did. You hightailed it through the door, and then he went in. And I followed him. You mighty lucky you had me with you."

"Thank you, Bubba. You're right; I'm lucky to have you. I wonder what he planned to do with me." I felt cold all over as I thought about it. Had he just been looking for a lone woman to grab, or did he plan on grabbing me specifically? Then I realized that was dumb thinking. If Eric had been alarmed enough to send a bodyguard, he must have known there was a threat, which pretty much ruled out me being targeted at random. Without comment, Bubba strode out the back door. He returned in just a minute.

"He's got him some duct tape and gags on the front seat of his car," Bubba said. "That's where his coat is. I brought it to put under his head." He bent to arrange the heavily padded camouflage jacket around the dead man's face and neck. Wrapping the head was a real good idea, since the man was leaking a little bit. When he had finished his task, Bubba licked his fingers.

Sam put an arm around me because I had started shaking.

"This is strange, though," I was saying, when the door to the hall from the bar began to open. I glimpsed Kevin Pryor's face. Kevin is a sweet guy, but he's a cop, and that's the last thing we needed.

"Sorry, toilet's back-flowing," I said, and pushed the door shut on his narrow, astonished, face. "Listen, fellas, why don't I hold this door shut while you two take this guy and put him in his car? Then we can figure out what to do with him." The floor of the hall would need swabbing. I discovered the hall door actually locked. I'd never realized that.

Sam was doubtful. "Sookie, don't you think that we should call the police?" he asked.

A year ago I would have been on the phone dialing 911 before the corpse even hit the floor. But that year had been one long learning curve. I caught Sam's eye and inclined my head toward Bubba. "How do you think he'd handle jail?" I murmured. Bubba was humming the opening line to "Blue Christmas." "Our hands are hardly strong enough to have done this," I pointed out.

After a moment of indecision, Sam nodded, resigned to the inevitable. "Okay, Bubba, let's you and me tote this guy out to his car."

I ran to get a mop while the men—well, the vampire and the shape-shifter—carried Biker Boy out the back door. By the time Sam and Bubba returned, bringing a gust of cold air in their wake, I had mopped the hall and the men's bathroom (as I would if there really had been an overflow). I sprayed some air freshener in the hall to improve the environment.

It was a good thing we'd acted quickly, because Kevin was pushing open the door as soon as I'd unlocked it.

"Everything okay back here?" he asked. Kevin is a runner, so he has almost no body fat, and he's not a big guy. He looks kind of like a sheep, and he still lives with his mom. But for all that, he's nobody's fool. In the past, whenever I'd listened to his thoughts, they were either on police work, or his black amazon of a partner, Kenya Jones. Right now, his thoughts ran more to the suspicious.

"I think we got it fixed," Sam said. "Watch your feet, we just mopped. Don't slip and sue me!" He smiled at Kevin.

"Someone in your office?" Kevin asked, nodding his head toward the closed door.

"One of Sookie's friends," Sam said.

"I better get out there and hustle some drinks," I said cheerfully, beaming at them both. I reached up to check that my ponytail was smooth, and then I made my Reeboks move. The bar was almost empty, and the woman I was replacing (Charlsie Tooten) looked relieved. "This is one slow night," she muttered to me. "The guys at table six have been nursing that pitcher for an hour, and Jane Bodehouse has tried to pick up every man who's come in. Kevin's been writing something in a notebook all night."

I glanced at the only female customer in the bar, trying to keep the distaste off my face. Every drinking establishment has its share of alcoholic customers, people who open and close the place. Jane Bodehouse was one of ours. Normally, Jane drank by herself at home, but every two weeks or so she'd take it into her head to come in and pick up a man. The pickup process was getting more and more iffy, since not only was Jane in her fifties, but lack of regular sleep and proper nutrition had been taking a toll for the past ten years.

This particular night, I noticed that when Jane had applied her makeup, she had missed the actual perimeters of her eyebrows and lips. The result was pretty unsettling. We'd have to call her son to come get her. I could tell at a glance she couldn't drive.

I nodded to Charlsie, and waved at Arlene, the other waitress, who was sitting at a table with her latest flame, Buck Foley. Things were really dead if Arlene was off her feet. Arlene waved back, her red curls bouncing.

"How're the kids?" I called, beginning to put away some of the glasses Charlsie had gotten out of the dishwasher. I felt like I was acting real normal until I noticed that my hands were shaking violently.

"Doing great. Coby made the All-A honor roll and Lisa won the spelling bee," she said with a broad smile. To anyone who believed that a four-times married woman couldn't be good mother, I would point at Arlene. I gave Buck a quick smile, too, in Arlene's honor. Buck is about the average kind of guy Arlene dates, which is not good enough for her.

"That's great! They're smart kids, like their mama," I said.

"Hey, did that guy find you?"

"What guy?" Though I had a feeling I already knew.

"That guy in the motorcycle gear. He asked me was I the waitress dating Bill Compton, since he'd got a delivery for that waitress."

"He didn't know my name?"

"No, and that's pretty weird, isn't it? Oh my God, Sookie, if he didn't know your name, how could he have come from Bill?"

Possibly Coby's smarts had come through his daddy, since it had taken Arlene this long to figure that out. I loved Arlene for her nature, not her brain.

"So, what did you tell him?" I asked, beaming at her. It was my nervous smile, not my real one. I don't always know when I'm wearing it.

"I told him I liked my men warm and breathing," she said, and laughed. Arlene was occasionally completely tactless, too. I reminded myself to reevaluate why she was my good friend. "No, I didn't really say that. I just told him you would be the blond who came in at nine."

Thanks, Arlene. So my attacker had known who I was because my best friend had identified me; he hadn't known my name or where I lived, just that I worked at Merlotte's and dated Bill Compton. That was a little reassuring, but not a lot.

Three hours dragged by. Sam came out, told me in a whisper that he'd given Bubba a magazine to look at and a bottle of Life Support to sip on, and began to poke around behind the bar. "How come that guy was driving a car instead of a motorcycle?" Sam muttered in a low voice. "How come his car's got a Mississippi license plate?" He hushed when Kevin came up to check that we were going to call Jane's son, Marvin. Sam phoned while Kevin stood there so he could relay the son's promise to be at Merlotte's in twenty minutes. Kevin pushed off after that, his notebook tucked under his arm. I wondered if Kevin was turning into a poet, or writing his resume.

The four men who'd been trying to ignore Jane while sipping their pitcher at the speed of a turtle finished their beer and left, each dropping a dollar on the table by way of tip. Big spenders. I'd never get my driveway regraveled with customers like these.

With only half an hour to wait, Arlene did her closing chores and asked if she could go on and leave with Buck. Her kids were still with her mom, so she and Buck might have the trailer to themselves for a little while.

"Bill coming home soon?" she asked me as she pulled on her coat. Buck was talking football with Sam.

I shrugged. He'd called me three nights before, telling me he'd gotten to "Seattle" safely and was meeting with—whomever he was supposed to meet with. The Caller ID had read "Unavailable." I felt like that said quite a lot about the whole situation. I felt like that was a bad sign.

"You . . . missing him?" Her voice was sly.

"What do you think?" I asked, with a little smile at the corners of my mouth. "You go on home, have a good time."

"Buck is very good at good times," she said, almost leering.

"Lucky you."

So Jane Bodehouse was the only customer in Merlotte's when Pam arrived. Jane hardly counted; she was so out of it.

Pam is a vampire, and she is co-owner of Fangtasia, a tourist bar in Shreveport. She's Eric's second in command. Pam is blond, probably two hundred-plus years old, and actually has a sense of humor—not a vampire trademark. If a vampire can be your friend, she was as close as I'd gotten.

She sat on a bar stool and faced me over the shining expanse of wood.

This was ominous. I had *never* seen Pam anywhere but Fangtasia. "What's up?" I said by way of greeting. I smiled at her, but I was tense all over.

"Where's Bubba?" she asked, in her precise voice. She looked over my shoulder. "Eric's going to be angry if Bubba didn't make it here." For the first time, I noticed that Pam had a faint accent, but I couldn't pin it down. Maybe just the inflections of antique English.

"Bubba's in the back, in Sam's office," I said, focusing on her face. I wished the ax would go on and fall. Sam came to stand beside me, and I introduced them. Pam gave him a more significant greeting than she would have given a plain human (whom she might not have acknowledged at all), since Sam was a shapeshifter. And I expected to see a flicker of interest, since Pam is omnivorous in matters of sex, and Sam is an attractive supernatural being. Though vampires aren't well-known for facial expressions, I decided that Pam's was definitely unhappy.

"What's the deal?" I asked, after a moment of silence.

Pam met my gaze. We're both blue-eyed blonds, but that's like saying two animals are both dogs. That's as far as any resemblance went. Pam's hair was straight and pale, and her eyes were very dark. Now they were full of trouble. She looked at Sam, her stare significant. Without a word, he went over to help Jane's son, a worn-looking man in his thirties, shift Jane to the car.

"Bill's missing," Pam said, shooting from the conversational hip.

"No, he's not. He's in Seattle," I said. Willfully obtuse. I had learned that word from my Word-A-Day calendar only that morning, and here I was getting to use it.

"He lied to you."

I absorbed that, made a "come on" gesture with my hand.

"He's been in Mississippi all this time. He drove to Jackson."

I stared down at the heavily polyurethane-coated wood of the bar. I'd pretty much figured Bill had lied to me, but hearing it said out loud, baldly, hurt like hell. He'd lied to me, and he was missing.

"So . . . what are you going to do to find him?" I asked, and hated how unsteady my voice was.

"We're looking. We're doing everything we can," Pam said. "Whoever got him may be after you, too. That's why Eric sent Bubba."

I couldn't answer. I was struggling to control myself.

Sam had returned, I suppose when he saw how upset I was. From about an inch behind my back, he said, "Someone tried to grab Sookie on her way into work tonight. Bubba saved her. The body's out behind the bar. We were going to move him after we'd closed."

"So quickly," Pam said. She sounded even unhappier. She gave Sam a once-over, nodded. He was a fellow supernatural being, though that was definitely second best to him being another vampire. "I'd better go over the car and see what I can find." Pam took it quite for granted that we'd dispose of the body ourselves rather than doing something more official. Vampires are having trouble accepting the authority of law enforcement and the obligation of citizens to notify the police when trouble arises. Though vamps can't join the armed services, they can become cops, and actually enjoy the hell out of the job. But vamp cops are often pariahs to the other undead.

I would a lot rather think about vampire cops than what Pam had just told me.

"When did Bill go missing?" Sam asked. His voice managed to stay level, but there was anger just under the surface.

"He was due in last night," Pam said. My head snapped up. I hadn't known that. Why hadn't Bill told me he was coming home? "He was going to drive into Bon Temps, phone us at Fangtasia to let us know he'd made it home, and meet with us tonight." This was practically babbling, for a vampire.

Pam punched in numbers on a cell phone; I could hear the little beeps. I listened to her resultant conversation with Eric. After relaying the facts, Pam told him, "She's sitting here. She's not speaking."

She pressed the phone into my hand. I automatically put it to my ear.

"Sookie, are you listening?" I knew Eric could hear the sounds of my hair moving over the receiver, the whisper of my breath.

"I can tell you are," he said. "Listen and obey me. For now, tell no one what's happened. Act just as normal. Live your life as you always do. One of us will be watching you all the time, whether you think so or not. Even in the day, we'll find some way to guard you. We will avenge Bill, and we will protect you."

Avenge Bill? So Eric was sure Bill was dead. Well, nonexistent.

"I didn't know he was supposed to be coming in last night," I said, as if that was the most important fact I'd learned.

"He had—bad news he was going to tell you," Pam said suddenly.

Eric overheard her and made a disgusted sound. "Tell Pam to shut up," he said, sounding overtly furious for the first time since I'd known him. I didn't see any need to relay the message, because I figured Pam had been able to hear him, too. Most vampires have very acute hearing.

"So you knew this bad news and you knew he was coming back," I said. Not only was Bill missing and possibly dead—permanently dead—but he had lied to me about where he was going and why, and he'd kept some important secret from me, something concerning me. The pain went so deep, I could not even feel the wound. But I knew I would later.

I handed the phone back to Pam, and I turned and left the bar.

I faltered as I was getting into my car. I should stay at Merlotte's to help dispose of the body. Sam wasn't a vampire, and he was only involved in this for my sake. This wasn't fair to him.

But after only a second's hesitation, I drove away. Bubba could help him, and Pam—Pam, who knew all, while I knew nothing.

Sure enough, I caught a glimpse of a white face in the woods when I got home. I almost called out to the watcher, invited the vampire in to at least sit on the couch during the night. But then I thought, No. I had to be by myself. None of this was any of my doing. I had no action to take. I had to remain passive, and I was ignorant through no will of my own.

I was as wounded and as angry as it was possible for me to be. Or at least I thought I was. Subsequent revelations would prove me wrong.

I stomped inside my house and locked the door behind me. A lock wouldn't keep the vampire out, of course, but lack of an invitation to enter would. The vampire could definitely keep any humans out, at least until dawn.

I put on my old long-sleeved blue nylon gown, and I sat at my kitchen table staring blankly at my hands. I wondered where Bill was now. Was he even walking the earth; or was he a pile of ashes in some barbecue pit? I thought of his dark brown hair, the thick feel of it beneath my fingers. I considered the secrecy of his planned return. After what seemed like a minute or two, I glanced at the clock on the stove. I'd been sitting at the table, staring into space, for over an hour.

I should go to bed. It was late, and cold, and sleeping would be the normal thing to do. But nothing in my future would be normal again. Oh, wait! If Bill were gone, my future *would* be normal.

No Bill. So, no vampires: no Eric, Pam, or Bubba.

No supernatural creatures: no Weres, shape-shifters, or maenads. I wouldn't have encountered them, either, if it hadn't been for my involvement with Bill. If he'd never come into Merlotte's, I'd just be waiting tables, listening to the unwanted thoughts of those around me: the petty greed, the lust, the disillusionment, the hopes, and the fantasies. Crazy Sookie, the village telepath of Bon Temps, Louisiana.

I'd been a virgin until Bill. Now the only sex I might possibly have would be with JB du Rone, who was so lovely that you could almost overlook the fact that he was dumb as a stump. He had so few thoughts that his companionship was nearly comfortable for me. I could even touch JB without receiving unpleasant pictures. But *Bill* . . . I found that my right hand was clenched in a fist, and I pounded it on the table so hard, it hurt like hell.

Bill had told me that if anything happened to him, I was to "go to" Eric. I'd never been sure if he was telling me that Eric would see to it that I received some financial legacy of Bill's, or that Eric would protect me from other vampires, or that I'd be Eric's . . . well, that I'd have to have the same relationship with Eric that I had with Bill. I'd told Bill I wasn't going to be passed around like a Christmas fruitcake.

But Eric had already come to me, so I didn't even have the chance to decide whether or not to follow Bill's last piece of advice.

I lost the trail of my thought. It had never been a clear one anyway.

*Oh, Bill, where are you?* I buried my face in my hands.

My head was throbbing with exhaustion, and even my cozy kitchen was chilly in this small hour. I rose to go to bed, though I knew I wouldn't sleep. I needed Bill with such gut-clenching intensity that I wondered if it was somehow abnormal, if I'd been enchanted by some supernatural power.

Though my telepathic ability provided immunity from the vampires' glamour, maybe I was vulnerable to another power? Or maybe I was just missing the only man I'd ever loved. I felt eviscerated, empty, and betrayed. I felt worse than I had when my grandmother had died, worse than when my parents had drowned. When my parents had died, I'd been very young, and maybe I hadn't fully comprehended, all at once, that they were permanently gone. It was hard to remember now. When my grandmother had died a few months ago, I had taken comfort in the ritual surrounding death in the South.

And I'd known they hadn't willingly left me.

I found myself standing in the kitchen doorway. I switched off the overhead light.

Once I was wrapped up in bed in the dark, I began crying, and I didn't stop for a long, long time. It was not a night to count my blessings. It was a night when every loss I'd ever had pressed hard on me. It did seem I'd had more bad luck than most people. Though I made a token attempt to fend off a deluge of self-pity, I wasn't too successful. It was pretty much twined in there with the misery of not knowing Bill's fate.

I wanted Bill to curl up against my back; I wanted his cool lips on my neck. I wanted his white hands running down my stomach. I wanted to talk to him. I wanted him to laugh off my terrible suspicions. I wanted to tell him about my day; about the stupid problem I was having with the gas company, and the new channels our cable company had added. I wanted to remind him that he needed a new washer on the sink in his bathroom, let him know that my brother, Jason, had found out he wasn't going to be a father after all (which was good, since he wasn't a husband, either).

The sweetest part of being a couple was sharing your life with someone else.

But my life, evidently, had not been good enough to share.

# Chapter Three

WHEN THE SUN came up, I'd managed a half hour of sleep. I started to rise and make some coffee, but there didn't seem to be much point. I just stayed in bed. The phone rang during the morning, but I didn't pick it up. The doorbell rang, but I didn't answer it.

At some point toward the middle of the afternoon, I realized that there was one thing I had to do, the task Bill had insisted on my accomplishing if he was delayed. This situation exactly fit what he'd told me.

Now I sleep in the largest bedroom, formerly my grandmother's. I wobbled across the hall to my former room. A couple of months before, Bill had taken out the floor of my old closet and made it into a trapdoor. He'd established a lighttight hidey-hole for himself in the crawl space under the house. He'd done a great job.

I made sure I couldn't be seen from the window before I opened the closet door. The floor of the closet was bare of everything but the carpet, which was an extension of the one cut to fit the room. After I'd retracted the flap that covered the closet floor, I ran a pocketknife around the flooring and eventually pried it up. I looked down into the black box below. It was full: Bill's computer, a box of disks, even his monitor and printer.

So Bill had foreseen this might happen, and he'd hidden his work before he'd left. He'd had some faith in me, no matter how faithless he might have been himself. I nodded, and rolled the carpet back into place, fitting it carefully into the corners. On the floor of the closet I put out-of-season things—shoe boxes containing summer shoes, a beach bag filled with big sunbathing towels and one of my many tubes of suntan lotion, and my folding chaise that I used for tanning. I stuck a huge umbrella back in the corner, and decided that the closet looked realistic enough. My sundresses hung from the bar, along with some very lightweight bathrobes and nightgowns. My flare of energy faded as I realized I'd finished the last service Bill had asked of me, and I had no way to let him know I had followed his wishes.

Half of me (pathetically) wanted to let him know I'd kept the faith; half of me wanted to get in the toolshed and sharpen me some stakes.

Too conflicted to form any course of action, I crawled back to my bed and hoisted myself in. Abandoning a lifetime of making the best of things, and being strong and cheerful and practical, I returned to wallowing in my grief and my overwhelming sense of betrayal.

When I woke, it was dark again, and Bill was in bed with me. Oh, thank God! Relief swept over me. Now all would be well. I felt his cool body behind me, and I rolled over, half asleep, and put my arms around him. He eased up my long nylon gown, and his hand stroked my leg. I put my head against his silent chest and nuzzled him. His arms tightened around me, he pressed firmly against me, and I sighed with joy, inserting a hand between us to unfasten his pants. Everything was back to normal.

Except he smelled different.

My eyes flew open, and I pushed back against rock-hard shoulders. I let out a little squeak of horror.

"It's me," said a familiar voice.

"Eric, what are you doing here?"

"Snuggling."

"You son of a bitch! I thought you were Bill! I thought he was back!"

"Sookie, you need a shower."

"What?"

"Your hair is dirty, and your breath could knock down a horse."

"Not that I care what you think," I said flatly.

"Go get cleaned up."

"Why?"

"Because we have to talk, and I'm pretty sure you don't want to have a long conversation in bed. Not that I have any objection to being in bed with you"—he pressed himself against me to prove how little he objected—"but I'd enjoy it more if I were with the hygienic Sookie I've come to know."

Possibly nothing he could have said would have gotten me out of the bed faster than that. The hot shower felt wonderful to my cold body, and my temper took care of warming up my insides. It wasn't the first time Eric had surprised me in my own home. I was going to have to rescind his invitation to enter. What had stopped me from that drastic step before—what stopped me now—was the idea that if I ever needed help, and he couldn't enter, I might be dead before I could yell, "Come in!"

I'd entered the bathroom carrying my jeans and underwear and a red-and-green Christmas sweater with reindeer on it, because that's what had been at the top of my drawer. You only get a month to wear the darn things, so I make the most of it. I used a blow-dryer on my hair, wishing Bill were there to comb it out for me.

He really enjoyed doing that, and I enjoyed letting him. At that mental image, I almost broke down again, but I stood with my head resting against the wall for a long moment while I gathered my resolve. I took a deep breath, turned to the mirror, and slapped on some makeup. My tan wasn't great this far into the cold season; but I still had a nice glow, thanks to the tanning bed at Bon Temps Video Rental.

I'm a summer person. I like the sun, and the short dresses, and the feeling you had many hours of light to do whatever you chose. Even Bill loved the smells of summer; he loved it when he could smell suntan oil and (he told me) the sun itself on my skin.

But the sweet part of winter was that the nights were much longer—at least, I'd thought so when Bill was around to share those nights with me. I threw my hairbrush across the bathroom. It made a satisfying clatter as it ricocheted into the tub. "You *bastard*!" I screamed at the top of my lungs. Hearing my voice saying such a thing out loud calmed me down as nothing else could have.

When I emerged from the bathroom, Eric was completely dressed. He had on a freebie T-shirt from one of the breweries that supplied Fangtasia ("This Blood's For You," it read) and blue jeans, and he had thoughtfully made the bed.

"Can Pam and Chow come in?" he asked.

I walked through the living room to the front door and opened it. The two vampires were sitting silently on the porch swing. They were in what I thought of as downtime. When vampires don't have anything in particular to do, they sort of go blank; retreat inside themselves, sitting or standing utterly immobile, eyes open but vacant. It seems to refresh them.

"Please come in," I said.

Pam and Chow entered slowly, looking around them

with interest, as if they were on a field trip. Louisiana farmhouse, circa early twenty-first century. The house had belonged to our family since it was built over a hundred and sixty years ago. When my brother, Jason, had struck out on his own, he'd moved into the place my parents had built when they'd married. I'd stayed here, with Gran, in this much-altered, much-renovated house; and she'd left it to me in her will.

The living room had been the total original house. Other additions, like the modern kitchen and the bathrooms, were relatively new. The next floor, which was much smaller than the ground level, had been added in the early 1900s to accommodate a generation of children who all survived. I rarely went up there these days. It was awfully hot upstairs in the summer, even with the window air conditioners.

All my furniture was aged, styleless, and comfortable—absolutely conventional. The living room had couches and chairs and a television and a VCR, and then you passed through a hall that had my large bedroom with its own bath on one side, and a hall bathroom and my former bedroom and some closets—linen, coat—on the other. Through that passage, you were into the kitchen/dining area, which had been added on soon after my grandparents' wedding. After the kitchen, there was a big roofed back porch, which I'd just had screened in. The porch housed a useful old bench, the washer and dryer, and a bunch of shelves.

There was a ceiling fan in every room and a fly swatter, too, hung in a discreet spot on a tiny nail. Gran wouldn't turn on the air conditioner unless she absolutely had to.

Though they didn't venture upstairs, no detail escaped Pam and Chow on the ground floor.

By the time they settled at the old pine table where Stackhouses had eaten for a few generations, I felt like

I lived in a museum that had just been cataloged. I opened the refrigerator and got out three bottles of TrueBlood, heated them up in the microwave, gave them a good shake, and plonked them down on the table in front of my guests.

Chow was still practically a stranger to me. He'd been working at Fangtasia only a few months. I assume he'd bought into the bar, as the previous bartender had. Chow had amazing tattoos, the dark blue Asian kind that are so intricate, they are like a set of fancy clothes. These were so different from my attacker's jailhouse decorations that it was hard to believe they were the same art form. I'd been told Chow's were Yakuza tattoos, but I had never had the nerve to ask him, especially since it wasn't exactly my business. However, if these were true Yakuza tats, Chow was not that old for a vampire. I'd looked up the Yakuza, and the tattooing was a (relatively) recent development in that criminal organization's long history. Chow had long black hair (no surprise there), and I'd heard from many sources that he was a tremendous draw at Fangtasia. Most evenings, he worked shirtless. Tonight, as a concession to the cold, he was wearing a zipped red vest.

I couldn't help but wonder if he ever really felt naked; his body was so thoroughly decorated. I wished I could ask him, but of course that was out of the question. He was the only person of Asian descent I had ever met, and no matter how you know individuals don't represent their whole race, you do kind of expect at least some of the generalizations to be valid. Chow did seem to have a strong sense of privacy. But far from being silent and inscrutable, he was chattering away with Pam, though in a language I couldn't understand. And he smiled at me in a disconcerting way. Okay, maybe he was too far from inscrutable. He was probably insulting the hell out of me, and I was too dumb to know it.

Pam was dressed, as always, in sort of middle-class anonymous clothes. This evening it was a pair of winter white knit pants and a blue sweater. Her blond hair was shining, straight and loose, down her back. She looked like Alice in Wonderland with fangs.

"Have you found out anything else about Bill?" I asked, when they'd all had a swallow of their drinks.

Eric said, "A little."

I folded my hands in my lap and waited.

"I know Bill's been kidnapped," he said, and the room swam around my head for a second. I took a deep breath to make it stop.

"Who by?" Grammar was the least of my worries.

"We aren't sure," Chow told me. "The witnesses are not agreeing." His English was accented, but very clear.

"Let me at them," I said. "If they're human, I'll find out."

"If they were under our dominion, that would be the logical thing to do," Eric said agreeably. "But, unfortunately, they're not."

Dominion, my foot. "Please explain." I was sure I was showing extraordinary patience under the circumstances.

"These humans owe allegiance to the king of Mississippi."

I knew my mouth was falling open, but I couldn't seem to stop it. "Excuse me," I said, after a long moment, "but I could have sworn you said . . . the king? Of Mississippi?"

Eric nodded without a trace of a smile.

I looked down, trying to keep a straight face. Even under the circumstances, it was impossible. I could feel my mouth twitch. "For real?" I asked helplessly. I don't know why it seemed even funnier that Mississippi had a king—after all, Louisiana had a queen—but it did. I reminded myself I wasn't supposed to know about the queen. Check.

The vampires looked at one another. They nodded in unison.

"Are you the king of Louisiana?" I asked Eric, giddy with all my mental effort to keep varying stories straight. I was laughing so hard that it was all I could do to keep upright in the chair. Possibly there was a note of hysteria.

"Oh, no," he said. "I am the sheriff of Area 5."

That really set me off. I had tears running down my face, and Chow was looking uneasy. I got up, made myself some Swiss Miss microwave hot chocolate, and stirred it with a spoon so it would cool off. I was calming down as I performed the little task, and by the time I returned to the table, I was almost sober.

"You never told me all this before," I said, by way of explanation. "You all have divided up America into kingdoms, is that right?"

Pam and Chow looked at Eric with some surprise, but he didn't regard them. "Yes," he said simply. "It has been so since vampires came to America. Of course, over the years the system's changed with the population. There were far fewer vampires in America for the first two hundred years, because the trip over was so perilous. It was hard to work out the length of the voyage with the available blood supply." Which would have been the crew, of course. "And the Louisiana Purchase made a great difference."

Well, of course it *would*. I stifled another bout of giggles. "And the kingdoms are divided into . . . ?"

"Areas. Used to be called fiefdoms, until we decided that was too behind the times. A sheriff controls each area. As you know, we live in Area 5 of the kingdom of Louisiana. Stan, whom you visited in Dallas, is sheriff of Area 6 in the kingdom of . . . in Texas."

I pictured Eric as the sheriff of Nottingham, and when that had lost amusement value, as Wyatt Earp. I was

definitely on the light-headed side. I really felt pretty bad
physically. I told myself to pack away my reaction to
this information, to focus on the immediate problem.
"So, Bill was kidnapped in daylight, I take it?"

Multiple nods all around.

"This kidnapping was witnessed by some humans
who live in the kingdom of Mississippi." I just loved to
say that. "And they're under the control of a vampire
king?"

"Russell Edgington. Yes, they live in his kingdom,
but a few of them will give me information. For a price."

"This king won't let you question them?"

"We haven't asked him yet. It could be Bill was taken
on his orders."

That raised a whole new crop of questions, but I told
myself to stay focused. "How can I get to them? Assuming I decide I want to."

"We've thought of a way you may be able to gather
information from humans in the area where Bill disappeared," said Eric. "Not just people I have bribed to let
me know what's happening there, but all the people that
associated with Russell. It's risky. I had to tell you what
I have, to make it work. And you may be unwilling.
Someone's already tried to get you once. Apparently,
whoever has Bill must not have much information about
you yet. But soon, Bill will talk. If you're anywhere
around when he breaks, they'll have you."

"They won't really need me then," I pointed out. "If
he's already broken."

"That's not necessarily true," Pam said. They did
some more of the enigmatic-gaze-swapping thing.

"Give me the whole story," I said. I noticed that Chow
had finished his blood, so I got up to get him some more.

"As Russell Edgington's people tell it, Betty Jo Pickard, Edgington's second in command, was supposed to
begin a flight to St. Louis yesterday. The humans re-

sponsible for taking her coffin to the airport took Bill's identical coffin by mistake. When they delivered the coffin to the hangar Anubis Airlines leases, they left it unguarded for perhaps ten minutes while they were filling out paperwork. During that time—they claim—someone wheeled the coffin, which was on a kind of gurney, out of the back of the hangar, loaded it onto a truck, and drove away."

"Someone who could penetrate Anubis security," I said, doubt heavy in my voice. Anubis Airlines had been established to transport vampires safely both day and night, and their guarantee of heavy security to guard the coffins of sleeping vampires was their big calling card. Of course, vampires don't have to sleep in coffins, but it sure is easy to ship them that way. There had been unfortunate "accidents" when vampires had tried to fly Delta. Some fanatic had gotten in the baggage hold and hacked open a couple of coffins with an ax. Northwest had suffered the same problem. Saving money suddenly didn't seem so attractive to the undead, who now flew Anubis almost exclusively.

"I'm thinking that someone could have mingled with Edgington's people, someone the Anubis employees thought was Edgington's, and Edgington's people thought belonged to Anubis. He could have wheeled Bill out as Edgington's people left, and the guards would be none the wiser."

"The Anubis people wouldn't ask to see papers? On a departing coffin?"

"They say they did see papers, Betty Jo Pickard's. She was on her way to Missouri to negotiate a trade agreement with the vampires of St. Louis." I had a blank moment of wondering what on earth the vampires of Mississippi could be trading with the vampires of Missouri, and then I decided I just didn't want to know.

"There was also extra confusion at the time," Pam was

saying. "A fire started under the tail of another Anubis plane, and the guards were distracted."

"Oh, accidentally-on-purpose."

"I think so," Chow said.

"So, why would anyone want to snatch Bill?" I asked. I was afraid I knew. I was hoping they'd provide me with something else. Thank God Bill had prepared for this moment.

"Bill's been working on a little special project," Eric said, his eyes on my face. "Do you know anything about that?"

More than I wanted to. Less than I ought to.

"What project?" I said. I've spent my whole life concealing my thoughts, and I called on all my skill now. That life depended on my sincerity.

Eric's gaze flickered over to Pam, to Chow. They both gave some infinitesimal signal. He focused on me again, and said, "That is a little hard to believe, Sookie."

"How come?" I asked, anger in my voice. When in doubt, attack. "When do any of you exactly spill your emotional guts to a human? And Bill is definitely one of you." I infused that with as much rage as I could muster.

They did that eye-flicker thing at one another again.

"You think we'll believe that Bill didn't tell you what he was working on?"

"Yes, I think so. Because he didn't." I had more or less figured it out all by myself anyway.

"Here's what I'm going to do," Eric said finally. He looked at me from across the table, his blue eyes as hard as marbles and just as warm. No more Mr. Nice Vampire. "I can't tell if you're lying or not, which is remarkable. For your sake, I hope you are telling the truth. I could torture you until you told me the truth, or until I was sure you had been telling me the truth from the beginning."

Oh, brother. I took a deep breath, blew it out, and tried to think of an appropriate prayer. *God, don't let me scream too loud* seemed kind of weak and negative. Besides, there was no one to hear me besides the vampires, no matter how loudly I shrieked. When the time came, I might as well let it rip.

"But," Eric continued thoughtfully, "that might damage you too badly for the other part of my plan. And really, it doesn't make that much difference if you know what Bill has been doing behind our backs or not."

Behind their backs? Oh, *shit*. And now I knew whom to blame for my very deep predicament. My own dear love, Bill Compton.

"That got a reaction," Pam observed.

"But not the one I expected," Eric said slowly.

"I'm not too happy about the torture option." I was in so much trouble, I couldn't even begin to add it up, and I was so overloaded with stress that I felt like my head was floating somewhere above my body. "And I miss Bill." Even though at the moment I would gladly kick his ass, I did miss him. And if I could just have ten minutes' conversation with him, how much better prepared I would be to face the coming days. Tears rolled down my face. But there was more they had to tell me; more I had to hear, whether I wanted to or not. "I do expect you to tell me why he lied about this trip, if you know. Pam mentioned bad news."

Eric looked at Pam with no love in his eyes at all.

"She's leaking again," Pam observed, sounding a little uncomfortable. "I think before she goes to Mississippi, she should know the truth. Besides, if she has been keeping secrets for Bill, this will . . ."

Make her spill the beans? Change her loyalty to Bill? Force her to realize she has to tell us?

It was obvious that Chow and Eric had been all for keeping me in ignorance and that they were acutely unhappy with Pam for hinting to me that, though I supposedly didn't know it, all was not well with Bill and me. But they both eyed Pam intently for a long minute, and then Eric nodded curtly.

"You and Chow wait outside," Eric said to Pam. She gave him a very pointed look, and then they walked out, leaving their drained bottles sitting on the table. Not even a thank-you for the blood. Didn't even rinse the bottles out. My head felt lighter and lighter as I contemplated poor vampire manners. I felt my eyelids flicker, and it occurred to me that I was on the edge of fainting. I am not one of these frail gals who keels over at every little thing, but I felt I was justified right now. Plus, I vaguely realized I hadn't eaten in over twenty-four hours.

"Don't you do it," Eric said. He sounded definite. I tried to concentrate on his voice, and I looked at him.

I nodded to indicate I was doing my best.

He moved over to my side of the table, turned the chair Pam had occupied until it faced me and was very close. He sat and leaned over to me, his big white hand covering both of mine, still folded neatly in my lap. If he closed his hand, he could crush all my fingers. I'd never work as a waitress again.

"I don't enjoy seeing you scared of me," he said, his face too close to mine. I could smell his cologne— Ulysse, I thought. "I have always been very fond of you."

He'd always wanted to have sex with me.

"Plus, I want to fuck you." He grinned, but at this moment it didn't do a thing to me. "When we kiss . . . it's very exciting." We had kissed in the line of duty, so to speak, and not as recreation. But it had been exciting. How not? He was gorgeous, and he'd had several hundred years to work on his smooching technique.

Eric got closer and closer. I wasn't sure if he was

going to bite me or kiss me. His fangs had run out. He was angry, or horny, or hungry, or all three. New vampires tended to lisp while they talked until they got used to their fangs; you couldn't even tell, with Eric. He'd had centuries of perfecting that technique, too.

"Somehow, that torture plan didn't make me feel very sexy," I told him.

"It did something for Chow, though," Eric whispered in my ear.

I wasn't shaking, but I should have been. "Could you cut to the chase here?" I asked. "Are you gonna torture me, or not? Are you my friend, or my enemy? Are you gonna find Bill, or let him rot?"

Eric laughed. It was short and unfunny, but it was better than him getting closer, at least at the moment. "Sookie, you are too much," he said, but not as though he found that particularly endearing. "I'm not going to torture you. For one thing, I would hate to ruin that beautiful skin; one day, I will see all of it."

I just hoped it was still on my body when that happened.

"You won't always be so afraid of me," he said, as if he were absolutely certain of the future. "And you won't always be as devoted to Bill as you are now. There is something I must tell you."

Here came the Big Bad. His cool fingers twined with mine, and without wanting to, I held his hand hard. I couldn't think of a word to say, at least a word that was safe. My eyes fixed on his.

"Bill was summoned to Mississippi," Eric told me, "by a vampire—a female—he'd known many years ago. I don't know if you've realized that vampires almost never mate with other vampires, for any longer than a rare one-night affair. We don't do this because it gives us power over each other forever, the mating and sharing of blood. This vampire . . ."

"Her name," I said.

"Lorena," he said reluctantly. Or maybe he wanted to tell me all along, and the reluctance was just for show. Who the heck knows, with a vampire.

He waited to see if I would speak, but I did not.

"She was in Mississippi. I am not sure if she regularly lives there, or if she went there to ensnare Bill. She had been living in Seattle for years, I know, because she and Bill lived there together for many years."

I had wondered why he'd picked Seattle as his fictitious destination. He hadn't just plucked it out of the air.

"But whatever her intention in asking him to meet her there . . . what excuse she gave him for not coming here . . . maybe he was just being careful of you . . ."

I wanted to die at that moment. I took a deep breath and looked down at our joined hands. I was too humiliated to look in Eric's eyes.

"He was—he became—instantly enthralled with her, all over again. After a few nights, he called Pam to say that he was coming home early without telling you, so he could arrange your future care before he saw you again."

"Future care?" I sounded like a crow.

"Bill wanted to make a financial arrangement for you."

The shock of it made me blanch. "Pension me off," I said numbly. No matter how well he had meant, Bill could not have offered me any greater offense. When he'd been in my life, it had never occurred to him to ask me how my finances were faring—though he could hardly *wait* to help his newly discovered descendants, the Bellefleurs.

But when he was going to be out of my life, and felt guilty for leaving pitiful, pitiable me—then he started worrying.

"He wanted . . ." Eric began, then stopped and looked

closely at my face. "Well, leave that for now. I would not have told you any of this, if Pam hadn't interfered. I would have sent you off in ignorance, because then it wouldn't have been words from my mouth that hurt you so badly. And I would not have had to plead with you, as I'm going to plead."

I made myself listen. I gripped Eric's hand as if it were a lifeline.

"What I'm going to do—and you have to understand, Sookie, my hide depends on this, too . . ."

I looked him straight in the face, and he saw the rush of my surprise.

"Yes, my job, and maybe my life, too, Sookie—not just yours, and Bill's. I'm sending you a contact tomorrow. He lives in Shreveport, but he has a second apartment in Jackson. He has friends among the supernatural community there, the vampires, shifters, and Weres. Through him you can meet some of them, and their human employees."

I was not completely in my head right now, but I felt like I'd understand all this when I played it back. So I nodded. His fingers stroked mine, over and over.

"This man is a Were," Eric said carelessly, "so he is scum. But he is more reliable than some others, and he owes me a big personal favor."

I absorbed that, nodded again. Eric's long fingers seemed almost warm.

"He'll take you out and about in the vampire community in Jackson, and you can pick brains there among human employees. I know it's a long shot, but if there's something to discover, if Russell Edgington did abduct Bill, you may pick up a hint. The man who tried to abduct you was from Jackson, going by the bills in his car, and he was a Were, as the wolf's head on his vest indicates. I don't know why they came after you. But I suspect it means Bill is alive, and they wanted to grab you to use as leverage over him."

"Then I guess they should have abducted *Lorena*," I said.

Eric's eyes widened in appreciation.

"Maybe they already have her," he said. "But maybe Bill has realized it is Lorena who betrayed him. He wouldn't have been taken if she hadn't revealed the secret he had told her."

I mulled that over, nodded yet again.

"Another puzzle is why she happened to be there at all," Eric said. "I think I would have known if she'd been a regular member of the Mississippi group. But I'll be thinking about that in my spare time." From his grim face, Eric had already put in considerable brain time on that question. "If this plan doesn't work within about three days, Sookie, we may have to kidnap one of the Mississippi vampires in return. This would almost certainly lead to a war, and a war—even with Mississippi—would be costly in lives and money. And in the end, they would kill Bill anyway."

Okay, the weight of the world was resting on my shoulders. Thanks, Eric. I needed more responsibility and pressure.

"But know this: If they have Bill—if he is still alive—we will get him back. And you will be together again, if that's what you want."

Big *if*.

"To answer your question: I am your friend, and that will last as long as I can be your friend without jeopardizing my own life. Or the future of my area."

Well, that laid it on the line. I appreciated his honesty. "As long as it's convenient for you, you mean," I said calmly, which was both unfair and inaccurate. However, I thought it was odd that my characterization of his attitude actually seemed to bother him. "Let me ask you something, Eric."

He raised his eyebrows to tell me he was waiting. His hands traveled up and down my arms, absently, as if he wasn't thinking of what he was doing. The movement reminded me of a man warming his hands at a fire.

"If I'm understanding you, Bill was working on a project for the . . ." I felt a wild bubble of laughter rising, and I ruthlessly suppressed it. "For the queen of Louisiana," I finished. "But you didn't know about it. Is this right?"

Eric stared at me for a long moment, while he thought about what to tell me. "She told me she had work for Bill to do," he said. "But not what it was, or why he had to be the one to do it, or when it would be complete."

That would miff almost any leader, having his underling co-opted like that. Especially if the leader was kept in ignorance. "So, why isn't this queen looking for Bill?" I asked, keeping my voice carefully neutral.

"She doesn't know he's gone."

"Why is that?"

"We haven't told her."

Sooner or later he'd quit answering. "Why not?"

"She would punish us."

"Why?" I was beginning to sound like a two-year-old.

"For letting something happen to Bill, when he was doing a special project for her."

"What would that punishment be?"

"Oh, with her it's difficult to tell." He gave a choked laugh. "Something very unpleasant."

Eric was even closer to me, his face almost touching my hair. He was inhaling, very delicately. Vampires rely on smell, and hearing, much more than sight, though their eyesight is extremely accurate. Eric had had my blood, so he could tell more about my emotions than a vampire who hadn't. All bloodsuckers are students of the human emotional system, since the most successful predators know the habits of their prey.

Eric actually rubbed his cheek against mine. He was like a cat in his enjoyment of contact.

"Eric." He'd given me more information than he knew.

"Mmm?"

"Really, what will the queen do to you if you can't produce Bill on the date her project is due?"

My question got the desired result. Eric pulled away from me and looked down at me with eyes bluer than mine and harder than mine and colder than the Arctic waste.

"Sookie, you really don't want to know," he said. "Producing his work would be good enough. Bill's actual presence would be a bonus."

I returned his look with eyes almost as cold as his. "And what will I get in return for doing this for you?" I asked.

Eric managed to look both surprised and pleased. "If Pam hadn't hinted to you about Bill, his safe return would have been enough and you would have jumped at the chance to help," Eric reminded me.

"But now I know about Lorena."

"And knowing, do you agree to do this for us?"

"Yes, on one condition."

Eric looked wary. "What would that be?" he asked.

"If something happens to me, I want you to take her out."

He gaped at me for at least a whole second before he roared with laughter. "I would have to pay a huge fine," he said when he'd quit chortling. "And I'd have to accomplish it first. That's easier said than done. She's three hundred years old."

"You've told me that what will happen to you if all

this comes unraveled would be pretty horrible," I reminded him.

"True."

"You've told me you desperately need me to do this for you."

"True."

"That's what I ask in return."

"You might make a decent vampire, Sookie," Eric said finally. "All right. Done. If anything happens to you, she'll never fuck Bill again."

"Oh, it's not just that."

"No?" Eric looked very skeptical, as well he might.

"It's because she betrayed him."

Eric's hard blue eyes met mine. "Tell me this, Sookie: Would you ask this of me if she were a human?" His wide, thin-lipped mouth, most often amused, was in a serious straight line.

"If she were a human, I'd take care of it myself," I said, and stood to show him to the door.

After Eric had driven away, I leaned against the door and laid my cheek against the wood. Did I mean what I'd told him? I'd long wondered if I were really a civilized person, though I kept striving to be one. I knew that at the moment I'd said I would take care of Lorena myself, I had meant it. There was something pretty savage inside me, and I'd always controlled it. My grandmother had not raised me to be a murderess.

As I plodded down the hall to my bedroom, I realized that my temper had been showing more and more lately. Ever since I'd gotten to know the vampires.

I couldn't figure out why that should be. They exerted tremendous control over themselves. Why should mine be slipping?

But that was enough introspection for one night.

I had to think about tomorrow.

# Chapter Four

Since it seemed I was going out of town, there was laundry to be done, and stuff in the refrigerator that needed throwing away. I wasn't particularly sleepy after spending so long in bed the preceding day and night, so I got out my suitcase, opened it, and tossed some clothes into the washer out on the freezing back porch. I didn't want to think about my own character any longer. I had plenty of other items to mull over.

Eric had certainly adopted a shotgun approach to bending me to his will. He'd bombarded me with many reasons to do what he wanted: intimidation, threat, seduction, an appeal for Bill's return, an appeal for his (and Pam's, and Chow's) life and/or well-being—to say nothing of my own health. "I might have to torture you, but I want to have sex with you; I need Bill, but I'm furious with him because he deceived me; I have to keep peace with Russell Edgington, but I have to get Bill back from him; Bill is my serf, but he's secretly working more for my boss."

Darn vampires. You can see why I'm glad their glamour doesn't affect me. It's one of the few positives my mind-reading ability has yielded me. Unfortunately, humans with psychic glitches are very attractive to the undead.

I certainly could not have foreseen any of this when I'd become attached to Bill. Bill had become almost as necessary to me as water; and not entirely because of my deep feelings for him, or my physical pleasure in his lovemaking. Bill was the only insurance I had against being annexed by another vampire, against my will.

After I'd run a couple of loads through the washer and dryer and folded the clothes, I felt much more relaxed. I was almost packed, and I'd put in a couple of romances and a mystery in case I got a little time to read. I am self-educated from genre books.

I stretched and yawned. There was a certain peace of mind to be found in having a plan, and my uneasy sleep of the past day and night had not refreshed me as much as I thought. I might be able to fall asleep easily.

Even without help from the vampires, I could maybe find Bill, I thought, as I brushed my teeth and climbed into bed. But breaking him out of whatever prison he was in and making a successful escape, that was another question. And then I'd have to decide what to do about our relationship.

I woke up at about four in the morning with an odd feeling there was an idea just waiting to be acknowledged. I'd had a thought at some point during the night; it was the kind of idea that you just know has been bubbling in your brain, waiting to boil over.

Sure enough, after a minute the idea resurfaced. What if Bill had not been abducted, but had defected? What if he'd become so enamored or addicted to Lorena that he'd decided to leave the Louisiana vampires and join with the Mississippi group? Immediately, I had doubts that that had been Bill's plan; it would be a very elaborate one, with the leakage of informants to Eric concerning Bill's abduction, the confirmed presence of Lorena in Mississippi. Surely there'd be a less dramatic, and simpler, way to arrange his disappearance.

I wondered if Eric, Chow, and Pam were even now searching Bill's house, which lay across the cemetery from mine. They weren't going to find what they were looking for. Maybe they'd come back here. They wouldn't have to get Bill back at all, if they could find the computer files the queen wanted so badly. I fell to sleep out of sheer exhaustion, thinking I heard Chow laugh outside.

Even the knowledge of Bill's betrayal did not stop me from searching for him in my dreams. I must have rolled over three times, reaching out to see if he'd slid into bed with me, as he often did. And every time, the other side of the bed was empty and cold.

However, that was better than finding Eric there instead.

I was up and showering at first light, and I'd made a pot of coffee before the knock at the front door came.

"Who is it?" I stood to one side of the door as I asked.

"Eric sent me," a gruff voice said.

I opened the door and looked up. And looked up some more.

He was huge. His eyes were green. His tousled hair was curly and thick and black as pitch. His brain buzzed and pulsed with energy; kind of a red effect. Werewolf.

"Come on in. You want some coffee?"

Whatever he'd expected, it wasn't what he was seeing. "You bet, chere. You got some eggs? Some sausage?"

"Sure." I led him to the kitchen. "I'm Sookie Stackhouse," I said, over my shoulder. I bent over to get the eggs out of the refrigerator. "You?"

"Alcide," he said, pronouncing it *Al-see,* with the *d* barely sounded. "Alcide Herveaux."

He watched me steadily while I lifted out the skillet—
my grandmother's old, blackened iron skillet. She'd gotten it when she got married, and fired it, like any woman
worth her salt would do. Now it was perfectly seasoned.
I turned the gas eye on at the stove. I cooked the sausage
first (for the grease), plopped it on a paper towel on a
plate and stuck it in the oven to keep warm. After asking
Alcide how he wanted the eggs, I scrambled them and
cooked them quickly, sliding them onto the warm plate.
He opened the right drawer for the silverware on the
first try, and poured himself some juice and coffee after
I silently pointed out which cabinet contained the cups.
He refilled my mug while he was at it.

He ate neatly. And he ate everything.

I plunged my hands into the hot, soapy water to clean
the few dishes. I washed the skillet last, dried it, and
rubbed some Crisco into the blackness, taking occasional
glances at my guest. The kitchen smelled comfortably
of breakfast and soapy water. It was a peculiarly peace-
ful moment.

This was anything but what I had expected when Eric
had told me someone who owed him a favor would be
my entrée into the Mississippi vampire milieu. As I
looked out the kitchen window at the cold landscape, I
realized that this was how I had envisioned my future;
on the few occasions I'd let myself imagine a man sharing my house.

This was the way life was supposed to be, for normal
people. It was morning, time to get up and work, time
for a woman to cook breakfast for a man, if he had to
go out and earn. This big rough man was eating real
food. He almost certainly had a pickup truck sitting out
in front of my house.

Of course, he was a werewolf. But a Were could live
a more close-to-human life than a vampire.

On the other hand, what I didn't know about Weres could fill a book.

He finished, put his plate in the water in the sink, and washed and dried it himself while I wiped the table. It was as smooth as if we'd choreographed it. He disappeared into the bathroom for a minute while I ran over my mental list of things that had to be done before I left. I needed to talk to Sam, that was the main thing. I'd called my brother the night before to tell him I'd be gone for a few days. Liz had been at Jason's, so he hadn't really thought a lot about my departure. He'd agreed to pick up my mail and my papers for me.

Alcide came to sit opposite me at the table. I was trying to think about how we should talk about our joint task; I was trying to anticipate any sore paws I might tread on. Maybe he was worrying about the same things. I can't read the minds of shape-shifters or werewolves with any consistency; they're supernatural creatures. I can reliably interpret moods, and pick up on the occasional clear idea. So the humans-with-a-difference are much less opaque to me than the vampires. Though I understand there's a contingent of shape-shifters and Weres who wants to change things, the fact of their existence still remains a secret. Until they see how publicity works out for the vampires, the supernaturals of the two-natured variety are ferocious about their privacy.

Werewolves are the tough guys of the shape-shifting world. They're shape-shifters by definition, but they're the only ones who have their own separate society, and they will not allow anyone else to be called "Were" in their hearing. Alcide Herveaux looked plenty tough. He was big as a boulder, with biceps that I could do pull-ups on. He would have to shave a second time if he planned on going out in the evening. He would fit right in on a construction site or a wharf.

He was a proper man.

"How are they forcing you to do this?" I asked.

"They have a marker of my dad's," he said. He put his massive hands on the table and leaned into them. "They own a casino in Shreveport, you know?"

"Sure." It was a popular weekend excursion for people in this area, to go over to Shreveport or up to Tunica (in Mississippi, right below Memphis) and rent a room for a couple of nights, play the slots, see a show or two, eat lots of buffet food.

"My dad got in too deep. He owns a surveying company—I work for him—but he likes to gamble." The green eyes smoldered with rage. "He got in too deep in the casino in Louisiana, so your vamps own his marker, his debt. If they call it in, our company will go under." Werewolves seemed to respect vampires about as much as vampires respect them. "So, to get the marker back, I have to help you hang around with the vamps in Jackson." He leaned back in the chair, looking me in the eyes. "That's not a hard thing, taking a pretty woman to Jackson and out barhopping. Now that I've met you, I'm glad to do it, to get my father out from under the debt. But why the hell you want to do that? You look like a real woman, not one of those sick bitches who get off on hanging around the vamps."

This was a refreshingly direct conversation, after my conference with the vampires. "I only hang around with one vampire, by choice," I said bitterly. "Bill, my—well, I don't know if he's even my boyfriend anymore. It seems the vampires of Jackson may have kidnapped him. Someone tried to grab me last night." I thought it only fair to let him know. "Since the kidnapper didn't seem to know my name, just that I worked at Merlotte's, I'll probably be safe in Jackson if no one figures out I'm the woman who goes with Bill. I have to tell you, the man who tried to grab me was a werewolf. And he had a Hinds County car plate." Jackson was in Hinds County.

"Wearing a gang vest?" Alcide asked. I nodded. Alcide looked thoughtful, which was a good thing. This was not a situation I took lightly, and it was a good sign that he didn't, either. "There's a small gang in Jackson made up of Weres. Some of the bigger shifters hang around the edges of this gang—the panther, the bear. They hire themselves out to the vamps on a pretty regular basis."

"There's one less of them now," I said.

After a moment's digestion of that information, my new companion gave me a long, challenging stare. "So, what good is a little human gal going to do against the vampires of Jackson? You a martial artist? You a great shot? You been in the Army?"

I had to smile. "No. You never heard my name?"

"You're famous?"

"Guess not." I was pleased that he didn't have any preconceptions about me. "I think I'll just let you find out about me."

"Long as you're not gonna turn into a snake." He stood up. "You're not a guy, are you?" That late-breaking thought made his eyes widen.

"No, Alcide. I'm a woman." I tried to say that matter-of-factly, but it was pretty hard.

"I was willing to put money on that." He grinned at me. "If you're not some kind of superwoman, what are you going to do when you know where your man is?"

"I'm going to call Eric, the . . ." Suddenly I realized that telling vampire secrets is a bad idea. "Eric is Bill's boss. He'll decide what to do after that."

Alcide looked skeptical. "I don't trust Eric. I don't trust any of 'em. He'll probably double-cross you."

"How?"

"He might use your man as leverage. He might demand restitution, since they have one of his men. He might use your man's abduction as an excuse to go to war, in which case your man will be executed tout de suite."

I had not thought that far. "Bill knows stuff," I said. "Important stuff."

"Good. That may keep him alive." Then he saw my face, and chagrin ran across his own. "Hey, Sookie, I'm sorry. I don't think before I talk sometimes. We'll get him back, though it makes me sick to think of a woman like you with one of those bloodsuckers."

This was painful, but oddly refreshing.

"Thanks, I guess," I said, attempting a smile. "What about you? Do you have a plan about how to introduce me to the vampires?"

"Yeah. There's a nightclub in Jackson, close to the capitol. It's for Supes and their dates only. No tourists. The vamps can't make it pay on their own, and it's a convenient meeting place for them, so they let us low-lifes share the fun." He grinned. His teeth were perfect— white and sharp. "It won't be suspicious if I go there. I always drop in when I'm in Jackson. You'll have to go as my date." He looked embarrassed. "Uh, I better tell you, you seem like you're a jeans kind of person like me—but this club, they like you to dress kind of party style." He feared I had no fancy dresses in my closet; I could read that clearly. And he didn't want me to be humiliated by appearing in the wrong clothes. What a man.

"Your girlfriend won't be crazy about this," I said, angling for information out of sheer curiosity.

"She lives in Jackson, as a matter of fact. But we broke up a couple of months ago," he said. "She took up with another shape-shifter. Guy turns into a damn owl."

Was she *nuts*? Of course, there'd be more to the story.

And of course, it fell into the category of "none of your business."

So without comment, I went to my room to pack my two party dresses and their accessories in a hanging bag. Both were purchases from Tara's Togs, managed (and now owned) by my friend Tara Thornton. Tara was real good about calling me when things went on clearance. Bill actually owned the building that housed Tara's Togs, and had told all the businesses housed in there to run a tab for me that he would pay, but I had resisted the temptation. Well, except for replacing clothes that Bill himself had ripped in our more thrilling moments.

I was very proud of both these dresses, since I'd never had anything like them before, and I zipped the bag shut with a smile.

Alcide stuck his head in the bedroom to ask if I was ready. He looked at the cream-and-yellow bed and curtains, and nodded approvingly. "I got to call my boss," I said. "Then we'll be good to go." I perched on the side of the bed and picked up the receiver.

Alcide propped himself against the wall by my closet door while I dialed Sam's personal number. His voice was sleepy when he answered, and I apologized for calling so early. "What's happening, Sookie?" he asked groggily.

"I have to go away for a few days," I said. "I'm sorry for not giving you more notice, but I called Sue Jennings last night to see if she'd work for me. She said yes, so I gave her my hours."

"Where are you going?" he asked.

"I have to go to Mississippi," I said. "Jackson."

"You got someone lined up to pick up your mail?"

"My brother. Thanks for asking."

"Plants to water?"

"None that won't live till I get back."

"Okay. Are you going by yourself?"

"No," I said hesitantly.

"With Bill?"

"No, he, uh, he hasn't shown up."

"Are you in trouble?"

"I'm just fine," I lied.

"Tell him a man's going with you," Alcide rumbled, and I gave him an exasperated look. He was leaning against the wall, and he took up an awful lot of it.

"Someone's there?" Sam's nothing if not quick on the uptake.

"Yes, Alcide Herveaux," I said, figuring it was a smart thing to tell someone who cared about me that I was leaving the area with this guy. First impressions can be absolutely false, and Alcide needed to be aware there was someone who would hold him accountable.

"Aha," Sam said. The name did not seem to be unfamiliar to him. "Let me talk to him."

"Why?" I can take a lot of paternalism, but I was about up to my ears.

"Hand over the damn phone." Sam almost never curses, so I made a face to show what I thought of his demand and gave the phone to Alcide. I stomped out to the living room and looked through the window. Yep. A Dodge Ram, extended cab. I was willing to bet it had everything on it that could be put on.

I'd rolled my suitcase out by its handle, and I'd slung my carrying bag over a chair by the door, so I just had to pull on my heavy jacket. I was glad Alcide had warned me about the dress-up rule for the bar, since it never would have occurred to me to pack anything fancy. Stupid vampires. Stupid dress code.

I was Sullen, with a capital S.

I wandered back down the hall, mentally reviewing the contents of my suitcase, while the two shape-shifters had (presumably) a "man talk." I glanced through the doorway of my bedroom to see that Alcide, with the phone to his ear, was perched on the side of my bed where I'd been sitting. He looked oddly at home there.

I paced restlessly back into the living room and stared out the window some more. Maybe the two were having shape-shifting talk. Though to Alcide, Sam (who generally shifted into a collie, though he was not limited to that form) would rank as a lightweight, at least they were from the same branch of the tree. Sam, on the other hand, would be a little leery of Alcide; werewolves had a bad rep.

Alcide strode down the hall, safety shoes clomping on the hardwood floor. "I promised him I'd take care of you," he said. "Now, we'll just hope that works out." He wasn't smiling.

I had been tuning up to be aggravated, but his last sentence was so realistic that the hot air went out of me as if I'd been punctured. In the complex relationship between vampire, Were, and human, there was a lot of leeway for something to go wrong somewhere. After all, my plan was thin, and the vampires' hold over Alcide was tenuous. Bill might not have been taken unwillingly; he might be happy being held captive by a king, as long as the vampire Lorena was on site. He might be enraged that I had come to find him.

He might be dead.

I locked the door behind me and followed Alcide as he stowed my things in the extended cab of the Ram.

The outside of the big truck gleamed, but inside, it was the littered vehicle of a man who spent his working life on the road; a hard hat, invoices, estimates, business cards, boots, a first-aid kit. At least there wasn't any food trash. As we bumped down my eroded driveway, I picked up a rubber-banded sheaf of brochures whose cover read, "Herveaux and Son, AAA Accurate Surveys." I eased out the top one and studied it carefully as Alcide drove the short distance to interstate 20 to go east to Monroe, Vicksburg, and then to Jackson.

I discovered that the Herveauxes, father and son, owned a bi-state surveying company, with offices in Jackson, Monroe, Shreveport, and Baton Rouge. The home office, as Alcide had told me, was in Shreveport. There was a photo inside of the two men, and the older Herveaux was just as impressive (in a senior way) as his son.

"Is your dad a werewolf, too?" I asked, after I'd digested the information and realized that the Herveaux family was at least prosperous, and possibly rich. They'd worked hard for it, though; and they'd keep working hard, unless the older Mr. Herveaux could control his gambling.

"Both my parents," Alcide said, after a pause.

"Oh, sorry." I wasn't sure what I was apologizing for, but it was safer than not.

"That's the only way to produce a Were child," he said, after a moment. I couldn't tell if he was explaining to be polite, or because he really thought I should know.

"So how come America's not full of werewolves and shapeshifters?" I asked, after I'd considered his statement.

"Like must marry like to produce another, which is not always doable. And each union only produces one child with the trait. Infant mortality is high."

"So, if you marry another werewolf, one of your kids will be a werebaby?"

"The condition will manifest itself at the onset of, ah, puberty."

"Oh, that's awful. Being a teenager is tough enough."

He smiled, not at me, but at the road. "Yeah, it does complicate things."

"So, your ex-girlfriend . . . she a shifter?"

"Yeah. I don't normally date shifters, but I guess I thought with her it would be different. Weres and shift-

ers are strongly attracted to each other. Animal magnetism, I guess," Alcide said, as an attempt at humor.

My boss, also a shifter, had been glad to make friends
with other shifters in the area. He had been hanging out
with a maenad ("dating" would be too sweet a word for
their relationship), but she'd moved on. Now, Sam was
hoping to find another compatible shifter. He felt more
comfortable with a strange human, like me, or another
shifter, than he did with regular women. When he'd told
me that, he'd meant it as a compliment, or maybe just
as a simple statement; but it had hurt me a little, though
my abnormality had been borne in on me since I was
very young.

Telepathy doesn't wait for puberty.

"How come?" I asked baldly. "How come you
thought it would be different?"

"She told me she was sterile. I found out she was on
birth control pills. Big difference. I'm not passing this
along. Even a shifter and a werewolf may have a child
who has to change at the full moon, though only kids
of a pure couple—both Weres or both shifters—can
change at will."

Food for thought, there. "So you normally date regular old girls. But doesn't it make it hard to date? Keeping secret such a big, ah, factor in your life?"

"Yeah," he admitted. "Dating regular girls can be a
pain. But I have to date someone." There was an edge
of desperation to his rumbly voice.

I gave that a long moment's contemplation, and then
I closed my eyes and counted to ten. I was missing Bill
in a most elemental and unexpected way. My first clue
had been the tug-below-the-waist I'd felt when I'd
watched my tape of *The Last of the Mohicans* the week
before and I'd fixated on Daniel Day-Lewis bounding
through the forest. If I could appear from behind a tree
before he saw Madeleine Stowe . . .

I was going to have to watch my step.

"So, if you bite someone, they won't turn into a were-wolf?" I decided to change the direction of my thoughts. Then I remembered the last time Bill had bitten me, and felt a rush of heat through . . . oh, *hell*.

"That's when you get your wolf-man. Like the ones in the movies. They die pretty quick, poor people. And that's not passed along, if they, ah, engender children in their human form. If it's when they're in their altered form, the baby is miscarried."

"How interesting." I could not think of one other thing to say.

"But there's that element of the supernatural, too, just like with vampires," Alcide said, still not looking in my direction. "The tie-in of genetics and the supernatural element, that's what no one seems to understand. We just can't tell the world we exist, like the vampires did. We'd be locked up in zoos, sterilized, ghettoized—because we're sometimes animals. Going public just seems to make the vampires glamorous and rich." He sounded more than a little bitter.

"So how come you're telling me all this, right off the bat? If it's such a big secret?" He had given me more information in ten minutes than I'd had from Bill in months.

"If I'm going to be spending a few days with you, it will make my life a lot easier if you know. I figure you have your own problems, and it seems the vampires have some power over you, too. I don't think you'll tell. And if the worst happens, and I've been utterly wrong about you, I'll ask Eric to pay you a visit and wipe out your memory." He shook his head in baffled irritation. "I don't know why, really. I just feel like I know you."

I couldn't think of a response to that, but I had to speak. Silence would lend too much importance to his last sentence. "I'm sorry the vampires have a hold on your dad. But I have to find Bill. If this is the only way I can do it, this is what I have to do. I at least owe him that much, even if . . ." My voice trailed off. I didn't want to finish the sentence. All the possible endings were too sad, too final.

He shrugged, a large movement on Alcide Herveaux. "Taking a pretty girl to a bar isn't that big a deal," he reassured me again, trying to bolster my spirits.

In his position, I might not have been so generous. "Is your dad a constant gambler?"

"Only since my mother died," Alcide said, after a long pause.

"I'm sorry." I kept my eyes off his face in case he needed some privacy. "I don't have either of my parents," I offered.

"They been gone long?"

"Since I was seven."

"Who raised you?"

"My grandmother raised me and my brother."

"She still living?"

"No. She died this year. She was murdered."

"Tough." He was matter-of-fact.

"Yeah." I had one more question. "Did both your parents tell you about yourself?"

"No. My grandfather told me when I was about thirteen. He'd noticed the signs. I just don't know orphaned Weres get through it without guidance."

"That would be really rough."

"We try to keep aware of all the Weres breeding in the area, so no one will go unwarned."

Even a secondhand warning would be better than no warning at all. But still, such a session would be a major trauma in anyone's life.

We stopped in Vicksburg to get gas. I offered to pay

for filling the tank, but Alcide told me firmly this could go on his books as a business expense, since he did in fact need to see some customers. He waved off my offer to pump the gas, too. He did accept the cup of coffee I bought him, with as many thanks as if it had been a new suit. It was a cold, bright day, and I took a brisk walk around the travel center to stretch my legs before climbing back into the cab of the truck.

Seeing the signs for the battlefield reminded me of one of the most taxing days I'd had as an adult. I found myself telling Alcide about my grandmother's favorite club, the Descendants of the Glorious Dead, and about their field trip to the battlefield two years before. I'd driven one car, Maxine Fortenberry (grandmother of one of my brother Jason's good buddies) another, and we'd toured at length. Each of the Descendants had brought a favorite text covering the siege, and an early stop at the visitors' center had gotten the Descendants all tanked up with maps and memorabilia. Despite the failure of Velda Cannon's Depends, we'd had a great time. We'd read every monument, we'd had a picnic lunch by the restored USS *Cairo*, and we'd gone home laden with souvenir booty and exhausted. We'd even gone into the Isle of Capri Casino for an hour of amazed staring, and some tentative slot machine feeding. It had been a very happy day for my grandmother, almost as happy a time as the evening she'd inveigled Bill into speaking at the Descendants meeting.

"Why did she want him to do that?" Alcide asked. He was smiling at my description of our supper stop at a Cracker Barrel.

"Bill's a vet," I said. "An Army vet, not an animal-doctor vet."

"So?" After a beat, he said, "You mean your boyfriend is a veteran of the *Civil War*?"

"Yeah. He was human then. He wasn't brought over until after the war. He had a wife and children." I could hardly keep calling him my boyfriend, since he'd been on the verge of leaving me for someone else.

"Who made him a vampire?" Alcide asked. We were in Jackson now, and he was making his way downtown to the apartment his company maintained.

"I don't know," I said. "He doesn't talk about it."

"That seems a little strange to me."

Actually, it seemed a little strange to me, too; but I figured it was something really personal, and when Bill wanted to tell me about it, he would. The relationship was very strong, I knew, between the older vampire and the one he'd "brought over."

"I guess he really isn't my boyfriend anymore," I admitted. Though "boyfriend" seemed a pretty pale term for what Bill had been to me.

"Oh, yeah?"

I flushed. I shouldn't have said anything. "But I still have to find him."

We were silent for a while after that. The last city I'd visited had been Dallas, and it was easy to see that Jackson was nowhere close to that size. (That was a big plus, as far as I was concerned.) Alcide pointed out the golden figure on the dome of the new capitol, and I admired it appropriately. I thought it was an eagle, but I wasn't sure, and I was a little embarrassed to ask. Did I need glasses? The building we were going to was close to the corner of High and State streets. It was not a new building; the brick had started out a golden tan, and now it was a grimy light brown.

"The apartments here are larger than they are in new buildings," Alcide said. "There's a small guest bedroom. Everything should be all ready for us. We use the apartment cleaning service."

I nodded silently. I could not remember if I'd ever been in an apartment building before. Then I realized I had, of course. There was a two-story U-shaped apartment building in Bon Temps. I had surely visited someone there; in the past seven years, almost every single person in Bon Temps had rented a place in Kingfisher Apartments at some point in his or her dating career.

Alcide's apartment, he told me, was on the top floor, the fifth. You drove in from the street down a ramp to park. There was a guard at the garage entrance, standing in a little booth. Alcide showed him a plastic pass. The heavyset guard, who had a cigarette hanging out of his mouth, barely glanced at the card Alcide held out before he pressed a button to raise the barrier. I wasn't too impressed with the security. I felt like I could whip that guy, myself. My brother, Jason, could pound him into the pavement.

We scrambled out of the truck and retrieved our bags from the rudimentary backseat. My hanging bag had fared pretty well. Without asking me, Alcide took my small suitcase. He led the way to a central block in the parking area, and I saw a gleaming elevator door. He punched the button, and it opened immediately. The elevator creaked its way up after Alcide punched the button marked with a 5. At least the elevator was very clean, and when the door swished open, so were the carpet and the hall beyond.

"They went condo, so we bought the place," Alcide said, as if it was no big deal. Yes, he and his dad had made some money. There were four apartments per floor, Alcide told me.

"Who are your neighbors?"

"Two state senators own 501, and I'm sure they've gone home for the holiday season," he said. "Mrs. Charles Osburgh the Third lives in 502, with her nurse. Mrs. Osburgh was a grand old lady until the past year.

I don't think she can walk anymore. Five-oh-three is empty right now, unless the realtor sold it this past two weeks." He unlocked the door to number 504, pushed it open, and gestured for me to enter ahead of him. I entered the silent warmth of the hall, which opened on my left into a kitchen enclosed by counters, not walls, so the eye was unobstructed in sweeping the living room/ dining area. There was a door immediately on my right, which probably opened onto a coat closet, and another a little farther down, which led into a small bedroom with a neatly made-up double bed. A door past that revealed a small bathroom with white-and-blue tiles and towels hung just so on the racks.

Across the living room, to my left, was a door that led into a larger bedroom. I peered inside briefly, not wanting to seem overly interested in Alcide's personal space. The bed in that room was a king. I wondered if Alcide and his dad did a lot of entertaining when they visited Jackson.

"The master bedroom has its own bath," Alcide explained. "I'd be glad to let you have the bigger room, but the phone's in there, and I'm expecting some business calls."

"The smaller bedroom is just fine," I said. I peeked around a little more after my bags were stowed in my room.

The apartment was a symphony in beige. Beige carpet, beige furniture. Sort of oriental bamboo-y patterned wallpaper with a beige background. It was very quiet and very clean.

As I hung my dresses in the closet, I wondered how many nights I'd have to go to the club. More than two, and I'd have to do some shopping. But that was impossible, at the least imprudent, on my budget. A familiar worry settled hard on my shoulders.

My grandmother hadn't had much to leave me, God

bless her, especially after her funeral expenses. The house had been a wonderful and unexpected gift.

The money she'd used to raise Jason and me, money that had come from an oil well that had petered out, was long gone. The fee I'd gotten paid for moonlighting for the Dallas vampires had mostly gone to buy the two dresses, pay my property taxes, and have a tree cut down because the previous winter's ice storm had loosened its roots and it had begun to lean too close to the house. A big branch had already fallen, damaging the tin roof a bit. Luckily, Jason and Hoyt Fortenberry had known enough about roofing to repair that for me.

I recalled the roofing truck outside of Belle Rive.

I sat on the bed abruptly. Where had that come from? Was I petty enough to be angry that my boyfriend had been thinking of a dozen different ways to be sure his descendants (the unfriendly and sometimes snooty Bellefleurs) prospered, while I, the love of his afterlife, worried herself to tears about her finances?

You bet, I was petty enough.

I should be ashamed of myself.

But later. My mind was not through toting up grievances.

As long as I was considering money (lack of), I wondered if it had even occurred to Eric when he dispatched me on this mission that since I'd be missing work, I wouldn't get paid. Since I wouldn't get paid, I couldn't pay the electric company, or the cable, or the phone, or my car insurance . . . though I had a moral obligation to find Bill, no matter what had happened to our relationship, right?

I flopped back on the bed and told myself that this would all work out. I knew, in the back of my mind, that all I had to do was sit down with Bill—assuming I ever got him back—and explain my situation to him, and he'd . . . he'd do something.

But I couldn't just take money from Bill. Of course, if we were married, it would be okay; husband and wife held all in common. But we couldn't get married. It was illegal.

And he hadn't asked me.

"Sookie?" a voice said from the doorway.

I blinked and sat up. Alcide was lounging against the jamb, his arms crossed over his chest.

"You okay?"

I nodded uncertainly.

"You missing him?"

I was too ashamed to mention my money troubles, and they weren't more important than Bill, of course. To simplify things, I nodded.

He sat beside me and put his arm around me. He was so warm. He smelled like Tide detergent, and Irish Spring soap, and man. I closed my eyes and counted to ten again.

"You miss him," he said, confirming. He reached across his body to take my left hand, and his right arm tightened around me.

*You don't* know *how I miss him,* I thought.

Apparently, once you got used to regular and spectacular sex, your body had a mind of its own (so to speak) when it was deprived of that recreation; to say nothing of missing the hugging and cuddling part. My body was begging me to knock Alcide Herveaux back onto the bed so it could have its way with him. *Right now.*

"I do miss him, no matter what problems we have," I said, and my voice came out tiny and shaky. I wouldn't open my eyes, because if I did, I might see on his face a tiny impulse, some little inclination, and that would be all it would take.

"What time do you think we should go to the club?" I asked, firmly steering in another direction.

He was so *warm*.

Other direction! "Would you like me to cook supper before we go?" Least I could do. I shot up off the bed like a bottle rocket; turned to face him with the most natural smile I could muster. Get out of close proximity, or jump his bones.

"Oh, let's go to the Mayflower Cafe. It looks like an old diner—it *is* an old diner—but you'll enjoy it. Everyone goes there—senators and carpenters, all kinds of people. They just serve beer, that okay?" I shrugged and nodded. That was fine with me. "I don't drink much," I told him.

"Me neither," he said. "Maybe because, every so often, my dad tends to drink too much. Then he makes bad decisions." Alcide seemed to regret having told me this. "After the Mayflower, we'll go to the club," Alcide said, much more briskly. "It gets dark real early these days, but the vamps don't show up till they've had some blood, picked up their dates, done some business. We should get there about ten. So we'll go out to eat about eight, if that suits you?"

"Sure, that'll be great." I was at a loss. It was only two in the afternoon. His apartment didn't need cleaning. There was no reason to cook. If I wanted to read, I had romance novels in my suitcase. But in my present condition, it was hardly likely to help my state of . . . mind.

"Listen, would it be okay if I ran out to visit some clients?" he asked.

"Oh, that would be fine." I thought it would be all to the good if he wasn't in my immediate vicinity. "You go do whatever you need to do. I have books to read, and there's the television." Maybe I could begin the mystery novel.

"If you want to . . . I don't know . . . my sister, Janice, owns a beauty shop about four blocks away, in one of the older neighborhoods. She married a local guy. You want to, you could walk over and get the works."

"Oh, I . . . well, that . . ." I didn't have the sophistication to think of a smooth and plausible refusal, when the glaring roadblock to such a treat was my lack of money.

Suddenly, comprehension crossed his face. "If you stopped by, it would give Janice the opportunity to look you over. After all, you're supposed to be my girlfriend, and she hated Debbie. She'd really enjoy a visit."

"You're being awful nice," I said, trying not to sound as confused and touched as I felt. "That's not what I expected."

"You're not what I expected, either," he said, and left his sister's shop number by the phone before heading out on his business.

# Chapter Five

JANICE HERVEAUX PHILLIPS (married two years, mother of one, I learned quickly) was exactly what I might have expected of a sister of Alcide's. She was tall, attractive, plainspoken, and confident; and she ran her business efficiently.

I seldom went into beauty parlors. My gran had always done her own home perms, and I had never colored my hair or done anything else to it, besides a trim now and then. When I confessed this to Janice, who'd noticed I was looking around me with the curiosity of the ignorant, her broad face split in a grin. "Then you'll need everything," she said with satisfaction.

"No, no, no," I protested anxiously. "Alcide—."

"Called me on his cell phone and made it clear I was to give you the works," Janice said. "And frankly, honey, anyone who helps him recover from that Debbie is my best friend."

I had to smile. "But I'll pay," I told her.

"No, your money's no good here," she said. "Even if you break up with Alcide tomorrow, just getting him through tonight will be worth it."

"Tonight?" I began to have a sinking feeling that once again, I didn't know everything there was to know.

"I happen to know that tonight that bitch is going to announce her engagement at that club they go to," Janice said.

Okay, this time what I didn't know was something pretty major. "She's marrying the—man she took up with after she dumped Alcide?" (I barely stopped myself from saying, "The shape-shifter?")

"Quick work, huh? What could he have that my brother doesn't have?"

"I can't imagine," I said with absolutely sincerity, earning a quick smile from Janice. There was sure to be a flaw in her brother somewhere—maybe Alcide came to the supper table in his underwear, or picked his nose in public.

"Well, if you find out, you let me know. Now, let's get you going." Janice glanced around her in a businesslike way. "Corinne is going to give you your pedicure and manicure, and Jarvis is going to do your hair. You sure have a great head of it," Janice said in a more personal way.

"All mine, all natural," I admitted.

"No color?"

"Nope."

"You're the lucky one," Janice said, shaking her head.

That was a minority opinion.

Janice herself was working on a client whose silver hair and gold jewelry proclaimed she was a woman of privilege, and while this cold-faced lady examined me with indifferent eyes, Janice fired off some instructions to her employees and went back to Ms. Big Bucks.

I had never been so pampered in my life. And everything was new to me. Corinne (manicures and pedicures), who was as plump and juicy as one of the sausages I'd cooked that morning, painted my toenails and fingernails screaming red to match the dress I was going to wear. The only male in the shop, Jarvis, had fingers as light and quick as butterflies. He was thin as a reed and artificially platinum blond. Entertaining me with a stream of chatter, he washed and set my hair and established me under the dryer. I was one chair down from the rich lady, but I got just as much attention. I had a *People* magazine to read, and Corinne brought me a Coke. It was so nice to have people urging me to relax.

I was feeling kind of roasted under the dryer when the timer binged. Jarvis got me out from under it and set me back in his chair. After consulting with Janice, he whipped his preheated curling iron from a sort of holster mounted on the wall, and painstakingly arranged my hair in loose curls trailing down my back. I looked spectacular. Looking spectacular makes you happy. This was the best I'd felt since Bill had left.

Janice came over to talk every moment she was able. I caught myself forgetting that I wasn't Alcide's real girlfriend, with a real chance of becoming Janice's sister-in-law. This kind of acceptance didn't come my way too often.

I was wishing I could repay her kindness in some way, when a chance presented itself. Jarvis's station mirrored Janice's, so my back was to Janice's customer's back. Left on my own while Jarvis went to get a bottle of the conditioner he thought I should try, I watched (in the mirror) Janice take off her earrings and put them in a little china dish. I might never have observed what happened next if I hadn't picked up a clear covetous thought from the rich lady's head, which was, simply, "Aha!" Janice walked away to get another towel, and in the clear reflection, I watched the silver-haired customer deftly sweep up the earrings and stuff them into her jacket pocket, while Janice's back was turned.

By the time I was finished, I'd figured out what to do.

I was just waiting to say good-bye to Jarvis, who'd had to go to the telephone; I knew he was talking to his mother, from the pictures I got from his head. So I slid out of my vinyl chair and walked over to the rich woman, who was writing a check for Janice.

" 'Scuse me," I said, smiling brilliantly. Janice looked a little startled, and the elegant woman looked snooty. This was a client who spent a lot of money here, and Janice wouldn't want to lose her. "You got a smear of hair gel on your jacket. If you'll please just slide out of it for a second, I'll get it right off."

She could hardly refuse. I grasped the jacket shoulders and gently tugged, and she automatically helped me slide the green-and-red plaid jacket down her arms. I carried it behind the screen that concealed the hair-washing area, and wiped at a perfectly clean area just for verisimilitude (a great word from my Word of the Day calendar). Of course, I also extracted the earrings and put them in my own pocket.

"There you are, good as new!" I beamed at her and helped her into the jacket.

"Thanks, Sookie," Janice said, too brightly. She suspected something was amiss.

"You're welcome!" I smiled steadily.

"Yes, of course," said the elegant woman, somewhat confusedly. "Well, I'll see you next week, Janice."

She clicked on her high heels all the way out the door, not looking back. When she was out of sight, I reached in my pocket and held out my hand to Janice. She opened her hand under mine, and I dropped the earrings into her palm.

"Good God almighty," Janice said, suddenly looking about five years older. "I forgot and left something where she could reach it."

"She does this all the time?"

"Yeah. That's why we're about the fifth beauty salon

she's patronized in the past ten years. The others put up with it for a while, but eventually she did that one thing too many. She's so rich, and so educated, and she was brought up right. I don't know why she does stuff like this."

We shrugged at each other, the vagaries of the white-collar well-to-do beyond our comprehension. It was a moment of perfect understanding. "I hope you don't lose her as a customer. I tried to be tactful," I said.

"And I really appreciate that. But I would have hated losing those earrings more than losing her as a client. My husband gave them to me. They tend to pinch after a while, and I didn't even think when I pulled them off."

I'd been thanked more than enough. I pulled on my own coat. "I better be off," I said. "I've really enjoyed the wonderful treat."

"Thank my brother," Janice said, her broad smile restored. "And, after all, you just paid for it." She held up the earrings.

I was smiling, too, as I left the warmth and camaraderie of the salon, but that didn't last too long. The thermometer had dropped and the sky was getting darker by the minute. I walked the distance back to the apartment building very briskly. After a chilly ride on a creaky elevator, I was glad to use the key Alcide had given me and step into the warmth. I switched on a lamp and turned on the television for a little company, and I huddled on the couch and thought about the pleasures of the afternoon. Once I'd thawed out, I realized Alcide must have turned down the thermostat. Though pleasant compared to the out-of-doors, the apartment was definitely on the cool side.

The sound of the key in the door roused me out of my reverie, and Alcide came in with a clipboard full of paperwork. He looked tired and preoccupied, but his face relaxed when he saw me waiting.

"Janice called me to tell me you'd come by," he said. His voice warmed up as he spoke. "She wanted me to say thank you again."

I shrugged. "I appreciate my hair and my new nails," I said. "I've never done that before."

"You've never been to a beauty shop before?"

"My grandmother went every now and then. I had my ends trimmed, once."

He looked as stunned as if I'd confessed I'd never seen a flush toilet.

To cover my embarrassment, I fanned my nails out for his admiration. I hadn't wanted very long ones, and these were the shortest ones Corinne could in all conscience manage, she had told me. "My toenails match," I told my host.

"Let's see," he said.

I untied my sneakers and pulled off my socks. I held out my feet. "Aren't they pretty?" I asked.

He was looking at me kind of funny. "They look great," he said quietly.

I glanced at the clock on top of the television. "I guess I better go get ready," I said, trying to figure out how to take a bath without affecting my hair and nails. I thought of Janice's news about Debbie. "You're really ready to dress up tonight, right?"

"Sure," he said gamely.

" 'Cause I'm going all out."

That interested him. "That would mean . . . ?"

"Wait and see." This was a nice guy, with a nice family, doing me a heavy-duty favor. Okay, he'd been coerced into it. But he was being extremely gracious to me, under any circumstances.

I ROLLED OUT of my room an hour later. Alcide was standing in the kitchen, pouring himself a Coke. It ran over the edge of the glass while he took me in.

That was a real compliment.

While Alcide mopped up the counter with a paper towel, he kept darting glances at me. I turned around slowly.

I was wearing red—screaming red, fire engine red. I was going to freeze most of the evening, because my dress didn't have any shoulders, though it did have long sleeves that you slid on separately. It zipped up the back. It flared below the hips, what there *was* below the hips. My grandmother would have flung herself across the doorsill to keep me from going out the door in this dress. I loved it. I had got it on extreme sale at Tara's Togs; I suspected Tara had kind of put it aside for me. Acting on a huge and unwise impulse, I'd bought the shoes and lipstick to go with it. And now the nails, thanks to Janice! I had a gray-and-black fringed silk shawl to wrap around myself, and a little bitty bag that matched my shoes. The bag was beaded.

"Turn around again," Alcide suggested a little hoarsely. He himself was wearing a conventional black suit with a white shirt and a green patterned tie that matched his eyes. Nothing, apparently, could tame his hair. Maybe he should have gone to Janice's beauty shop instead of me. He looked handsome and rough, though "attractive" might be a more accurate word than "handsome."

I rotated slowly. I wasn't confident enough to keep my eyebrows from arching in a silent question as I completed my turn.

"You look *mouthwatering*," he said sincerely. I released a breath I hadn't realized I'd been holding.

"Thanks," I said, trying not to beam like an idiot.

I had a trying time getting into Alcide's truck, what with the shortness of the dress and the highness of the heels, but with Alcide giving me a tactical boost, I managed.

Our destination was a small place on the corner of Capitol and Roach. It wasn't impressive from the outside, but the Mayflower Cafe was as interesting as Alcide had predicted. Some of the people at the tables scattered on the black-and-white tile floor were dressed to the nines, like Alcide and me. Some of them were wearing flannel and denim. Some had brought their own wine or liquor. I was glad we weren't drinking; Alcide had one beer, and that was it. I had iced tea. The food was really good, but not fancy. Dinner was long, drawn-out, and interesting. Lots of people knew Alcide, and they came by the table to say hello to him and to find out who I was. Some of these visitors were involved in the state government, some were in the building trade like Alcide, and some appeared to be friends of Alcide's dad's.

A few of them were not law-abiding men at all; even though I've always lived in Bon Temps, I know hoods when I see the product of their brains. I'm not saying they were thinking about bumping off anyone, or bribing senators, or anything specific like that. Their thoughts were greedy—greedy of money, greedy of me, and in one case, greedy of Alcide (to which he was completely oblivious, I could tell).

But most of all, these men—all of them—were greedy for power. I guess in a state capital, that lust for power was inevitable, even in as poverty-plagued a state as Mississippi.

The women with the greediest men were almost all extremely well groomed and very expensively dressed. For this one evening, I could match them, and I held my head up. One of them thought I looked like a high-priced whore, but I decided that was a compliment, at least for tonight. At least she thought I was expensive. One woman, a banker, knew Debbie the-former-girlfriend, and she examined me from head to toe, thinking Debbie would want a detailed description.

None of these people, of course, knew one thing about me. It was wonderful to be among people who had no idea of my background and upbringing, my occupation or my abilities. Determined to enjoy the feeling, I concentrated on not speaking unless I was spoken to, not spilling any food on my beautiful dress, and minding my manners, both table and social. While I was enjoying myself, I figured it would be a pity if I caused Alcide any embarrassment, since I was entering his life so briefly.

Alcide snatched the bill before I could reach it, and scowled at me when I opened my mouth to protest. I finally gave a little bob of my head. After that silent struggle, I was glad to observe that Alcide was a generous tipper. That raised him in my estimation. To tell the truth, he was entirely too high in my estimation already. I was on the alert to pick out something negative about the man. When we got back in Alcide's pickup— this time he gave me even more help when he boosted me up to the seat, and I was pretty confident he enjoyed the procedure—we were both quiet and thoughtful.

"You didn't talk much at supper," he said. "You didn't have a good time?"

"Oh, sure, I did. I just didn't think it was a real good time to start broadcasting any opinions."

"What did you think of Jake O'Malley?" O'Malley, a man in his early sixties with thick steel-colored eyebrows, had stood talking to Alcide for at least five minutes, all the while stealing little sideways glances at my boobs.

"I think he's planning on screwing you six ways from Sunday."

It was lucky we hadn't pulled away from the curb yet.

Alcide switched on the overhead light and looked at me. His face was grim. "What are you talking about?" he asked.

"He's going to underbid you on the next job, because he's bribed one of the women in your office—Thomasina something?—to let him know what you all's bid is. And then—"

"What?"

I was glad the heater was running full blast. When werewolves got mad, you could feel it in the air around you. I had so hoped I wouldn't have to explain myself to Alcide. It had been so neat, being unknown.

"You are . . . what?" he asked, to make sure I understood him.

"Telepath," I said, kind of mumbling.

A long silence fell, while Alcide digested this.

"Did you hear *anything* good?" he asked, finally.

"Sure. Mrs. O'Malley wants to jump your bones," I told him, smiling brightly. I had to remind myself not to pull at my hair.

"That's good?"

"Comparatively," I said. "Better to be screwed physically than financially." Mrs. O'Malley was at least twenty years younger than Mr. O'Malley, and she was the most groomed person I'd ever seen. I was betting she brushed her eyebrows a hundred strokes a night.

He shook his head. I had no clear picture of what he was thinking. "What about me, you read me?"

Aha. "Shape-shifters are not so easy," I said. "I can't pick out a clear line of thought, more a general mood, intentions, sort of. I guess if you thought directly at me, I'd get it. You want to try? Think something at me."

*The dishes I use at the apartment have a border of yellow roses.*

"I wouldn't call them roses," I said doubtfully. "More like zinnias, if you ask me."

I could feel his withdrawal, his wariness. I sighed. Same old, same old. It sort of hurt, since I liked him. "But just to pick your own thoughts out of your head, that's a murky area," I said. "I can't consistently do that, with Weres and shifters." (A few Supes were fairly easy to read, but I saw no need to bring that up at this point in time.)

"Thank God."

"Oh?" I said archly, in an attempt to lighten the mood. "What are you afraid I'll read?"

Alcide actually grinned at me before he turned off the dome light and we pulled out of our parking space. "Never mind," he said, almost absently. "Never mind. So what you're going to be doing tonight is reading minds, to try to pick up clues about your vampire's whereabouts?"

"That's right. I can't read vampires; they don't seem to put out any brainwaves. That's just how I put it. I don't know how I do this, or if there's a scientific way to phrase it." I wasn't exactly lying: Undead minds really were unreadable—except for a little split second's glimpse every now and then (which hardly counted, and no one could know about). If vampires thought I could read their minds, not even Bill could save me. If he would.

Every time I forgot for a second that our relationship had radically changed, it hurt all over again to be reminded.

"So what's your plan?"

"I'm aiming for humans dating or serving local vampires. Humans were the actual abductors. He was snatched in daytime. At least, that's what they told Eric."

"I should have asked you about this earlier," he said, mostly to himself. "Just in case I hear something the regular way—through my ears—maybe you should tell me the circumstances."

As we drove by what Alcide said was the old train station, I gave him a quick summary. I caught a glimpse of a street sign reading "Amite" as we pulled up to an awning that stretched over a deserted length of sidewalk in the outskirts of downtown Jackson. The area directly under the awning was lit with a brilliant and cold light. Somehow that length of sidewalk seemed creepily ominous, especially since the rest of the street was dark. Uneasiness crawled down my back. I felt a deep reluctance to stop at that bit of sidewalk.

It was a stupid feeling, I told myself. It was just a stretch of cement. No beasts were in sight. After the businesses closed at five, downtown Jackson was not exactly teeming, even under ordinary circumstances. I was willing to bet that most of the sidewalks in the whole state of Mississippi were bare on this cold December night.

But there was something ominous in the air, a watchfulness laced with a charge of malice. The eyes observing us were invisible; but they were observing us, nonetheless. When Alcide climbed out of the truck and came around to help me down, I noticed that he left the keys in the ignition. I swung my legs outward and put my hands on his shoulders, my long silk stole wound firmly around me and trailing behind, fringe trembling in a gust of chilled air. I pushed off as he lifted, and then I was on the sidewalk.

The truck drove away.

I looked at Alcide sideways, to see if this was startling to him, but he looked quite matter-of-fact. "Vehicles parked in front would attract attention from the general public," he told me, his voice hushed in the vast silence of that coldly lit bit of pavement.

"They can come in? Regular people?" I asked, nodding toward the single metal door. It looked as uninviting as a door can look. There was no name anywhere on it, or on the building, for that matter. No Christmas decorations, either. (Of course, vampires don't observe holidays, except for Halloween. It's the ancient festival of Samhain dressed up in trappings that the vamps find delightful. So Halloween's a great favorite, and it's celebrated worldwide in the vamp community.)

"Sure, if they want to pay a twenty-dollar cover charge to drink the worst drinks in five states. Served by the rudest waiters. Very slowly."

I tried to smother my smile. This was not a smiley kind of place. "And if they stick that out?"

"There's no floor show, no one speaks to them, and if they last much longer, they find themselves out on the sidewalk getting into their car with no memory of how they got there."

He grasped the handle of the door and pulled it open. The dread that soaked the air did not seem to affect Alcide.

We stepped into a tiny hall that was blocked by another door after about four feet. There, again, I knew we were being watched, though I couldn't see a camera or a peephole anywhere.

"What's the name of this place?" I whispered.

"The vamp that owns it calls it Josephine's," he said, just as quietly. "But Weres call it Club Dead."

I thought about laughing, but the inner door opened just then.

The doorman was a goblin.

I had never seen one before, but the word "goblin" popped into my mind as if I had a supernatural dictionary printed on the inside of my eyeballs. He was very short and very cranky-looking, with a knobby face and broad hands. His eyes were full of fire and malignance. He glared up at us as if customers were the last things he needed.

Why any ordinary person would walk into Josephine's

after the cumulative effect of the haunted sidewalk, the vanishing vehicle, and the goblin at the door . . . well, some people are just born asking to be killed, I guess.

"Mr. Herveaux," the goblin said slowly, in a deep, growly voice. "Good to have you back. Your companion is . . . ?"

"Miss Stackhouse," Alcide said. "Sookie, this is Mr. Hob." The goblin examined me with glowing eyes. He looked faintly troubled, as if he couldn't quite fit me into a slot; but after a second, he stood aside to let us pass.

Josephine's was not very crowded. Of course, it was somewhat early for its patrons. After the eerie build-up, the large room looked almost disappointingly like any other bar. The serving area itself was in the middle of the room, a large square bar with a lift-up panel for the staff to go to and fro. I wondered if the owner had been watching reruns of *Cheers*. The glasses hung down, suspended on racks, and there were artificial plants and low music and dim lighting. There were polished bar stools set evenly all around the square. To the left of the bar was a small dance floor, and even farther left was a tiny stage for a band or a disc jockey. On the other three sides of the square were the usual small tables, about half of which were in use.

Then I spotted the list of ambiguous rules on the wall, rules designed to be understood by the regular habitués, but not by the occasional tourist. "No Changing on the Premises," one said sternly. (Weres and shifters could not switch from animal to human when they were at the bar; well, I could understand that.) "No Biting of Any Kind," said another. "No Live Snacks," read a third. Ick.

The vampires were scattered throughout the bar, some with others of their own kind, some with humans. There was a raucous party of shifters in the southeast corner, where several tables had been drawn together to accommodate the size of the party. The center of this group appeared to be a tall young woman with gleaming short black hair, an athletic build, and a long, narrow face. She was draped over a square man of her own age, which I guessed to be about twenty-eight. He had round eyes and a flat nose and the softest looking hair I'd ever seen—it was almost baby fine, and so light a blond, it was nearly white. I wondered if this were the engagement party, and I wondered if Alcide had known it was to take place. His attention was definitely focused on that group.

Naturally, I immediately checked out what the other women in the bar were wearing. The female vampires and the women with male vampires were dressed about at my level. The shifter females tended to dress down a bit more. The black-haired woman I'd pegged for Debbie was wearing a gold silk blouse and skintight brown leather pants, with boots. She laughed at some comment of the blond man's, and I felt Alcide's arm grow rigid under my fingers. Yep, this must be the ex-girlfriend, Debbie. Her good time had certainly escalated since she'd glimpsed Alcide's entrance.

*Phony bitch*, I decided in the time it takes to snap your fingers, and I made up my mind to behave accordingly. The goblin Hob led the way to an empty table within view of the happy party, and held out a chair for me. I nodded to him politely, and unwound my wrap, folding it and tossing it onto an empty chair. Alcide sat in the chair to my right, so he could put his back to the corner where the shifters were having such a raucous good time.

A bone-thin vampire came to take our order. Alcide asked my pleasure with an inclination of his head. "A champagne cocktail," I said, having no idea what one tasted like. I'd never gone to the trouble to mix myself one at Merlotte's, but now that I was in someone else's

bar, I thought I'd give it a shot. Alcide ordered a Hei-
neken. Debbie was casting many glances our way, so I
leaned forward and smoothed back a lock of Alcide's
curly black hair. He looked surprised, though of course
Debbie couldn't see that.

"Sookie?" he said, rather doubtfully.

I smiled at him, not my nervous smile—because I
wasn't, for once. Thanks to Bill, I now had a little con-
fidence about my own physical attractiveness. "Hey, I'm
your date, remember? I'm acting date-like," I told him.

The thin vampire brought our drinks just then, and I
clinked my glass against his bottle. "To our joint venture," I said, and his eyes lit up. We sipped.

I loved champagne cocktails.

"Tell me more about your family," I said, because I
enjoyed listening to his rumbly voice. I would have to
wait until there were more humans in the bar before I
began listening in to others' thoughts.

Alcide obligingly began telling me about how poor
his dad had been when he started his surveying business,
and how long it had taken for him to prosper. He was
just beginning to tell me about his mother when Debbie
sashayed up.

It had only been a matter of time.

"Hello, Alcide," she purred. Since he hadn't been able
to see her coming, his strong face quivered. "Who's your
new friend? Did you borrow her for the evening?"

"Oh, longer than that," I said clearly, and smiled at
Debbie, a smile that matched her own for sincerity.

"Really?" If her eyebrows had crawled any higher,
they'd have been in heaven.

"Sookie is a good friend," Alcide said impassively.

"Oh?" Debbie doubted his word. "It wasn't too long
ago you told me you'd never have another 'friend' if
you couldn't have . . . Well." She smirked.

I covered Alcide's huge hand with my own and gave
her a look that implied much.

"Tell me," Debbie said, her lips curling in a skeptical way, "how do you like that birthmark of Alcide's?"

Who could have predicted she was willing to be a bitch so openly? Most women try to hide it, at least from strangers.

*It's on my right butt cheek. It's shaped like a rabbit.* Well, how nice. Alcide had remembered what I'd said, and he'd thought directly at me.

"I love bunnies," I said, still smiling, my hand drifting down Alcide's back to caress, very lightly, the top of his right buttock.

For a second, I saw sheer rage on Debbie's face. She was so focused, so controlled, that her mind was a lot less opaque than most shifters'. She was thinking about her owl fiancé, about how he wasn't as good in the sack as Alcide, but he had a lot of ready cash and he was willing to have children, which Alcide wasn't. And she was stronger than the owl, able to dominate him.

She was no demon (of course, her fiancé would have a really short shelf life if she *were*) but she was no sweetie, either.

Debbie still could have recovered the situation, but her discovery that I knew Alcide's little secret made her nuts. She made a big mistake.

She raked me over with a glare that would have paralyzed a lion. "Looks like you went to Janice's salon today," she said, taking in the casually tumbled curls, the fingernails. Her own straight black hair had been cut in asymmetrical clumps, tiny locks of different lengths, making her look a little like a dog in a very good show, maybe an Afghan. Her narrow face increased the resemblance. "Janice never sends anyone out looking like they live in this century."

Alcide opened his mouth, rage tensing all his muscles. I laid my hand on his arm.

"What do *you* think of my hair?" I asked softly, moving my head so it slithered over my bare shoulders. I took his hand and held it gently to the curls falling over my chest. Hey, I was pretty good at this! Sookie the sex kitten.

Alcide caught his breath. His fingers trailed through the length of my hair, and his knuckles brushed my collarbone. "I think it's beautiful," he said, and his voice was both sincere and husky.

I smiled at him.

"I guess instead of borrowing you, he rented you," Debbie said, goaded into irreparable error.

It was a terrible insult, to both of us. It took every bit of resolution I had to hang on to a ladylike self-control. I felt the primitive self, the truer me, swim nearly to the surface. We sat staring at the shifter, and she blanched at our silence. "Okay, I shouldn't have said that," she said nervously. "Just forget it."

Because she was a shifter, she'd beat me in a fair fight. Of course, I had no intention of fighting fair, if it came to that.

I leaned over and touched one red fingertip to her leather pants. "Wearing Cousin Elsie?" I asked.

Unexpectedly, Alcide burst into laughter. I smiled at him as he doubled over, and when I looked up, Debbie was stalking back to her party, who had fallen silent during our exchange.

I reminded myself to skip going to the ladies' room alone this evening.

BY THE TIME we ordered our second drinks, the place was full. Some Were friends of Alcide's came in, a large group—Weres like to travel in packs, I understand. Shifters, it depended on the animal they most often shifted to. Despite their theoretical versatility, Sam had told me that shape-shifters most often changed to the same animal every time, some creature they had a special affinity for. And they might call themselves by that animal: weredog, or werebat, or weretiger. But never just "Weres"—that term was reserved for the wolves. The true werewolves scorned such variance in form, and they didn't think much of shifters in general. They, the werewolves, considered themselves the cream of the shapeshifting world.

Shifters, on the other hand, Alcide explained, thought of werewolves as the thugs of the supernatural scene. "And you do find a lot of us in the building trades," he said, as if he were trying hard to be fair. "Lots of Weres are mechanics, or brick masons, or plumbers, or cooks."

"Useful occupations," I said.

"Yes," he agreed. "But not exactly white-collar. So though we all cooperate with each other, to some extent, there's a lot of class discrimination."

A small group of Weres in motorcycle gear strode in. They wore the same sort of leather vest with wolf's heads on the back that had been worn by the man who'd attacked me at Merlotte's. I wondered if they'd started searching for their comrade yet. I wondered if they had a clearer idea of who they were looking for, what they'd do if they realized who I was. The four men ordered several pitchers of beer and began talking very secretively, heads close together and chairs pulled right up to the table.

A deejay—he appeared to be a vampire—began to play records at the perfect level; you could be sure what the song was, but you could still talk.

"Let's dance," Alcide suggested.

I hadn't expected that; but it would put me closer to the vampires and their humans, so I accepted. Alcide held my chair for me, and took my hand as we went over to the minuscule dance floor. The vampire changed the music from some heavy metal thing to Sarah Mc-

Lachlan's "Good Enough," which is slow, but with a beat.

I can't sing, but I can dance; as it happened, Alcide could, too.

The good thing about dancing is that you don't have to talk for a while, if you feel chatted out. The bad thing is it makes you hyperconscious of your partner's body. I had already been uncomfortably aware of Alcide's— excuse me—animal magnetism. Now, so close to him, swaying in rhythm with him, following his every move, I found myself in a kind of trance. When the song was over, we stayed on the little dance floor, and I kept my eyes on the floor. When the next song started up, a faster piece of music—though for the life of me I couldn't have told you what—we began dancing again, and I spun and dipped and moved with the werewolf.

Then the muscular squat man sitting at a bar stool behind us said to his vampire companion, "He hasn't talked yet. And Harvey called today. He said they searched the house and didn't find anything."

"Public place," said his companion, in a sharp voice. The vampire was a very small man—perhaps he'd become a vampire when men were shorter.

I knew they were talking about Bill, because the human was thinking of Bill when he said, "He hasn't talked." And the human was an exceptional broadcaster, both sound and visuals coming through clearly.

When Alcide tried to lead me away from their orbit, I resisted his lead. Looking up into his surprised face, I cut my eyes toward the couple. Comprehension filtered into his eyes, but he didn't look happy.

Dancing and trying to read another person's mind at the same time is not something I'd recommend. I was straining mentally, and my heart was pounding with shock at the glimpse of Bill's image. Luckily, Alcide excused himself to go to the men's room just then, park-

ing me on a stool at the bar right by the vampire. I tried
to keep looking around at different dancers, at the deejay, at anything but the man to the vampire's left, the
man whose mind I was trying to pick through.

He was thinking about what he'd done during the day;
he'd been trying to keep someone awake, someone who
really needed to sleep—a vampire. Bill.

Keeping a vampire awake during the day was the
worst kind of torture. It was difficult to do, too. The
compulsion to sleep when the sun came up was imper-
ative, and the sleep itself was like death.

Somehow, it had never crossed my mind—I guess
since I'm an American—that the vampires who had
snatched Bill might be resorting to evil means to get him
to talk. If they wanted the information, naturally they
weren't just going to wait around until Bill felt like telling them. Stupid me—dumb, dumb, dumb. Even knowing Bill had betrayed me, even knowing he had thought
of leaving me for his vampire lover, I was struck deep
with pain for him.

Engrossed in my unhappy thoughts, I didn't recognize
trouble when it was standing right beside me. Until it
grabbed me by the arm.

One of the Were gang members, a big dark-haired
man, very heavy and very smelly, had grabbed hold of
my arm. He was getting his greasy fingerprints all over
my beautiful red sleeves, and I tried to pull away from
him.

"Come to our table and let us get to know you, sweet
thing," he said, grinning at me. He had a couple of earrings in one ear. I wondered what happened to them
during the full moon. But almost immediately, I realized
I had more serious problems to solve. The expression
on his face was too frank; men just didn't look at women
that way unless those women were standing on a street

corner in hot pants and a bra: in other words, he thought I was a sure thing.

"No, thank you," I said politely. I had a weary, wary feeling that this wasn't going to be the end of it, but I might as well try. I'd had plenty of experience at Merlotte's with pushy guys, but I always had backup at Merlotte's. Sam wouldn't tolerate the servers being pawed or insulted.

"Sure, darlin'. You want to come see us," he said insistently.

For the first time in my life, I wished Bubba were with me.

I was getting far too used to people who bothered me meeting a bad end. And maybe I was getting too accustomed to having some of my problems solved by others.

I thought of scaring the Were by reading his mind. It would have been an easy read—he was wide open, for a Were. But not only were his thoughts boring and unsurprising (lust, aggression), if his gang was charged with searching for the girlfriend of Bill the vampire, and they knew she was a barmaid and a telepath, and they found a telepath, well . . .

"No, I don't want to come sit with you," I said definitely. "Leave me alone." I slid off the stool so I wouldn't be trapped in one position.

"You don't have no man here. We're real men, honey." With his free hand, he cupped himself. Oh, charming. That really made me horny. "We'll keep you happy."

"You couldn't make me happy if you were Santa Claus," I said, stomping on his instep with all my strength. If he hadn't been wearing motorcycle boots, it might have been effective. As it was, I came close to breaking the heel of my shoe. I was mentally cursing my false nails because they made it hard to form a fist. I was going to hit him in the nose with my free hand; a blow to the nose really hurts badly. He'd have to let go.

He snarled at me, really snarled, when my heel hit his instep, but he didn't loosen his grip. His free hand seized my bare shoulder, and his fingers dug in.

I'd been trying to be quiet, hoping to resolve this without hubbub, but I was past that point right now. "Let *go*!" I yelled, as I made a heroic attempt to knee him in the balls. His thighs were heavy and his stance narrow, so I couldn't get a good shot. But I did make him flinch, and though his nails gouged my shoulder, he let go.

Part of this was due to the fact that Alcide had a hold on the scruff of his neck. And Mr. Hob stepped in, just as the other gang members surged around the bar to come to the aid of their buddy. The goblin who'd ushered us into the club doubled as the bouncer, it happened. Though he looked like a very small man on the outside, he wrapped his arms around the biker's waist and lifted him with ease. The biker began shrieking, and the smell of burned flesh began to circulate in the bar. The rail-thin bartender switched on a heavy-duty exhaust fan, which helped a lot, but we could hear the screams of the biker all the way down a narrow dark hall I hadn't noticed before. It must lead to the rear exit of the building. Then there was a big clang, a yell, and the same clang sounding again. Clearly, the back door of the bar had been opened and the offender tossed outside.

Alcide swung around to face the biker's friends, while I stood shaking with reaction behind him. I was bleeding from the imprints of the biker's fingernails in the flesh of my shoulder. I needed some Neosporin, which was what my grandmother had put on every injury when I'd objected to Campho-Phenique. But any little first-aid concerns were going to have to wait: It looked as though we faced another fight. I glanced around for a weapon, and saw the bartender had gotten a baseball bat out and laid it on the bar. She was keeping a wary eye on the situation. I seized the bat and went to stand beside Alcide. I swung the bat into position and waited for the next move. As my brother, Jason, had taught me—based on his many fights in bars, I'm afraid—I picked out one man in particular, pictured myself swinging the bat and bringing it to strike on his knee, which was more accessible to me than his head. That would bring him down, sure enough.

Then someone stepped into the no-man's-land between Alcide and me and the Weres. It was the small vampire, the one who'd been talking with the human whose mind had been such a source of unpleasant information.

Maybe five feet five with his shoes on, he was also slight of build. When he'd died, he'd been in his early twenties, I guessed. Clean-shaven and very pale, he had eyes the color of bitter chocolate, a jarring contrast with his red hair.

"Miss, I apologize for this unpleasantness," he said, his voice soft and his accent heavily Southern. I hadn't heard an accent that thick since my great-grandmother had died twenty years ago.

"I'm sorry the peace of the bar has been disturbed," I said, summoning up as much dignity as I could while gripping a baseball bat. I'd instinctively kicked off my heels so I could fight. I straightened up from my fighting stance, and inclined my head to him, acknowledging his authority.

"You men should leave now," the little man said, turning to the group of Weres, "after apologizing to this lady and her escort."

They milled around uneasily, but none wanted to be the first to back down. One of them who was apparently younger and dumber than the others, was a blond with a heavy beard and a bandanna around his head in a particularly stupid-looking style. He had the fire of battle in his eyes; his pride couldn't handle the whole situation. The biker telegraphed his move before he'd even begun it, and quick as lightning I held out the bat to the vampire, who snatched it in a move so fast, I couldn't even glimpse it. He used it to break the werewolf's leg.

The bar was absolutely silent as the screaming biker was carried out by his friends. The Weres chorused, "Sorry, sorry," as they lifted the blond and removed him from of the bar.

Then the music started again, the small vampire returned the bat to the bartender, Alcide began checking me over for damage, and I began shaking.

"I'm fine," I said, pretty much just wanting everyone to look somewhere else.

"But you're bleeding, my dear," said the vampire.

It was true; my shoulder was trailing blood from the biker's fingernails. I knew etiquette. I leaned toward the vampire, offering him the blood.

"Thank you," he said instantly, and his tongue flicked out. I knew I would heal better and quicker with his saliva anyway, so I held quite still, though to tell the truth, it was like letting someone feel me up in public. Despite my discomfort, I smiled, though I know it can't have been a comfortable smile. Alcide held my hand, which was reassuring.

"Sorry I didn't come out quicker," he said.

"Not something you can predict." Lick, lick, lick. Oh, come on, I had to have stopped bleeding by now.

The vampire straightened, ran his tongue over his lips, and smiled at me. "That was quite an experience. May I introduce myself? I'm Russell Edgington."

Russell Edgington, the king of Mississippi; from the reaction of the bikers, I had suspected as much. "Pleased to meet you," I said politely, wondering if I should curtsey. But he hadn't introduced himself by his title. "I'm

Sookie Stackhouse, and this is my friend Alcide Herveaux."

"I've known the Herveaux family for years," the king of Mississippi said. "Good to see you, Alcide. How's that father of yours?" We might have been standing in the Sunday sunlight outside the First Presbyterian Church, rather than in a vampire bar at midnight.

"Fine, thank you," Alcide said, somewhat stiffly. "We're sorry there was trouble."

"Not your fault," the vampire said graciously. "Men sometimes have to leave their ladies alone, and ladies are not responsible for the bad manners of fools." Edgington actually bowed to me. I had no idea what to do in response, but an even deeper head-inclination seemed safe. "You're like a rose blooming in an untended garden, my dear."

*And you're full of bull hockey.* "Thank you, Mr. Edgington," I said, casting my eyes down lest he read the skepticism in them. Maybe I should have called him "Your Highness"? "Alcide, I'm afraid I need to call it a night," I said, trying to sound soft and gentle and shaken. It was a little too easy.

"Of course, darlin'," he said instantly. "Let me get your wrap and purse." He began making his way to our table immediately, God bless him.

"Now, Miss Stackhouse, we want you to come back tomorrow night," Russell Edgington said. His human friend stood behind Edgington, his hands resting on Edgington's shoulders. The small vampire reached up and patted one of those hands. "We don't want you scared off by the bad manners of one individual."

"Thanks, I'll mention that to Alcide," I said, not letting any enthusiasm leak into my voice. I hoped I appeared subservient to Alcide without being spineless. Spineless people didn't last long around vampires. Russell Edgington believed he was projecting the appearance of an old-style Southern gentleman, and if that was his thing, I might as well feed it.

Alcide returned, and his face was grim. "I'm afraid your wrap had an accident," he said, and I realized he was furious. "Debbie, I guess."

My beautiful silk shawl had a big hole burned in it. I tried to keep my face impassive, but I didn't manage very well. Tears actually welled up in my eyes, I suppose because the incident with the biker had shaken me already.

Edgington, of course, was soaking this all in.

"Better the shawl than me," I said, attempting a shrug. I made the corners of my mouth turn up. At least my little purse appeared intact, though I hadn't had any more in it than a compact and a lipstick, and enough cash to pay for supper. To my intense embarrassment, Alcide shrugged out of his suit coat and held it for me to slide into. I began to protest, but the look on his face said he wasn't going to take no for an answer.

"Good night, Miss Stackhouse," the vampire said. "Herveaux, see you tomorrow night? Does your business keep you in Jackson?"

"Yes, it does," Alcide said pleasantly. "It was good to talk to you, Russell."

THE TRUCK WAS outside the club when we emerged. The sidewalk seemed no less full of menace than it had when we arrived. I wondered how all these effects were achieved, but I was too depressed to question my escort.

"You shouldn't have given me your coat, you must be freezing," I said, after we'd driven a couple of blocks.

"I have on more clothes than you," Alcide said.

He wasn't shivering like I was, even without his coat. I huddled in it, enjoying the silk lining, and the warmth, and his smell.

"I should never have left you by yourself with those jerks in the club."

"Everyone has to go to the bathroom," I said mildly.

"I should have asked someone else to sit with you."

"I'm a big girl. I don't need a perpetual guard. I handle little incidents like that all the time at the bar." If I sounded weary of it, I was. You just don't get to see the best side of men when you're a barmaid; even at a place like Merlotte's, where the owner watches out for his servers and almost all the clientele is local.

"Then you shouldn't be working there." Alcide sounded very definite.

"Okay, marry me and take me away from all this," I said, deadpan, and got a frightened look in return. I grinned at him. "I have to make my living, Alcide. And mostly, I like my job."

He looked unconvinced and thoughtful. It was time to change the subject.

"They've got Bill," I said.

"You know for sure."

"Yeah."

"Why? What does he know that Edgington would want to know so badly, badly enough to risk a war?"

"I can't tell you."

"But you do know?"

To tell him would be to say I trusted him. I was in the same kind of danger as Bill if it was known that I knew what he knew. And I'd break a lot faster.

"Yes," I said. "I know."

# *Chapter Six*

WE WERE SILENT in the elevator. As Alcide unlocked his apartment, I leaned against the wall. I was a mess: tired, conflicted, and agitated by the fracas with the biker and Debbie's vandalism.

I felt like apologizing, but I didn't know what for.

"Good night," I said, at the door to my room. "Oh, here. Thanks." I shrugged out of his coat and held it out to him. He hung it over the back of one of the bar stools at the eat-in counter.

"Need help with your zipper?" he asked.

"It would be great if you could get it started." I turned my back to him. He'd zipped it up the last couple of inches when I was getting dressed, and I appreciated his thinking of this before he vanished into his room.

I felt his big fingers against my back, and the little hiss of the zipper. Then something unexpected happened; I felt him touch me again.

I shivered all over as his fingers trailed down my skin.

I didn't know what to do.

I didn't know what I wanted to do.

I made myself turn to face him. His face was as uncertain as mine.

"Worst possible time," I said. "You're on the rebound. I'm looking for my boyfriend; granted, he's my unfaithful boyfriend, but still . . ."

"Bad timing," he agreed, and his hands settled on my shoulders. Then he bent down and kissed me. It took about a half a second for my arms to go around his waist and his tongue to slide into my mouth. He kissed soft. I wanted to run my fingers through his hair and find out how broad his chest was and if his butt was really as high and round as it looked in his pants . . . oh, hell. I gently pushed back.

"Bad timing," I said. I flushed, realizing that with my dress half unzipped, Alcide could see my bra and the tops of my bosom easily. Well, it was good I had a pretty bra on.

"Oh, God," he said, having gotten an eyeful. He made a supreme effort and squeezed those green eyes shut. "Bad timing," he agreed again. "Though I can hope that, real soon, it might seem like better timing."

I smiled. "Who knows?" I said, and stepped back into my room while I could still make myself move in that direction. After shutting the door gently, I hung up the red dress, pleased it still looked good and unstained. The sleeves were a disaster, with greasy fingerprints and a little blood on them. I sighed regretfully.

I'd have to flit from door to door to use the bathroom. I didn't want to be a tease, and my robe was definitely short, nylon, and pink. So I scooted, because I could hear Alcide rummaging around in the kitchen. What with one thing and another, I was in the little bathroom for a while. When I came out, all the lights in the apartment were off except the one in my bedroom. I closed the shades, feeling a little silly doing so since no other building on the block was five stories high. I put on my pink nightgown, and crawled in the bed to read a chapter of my romance by way of calming down. It was the one where the heroine finally beds the hero, so it didn't work too well, but I did stop thinking about the biker's skin burning from contact with the goblin, and about Debbie's malicious narrow face. And about the idea of Bill being tortured.

The love scene (actually, the sex scene) steered my mind more toward Alcide's warm mouth.

I switched off the bedside lamp after I'd put my bookmark in my book. I snuggled down in the bed and piled the covers high on top of me, and felt—finally—warm and safe.

Someone knocked at my window.

I let out a little shriek. Then, figuring who it must be, I yanked on my robe, belted it, and opened the shades.

Sure enough, Eric was floating just outside. I switched on the lamp again, and struggled with the unfamiliar window.

"What the hell do you want?" I was saying, as Alcide dashed into the room.

I barely spared him a glance over my shoulder. "You better leave me alone and let me get some sleep," I told Eric, not caring if I sounded like an old scold, "and you better stop showing up outside places in the middle of the night and expecting me to let you in!"

"Sookie, let me in," Eric said.

"No! Well, actually, this is Alcide's place. Alcide, what you want to do?"

I turned to look at him for the first time, and tried not to let my mouth fall open. Alcide slept in those long drawstring pants, period. Whoa. If he'd been shirtless thirty minutes before, the timing might have seemed just perfect.

"What do you want, Eric?" Alcide asked, much more calmly than I had done.

"We need to talk," Eric said, sounding impatient.

"If I let him in now, can I rescind it?" Alcide asked me.

"Sure." I grinned at Eric. "Any moment, you can rescind it."

"Okay. You can come in, Eric." Alcide took the screen off the window, and Eric slid in feetfirst. I eased the window shut behind him. Now I was cold again. There was gooseflesh all over Alcide's chest, too, and his nipples . . . I forced myself to keep an eye on Eric.

Eric gave both of us a sharp look, his blue eyes as brilliant as sapphires in the lamplight. "What have you found out, Sookie?"

"The vampires here do have him."

Eric's eyes may have widened a little, but that was his only reaction. He appeared to be thinking intently.

"Isn't it a little dangerous for you to be on Edgington's turf, unannounced?" Alcide asked. He was doing his leaning-against-the-wall thing again. He and Eric were both big men and the room really seemed crowded all of a sudden. Maybe their egos were using up all the oxygen.

"Oh, yes," Eric said. "Very dangerous." He smiled radiantly.

I wondered if they'd notice if I went back to bed. I yawned. Two pairs of eyes swung to focus on me. "Anything else you need, Eric?" I asked.

"Do you have anything else to report?"

"Yes, they've tortured him."

"Then they won't let him go."

Of course not. You wouldn't let loose a vampire you'd tortured. You'd be looking over your shoulder for the rest of your life. I hadn't thought that through, but I could see its truth.

"You're going to attack?" I wanted to be nowhere around Jackson when that happened.

"Let me think on it," Eric said. "You are going back to the bar tomorrow night?"

"Yes, Russell invited us specifically."

"Sookie attracted his attention tonight," Alcide said.

"But that's perfect!" Eric said. "Tomorrow night, sit with the Edgington crew and pick their brains, Sookie."

"Well, that would never have occurred to me, Eric," I said, wonderingly. "Gosh, I'm glad you woke me up tonight to explain that to me."

"No problem," Eric said. "Anytime you want me to wake you up, Sookie, you have only to say."

I sighed. "Go away, Eric. Good night again, Alcide."

Alcide straightened, waiting for Eric to go back out the window. Eric waited for Alcide to leave.

"I rescind your invitation into my apartment," Alcide said, and abruptly Eric walked to the window, reopened it, and launched himself out. He was scowling. Once outside, he regained his composure and smiled at us, waving as he vanished downward.

Alcide slammed the window shut and let the blinds back down.

"No, there are lots of men who don't like me at all," I told him. He'd been easy to read that time, all right.

He gave me an odd look. "Is that so?"

"Yes, it is."

"If you say so."

"Most people, regular people, that is . . . they think I'm nuts."

"Is that right?"

"Yes, that's right! And it makes them very nervous to have me serve them."

He began laughing, a reaction that was so far from what I had intended that I had no idea what to say next.

He left the room, still more or less chuckling to himself.

Well, that had been weird. I turned out the lamp and

took off the robe, tossing it across the foot of the bed. I snuggled between the sheets again, the blanket and spread pulled up to my chin. It was cold and bleak outside, but here I was, finally, warm and safe and alone.

Really, really alone.


THE NEXT MORNING, Alcide was already gone when I got up. Construction and surveying people get going early, naturally, and I was used to sleeping late because of my job at the bar and because I hung around with a vampire. If I wanted to spend time with Bill, it had to be at night, obviously.

There was a note propped up on the coffeepot. I had a slight headache since I am not used to alcohol and I'd had two drinks the night before—the headache was not quite a hangover, but I wasn't my normal cheerful self, either. I squinted at the tiny printing.

"Running errands. Make yourself at home. I'll be back in the afternoon."

For a minute I felt disappointed and deflated. Then I got a hold of myself. It wasn't like he'd called me up and scheduled this as a romantic weekend, or like we really knew each other. Alcide had had my company foisted on him. I shrugged, and poured myself a cup of coffee. I made some toast and turned on the news. After I'd watched one cycle of CNN headlines, I decided to shower. I took my time. What else was there to do?

I was in danger of experiencing an almost unknown state—boredom.

At home, there was always something to do, though it might not be something I particularly enjoyed. If you have a house, there's always some little job waiting for your attention. And when I was in Bon Temps, there was the library to go to, or the dollar store, or the grocery. Since I'd taken up with Bill, I'd also been running errands for him that could only be done in the daytime when offices were open.

As Bill crossed my mind, I was plucking a stray hair from my eyebrow line, leaning over the sink to peer in the bathroom mirror. I had to lay down the tweezers and sit on the edge of the tub. My feelings for Bill were so confused and conflicting, I had no hope of sorting them out anytime soon. But knowing he was in pain, in trouble, and I didn't know how to find him—that was a lot to bear. I had never supposed that our romance would go smoothly. It was an interspecies relationship, after all. And Bill was a lot older than me. But this aching chasm I felt now that he was gone—that, I hadn't ever imagined.

I pulled on some jeans and a sweater and made my bed. I lined up all my makeup in the bathroom I was using, and hung the towel just so. I would have straightened up Alcide's room if I hadn't felt it would be sort of impertinent to handle his things. So I read a few chapters of my book, and then decided I simply could not sit in the apartment any longer.

I left a note for Alcide telling him I was taking a walk, and then I rode down in the elevator with a man in casual clothes, lugging a golf bag. I refrained from saying, "Going to play golf?" and confined myself to mentioning that it was a good day to be outside. It was bright and sunny, clear as a bell, and probably in the fifties. It was a happy day, with all the Christmas decorations looking bright in the sun, and lots of shopping traffic.

I wondered if Bill would be home for Christmas. I wondered if Bill could go to church with me on Christmas Eve, or if he would. I thought of the new Skil saw I'd gotten Jason; I'd had it on layaway at Sears in Monroe for months, and just picked it up a week ago. I had gotten a toy for each of Arlene's kids, and a sweater for Arlene. I really didn't have anyone else to buy a gift for, and that was pathetic. I decided I'd get Sam a CD this year. The idea cheered me. I love to give presents. This would have been my first Christmas with a boyfriend . . .

Oh, hell, I'd come full cycle, just like *Headline News*.

"Sookie!" called a voice.

Startled out of my dreary round of thoughts, I looked around to see that Janice was waving at me out of the door of her shop, on the other side of the street. I'd unconsciously walked the direction I knew. I waved back at her.

"Come on over!" she said.

I went down to the corner and crossed with the light. The shop was busy, and Jarvis and Corinne had their hands full with customers.

"Christmas parties tonight," Janice explained, while her hands were busy rolling up a young matron's black shoulder-length hair. "We're not usually open after noon on Saturdays." The young woman, whose hands were decorated with an impressive set of diamond rings, kept riffling through a copy of *Southern Living* while Janice worked on her head.

"Does this sound good?" she asked Janice. "Ginger meatballs?" One glowing fingernail pointed to the recipe.

"Kind of oriental?" Janice asked.

"Um, sort of." She read the recipe intently. "No one else would be serving them," she muttered. "You could stick toothpicks in 'em."

"Sookie, what are you doing today?" Janice asked, when she was sure her customer was thinking about ground beef.

"Just hanging out," I said. I shrugged. "Your brother's out running errands, his note said."

"He left you a note to tell you what he was doing? Girl, you should be proud. That man hasn't set pen to paper since high school." She gave me a sideways look and grinned. "You all have a good time last night?"

I thought it over. "Ah, it was okay," I said hesitantly. The dancing had been fun, anyway.

Janice burst out laughing. "If you have to think about it that hard, it must not have been a perfect evening."

"Well, no," I admitted. "There was like a little fight in the bar, and a man had to be evicted. And then, Debbie was there."

"How did her engagement party go?"

"There was quite a crowd at her table," I said. "But she came over after a while and asked a lot of questions." I smiled reminiscently. "She sure didn't like seeing Alcide with someone else!"

Janice laughed again.

"Who got engaged?" asked her customer, having decided against the recipe.

"Oh, Debbie Pelt? Used to go with my brother?" Janice said.

"I know her," said the black-haired woman, pleasure in her voice. "She used to date your brother, Alcide? And now she's marrying someone else?"

"Marrying Charles Clausen," Janice said, nodding gravely. "You know him?"

"Sure I do! We went to high school together. He's marrying Debbie Pelt? Well, better him than your brother," Black Hair said confidentially.

"I'd already figured that out," Janice said. "You know something I don't know, though?"

"That Debbie, she's into some weird stuff," Black Hair said, raising her eyebrows to mark deep significance.

"Like what?" I asked, hardly breathing as I waited to hear what would come out. Could it be that this woman actually knew about shape-shifting, about werewolves?

My eyes met Janice's and I saw the same apprehension in them.

Janice knew about her brother. She knew about his world.

And she knew I did, too.

"Devil worship, they say," Black Hair said. "Witchcraft."

We both gaped at her reflection in the mirror. She had gotten the reaction she'd been looking for. She gave a satisfied nod. Devil worship and witchcraft weren't synonymous, but I wasn't going to argue with this woman; this was the wrong time and place.

"Yes, ma'am, that's what I hear. At every full moon, she and some friends of hers go out in the woods and do stuff. No one seems to know exactly what," she admitted.

Janice and I exhaled simultaneously.

"Oh, my goodness," I said weakly.

"Then my brother's well out of a relationship with her. We don't hold with such doings," Janice said righteously.

"Of course not," I agreed.

We didn't meet each other's eyes.

After that little passage, I made motions about leaving, but Janice asked me what I was wearing that night.

"Oh, it's kind of a champagne color," I said. "Kind of a shiny beige."

"Then the red nails won't do," Janice said. "Corinne!"

Despite all my protests, I left the shop with bronze finger- and toenails, and Jarvis worked on my hair again. I tried to pay Janice, but the most she would let me do was tip her employees.

"I've never been pampered so much in my life," I told her.

"What do you do, Sookie?" Somehow that hadn't come up the day before.

"I'm a barmaid," I said.

"That *is* a change from Debbie," Janice said. She looked thoughtful.

"Oh, yeah? What does Debbie do?"

"She's a legal assistant."

Debbie definitely had an educational edge. I'd never been able to manage college; financially, it would have been rough, though I could've found a way, I guess. But my disability had made it hard enough to get out of high school. A telepathic teenager has an extremely hard time of it, let me tell you. And I had so little control then. Every day had been full of dramas—the dramas of other kids. Trying to concentrate on listening in class, taking tests in a roomful of buzzing brains . . . the only thing I'd ever excelled in was homework.

Janice didn't seem to be too concerned that I was a barmaid, which was an occupation not guaranteed to impress the families of those you dated.

I had to remind myself all over again that this setup with Alcide was a temporary arrangement he'd never asked for, and that after I'd discovered Bill's whereabouts—right, Sookie, remember Bill, your *boyfriend*?—I'd never see Alcide again. Oh, he might drop into Merlotte's, if he felt like getting off the interstate on his way from Shreveport to Jackson, but that would be all.

Janice was genuinely hoping I would be a permanent member of her family. That was so nice of her. I liked her a lot. I almost found myself wishing that Alcide really liked me, that there was a real chance of Janice being my sister-in-law.

They say there's no harm in daydreaming, but there is.

# Chapter Seven

ALCIDE WAS WAITING for me when I got back. A pile of wrapped presents on the kitchen counter showed me how he'd spent at least part of his morning. Alcide had been completing his Christmas shopping.

Judging from his self-conscious look (Mr. Subtle, he wasn't), he'd done something he wasn't sure I'd like. Whatever it was, he wasn't ready to reveal it to me, so I tried to be polite and stay out of his head. As I was passing through the short hall formed by the bedroom wall and the kitchen counter, I sniffed something less than pleasant. Maybe the garbage needed to be tossed? What garbage could we have generated in our short stay that would produce that faint, unpleasant odor? But the past pleasure of my chat with Janice and the present pleasure of seeing Alcide made it easy to forget.

"You look nice," he said.

"I stopped in to see Janice." I was worried for fear he would think I was imposing on his sister's generosity. "She has a way of getting you to accept things you had no intention of accepting."

"She's good," he said simply. "She's known about me

since we were in high school, and she's never told a soul."

"I could tell."

"How—? Oh, yeah." He shook his head. "You seem like the most regular person I ever met, and it's hard to remember you've got all this extra stuff."

No one had ever put it quite like that.

"When you were coming in, did you smell something strange by—" he began, but then the doorbell rang.

Alcide went to answer it while I took off my coat.

He sounded pleased, and I turned to face the door with a smile. The young man coming in didn't seem surprised to see me, and Alcide introduced him as Janice's husband, Dell Phillips. I shook his hand, expecting to be as pleased with him as I was with Janice.

He touched me as briefly as possible, and then he ignored me. "I wondered if you could come by this afternoon and help me set up our outside Christmas lights," Dell said—to Alcide, and Alcide only.

"Where's Tommy?" Alcide asked. He looked disappointed. "You didn't bring him by to see me?" Tommy was Janice's baby.

Dell looked at me, and shook his head. "You've got a woman here, it didn't seem right. He's with my mom."

The comment was so unexpected, all I could do was stand in silence. Dell's attitude had caught Alcide flat-footed, too. "Dell," he said, "don't be rude to my friend."

"She's staying in your apartment, that says more than friend," Dell said matter-of-factly. "Sorry, miss, this just isn't right."

"Judge not, that ye be not judged," I told him, hoping I didn't sound as furious as my clenched stomach told me I was. It felt wrong to quote the Bible when you were in a towering rage. I went into the guest bedroom and shut the door.

After I heard Dell Phillips leave, Alcide knocked on the door.

"You want to play Scrabble?" he asked.

I blinked. "Sure."

"When I was shopping for Tommy, I picked up a game."

He'd already put it on the coffee table in front of the couch, but he hadn't been confident enough to unwrap it and set it up.

"I'll pour us a Coke," I said. Not for the first time, I noticed that the apartment was quite cool, though of course it was much warmer than outside. I wished I had brought a light sweater to put on, and I wondered if it would offend Alcide if I asked him to turn the heat up. Then I remembered how warm his skin was, and I figured he was one of those people who runs kind of hot. Or maybe all Weres were like that? I pulled on the sweatshirt I'd worn yesterday, being very careful when I eased it over my hair.

Alcide had folded himself onto the floor on one side of the table, and I settled on the other. It had been a long time since either of us played Scrabble, so we studied the rules for a while before we began the game.

Alcide had graduated from Louisiana Tech. I'd never been to college, but I read a lot, so we were about even on the extent of our vocabulary. Alcide was the better strategist. I seemed to think a little faster.

I scored big with "quirt," and he stuck his tongue out at me. I laughed, and he said, "Don't read my mind, that would be cheating."

"Of course I wouldn't do any such thing," I said demurely, and he scowled at me.

I lost—but only by twelve points. After a pleasantly quarrelsome rehash of the game, Alcide got up and took our glasses over to the kitchen. He put them down and began to search through the cabinets, while I stored the game pieces and replaced the lid.

"Where you want me to put this?" I asked.

"Oh, in the closet by the door. There are a couple of shelves in there."

I tucked the box under one arm and went to the closet. The smell I'd noticed earlier seemed to be stronger.

"You know, Alcide," I said, hoping I wasn't being tacky, "there's something that smells almost rotten, right around here."

"I'd noticed it, too. That's why I'm over here looking through the cabinets. Maybe there's a dead mouse?"

As I spoke, I was turning the doorknob.

I discovered the source of the smell.

"Oh, no," I said. "Oh, *nononono*."

"Don't tell me a rat got in there and died," Alcide said.

"Not a rat," I said. "A werewolf."

The closet had a shelf above a hanging bar, and it was a small closet, intended only for visitors' coats. Now it was filled by the swarthy man from Club Dead, the man who'd grabbed me by the shoulder. He was really dead. He'd been dead for several hours.

I didn't seem to be able to look away.

Alcide's presence at my back was an unexpected comfort. He stared over my head, his hands gripping my shoulders.

"No blood," I said in a jittery voice.

"His neck." Alcide was at least as shaken as I was.

His head really was resting on his shoulder, while still attached to his body. Ick, ick, ick. I gulped hard. "We should call the police," I said, not sounding very positive about the process. I noted the way the body had been stuffed into the closet. The dead man was almost standing up. I figured he'd been shoved in, and then whoever had done the shoving had forced the door closed. He'd sort of hardened in position.

"But if we call the police . . ." Alcide's voice trailed off. He took a deep breath. "They'll never believe we didn't do it. They'll interview his friends, and his friends will tell them he was at Club Dead last night, and they'll check it out. They'll find out he got into trouble for bothering you. No one will believe we didn't have a hand in killing him."

"On the other hand," I said slowly, thinking out loud, "do you think they'd mention a word about Club Dead?"

Alcide pondered that. He ran his thumb over his mouth while he thought. "You may be right. And if they couldn't bring up Club Dead, how could they describe the, uh, confrontation? You know what they'd do? They'd want to take care of the problem themselves."

That was an *excellent* point. I was sold: no police. "Then we need to dispose of him," I said, getting down to brass tacks. "How are we gonna do that?"

Alcide was a practical man. He was used to solving problems, starting with the biggest.

"We need to take him out to the country somewhere. To do that, we have to get him down to the garage," he said after a few moments' thought. "To do that, we have to wrap him up."

"The shower curtain," I suggested, nodding my head in the direction of the bathroom I'd used. "Um, can we close the closet and go somewhere else while we work this out?"

"Sure," Alcide said, suddenly as anxious as I was to stop looking at the gruesome sight before us.

So we stood in the middle of the living room and had a planning session. The first thing I did was turn off the heat in the apartment altogether, and open all the windows. The body had not made its presence known earlier only because Alcide liked the temperature kept cool, and because the closet door fit well. Now we had to disperse the faint but pervasive smell.

"It's five flights down, and I don't think I can carry him that far," Alcide said. "He needs to go at least some of the distance in the elevator. That's the most dangerous part."

We kept discussing and refining, until we felt we had a workable procedure. Alcide asked me twice if I was okay, and I reassured him both times; it finally dawned on me that he was thinking I might break into hysterics, or faint.

"I've never been able to afford to be too finicky," I said. "That's not my nature." If Alcide expected or wanted me to ask for smelling salts, or to beg him to save little me from the big bad wolf, he had the wrong woman.

I might be determined to keep my head, but that's not to say I felt exactly calm. I was so jittery when I went to get the shower curtain that I had to restrain myself from ripping it from the clear plastic rings. Slow and steady, I told myself fiercely. Breathe in, breathe out, get the shower curtain, spread it on the hall floor.

It was blue and green with yellow fish swimming serenely in even rows.

Alcide had gone downstairs to the parking garage to move his truck as close to the stair door as possible. He'd thoughtfully brought a pair of work gloves back up with him. While he pulled them on, he took a deep breath—maybe a mistake, considering the body's proximity. His face a frozen mask of determination, Alcide gripped the corpse's shoulders and gave a yank.

The results were dramatic beyond our imagining. In one stiff piece, the biker toppled out of the closet. Alcide had to leap to his right to avoid the falling body, which banged against the kitchen counter and then fell sideways onto the shower curtain.

"Wow," I said in a shaky voice, looking down at the result. "That turned out well."

The body was lying almost exactly as we wanted it. Alcide and I gave each other a sharp nod and knelt at each end. Acting in concert, we took one side of the plastic curtain and flipped it over the body, then the other. We both relaxed when the man's face was covered. Alcide had also brought up a roll of duct tape—real men always have duct tape in their trucks—and we used it to seal the wrapped body in the curtain. Then we folded the ends over, and taped them. Luckily, though a hefty guy, the Were hadn't been very tall.

We stood up and let ourselves have a little moment of recovery. Alcide spoke first. "It looks like a big green burrito," he observed.

I slapped a hand over my mouth to stifle a fit of the giggles.

Alcide's eyes were startled as he stared at me over the wrapped corpse. Suddenly, he laughed, too.

After we'd settled down, I asked, "You ready for phase two?"

He nodded, and I pulled on my coat and scooted past the body and Alcide. I went out to the elevator, closing the apartment door behind me very quickly, just in case someone passed by.

The minute I punched the button, a man appeared around the corner and came to stand by the elevator door. Perhaps he was a relative of old Mrs. Osburgh, or maybe one of the senators was making a flying trip back to Jackson. Whoever he was, he was well dressed and in his sixties, and he was polite enough to feel the obligation of making conversation.

"It's really cold today, isn't it?"

"Yes, but not as cold as yesterday." I stared at the closed doors, willing them to open so he would be gone.

"Did you just move in?"

I had never been so irritated with a courteous person before. "I'm visiting," I said, in the kind of flat voice that should indicate the conversation is closed.

"Oh," he said cheerfully. "Who?"

Luckily the elevator chose that moment to arrive and its doors snicked open just in time to save this too-genial man from getting his head snapped off. He gestured with a sweep of his hand, wanting me to precede him, but I took a step back, said, "Oh my gosh, I forgot my keys!" and walked briskly off without a backward glance. I went to the door of the apartment next to Alcide's, the one he'd told me was empty, and I knocked on the door. I heard the elevator doors close behind me, and I breathed a sigh of relief.

When I figured Mr. Chatty had had time to get to his car and drive out of the garage—unless he was talking the ears off the security guard—I recalled the elevator. It was Saturday, and there was no telling what people's schedules would be like. According to Alcide, many of the condos had been bought as an investment and were subleased to legislators, most of who would be gone for the pre-holidays. The year-round tenants, however, would be moving around in atypical ways, since it was not only the weekend, but also only two weekends before Christmas. When the creaky contraption came back to the fifth floor, it was empty.

I dashed back to 504, knocked twice on the door, and dashed back to the elevator to hold the doors open. Preceded by the legs of the corpse, Alcide emerged from the apartment. He moved as quickly as a man can while he's carrying a stiff body over his shoulder.

This was our most vulnerable moment. Alcide's bundle looked like nothing on this earth but a corpse wrapped in a shower curtain. The plastic kept the smell down, but it was still noticeable in the small enclosure. We made it down one floor safely, then the next. At the third floor, our nerve ran out. We stopped the elevator, and to our great relief it opened onto an empty corridor. I darted out and over to the stair door, holding it open for Alcide. Then I scampered down the stairs ahead of him, and looked through the pane of glass in the door to the garage.

"Whoa," I said, holding my hand up. A middle-aged woman and a teenage girl were unloading packages from the trunk of their Toyota, simultaneously having a vigorous disagreement. The girl had been invited to an all-night party. No, her mother said.

She had to go, all her friends would be there. No, her mother said.

But Mom, everyone else's mom was letting them go. No, her mother said.

"Please don't decide to take the stairs," I whispered.

But the argument raged on as they got in the elevator. I clearly heard the girl break her train of complaint long enough to say, "Ew, something smells in here!" before the doors closed.

"What's happening?" Alcide whispered.

"Nothing. Let's see if that lasts a minute longer."

It did, and I stepped out of the door and over to Alcide's truck, darting glances from side to side to make sure I was really alone. We weren't quite in sight of the security guard, who was in his little glass hut up the slope of the ramp.

I unlocked the back of Alcide's pickup; fortunately, his pickup bed had a cover. With one more comprehensive look around the garage, I hurried back to the stair door and rapped on it. After a second, I pulled it open.

Alcide shot out and over to his truck faster than I would have believed he could move, burdened as he was. We pushed as hard as we could, and the body slowly retreated into the truck bed. With tremendous relief, we slammed the tailgate shut and locked it.

"Phase two complete," Alcide said with an air that I would have called giddy if he hadn't been such a big man.

Driving through the streets of a city with a body in your vehicle is a terrifying exercise in paranoia.

"Obey every single traffic rule," I reminded Alcide, unhappy with how tense my voice sounded.

"Okay, okay," he growled, his voice equally tense.

"Do you think those people in that Jimmy are looking at us?"

"No."

It would obviously be a good thing for me to keep quiet, so I did. We got back on I-20, the same way we'd entered Jackson, and drove until there was no city, only farmland.

When we got to the Bolton exit, Alcide said, "This looks good."

"Sure," I said. I didn't think I could stand driving around with the body any longer. The land between Jackson and Vicksburg is pretty low and flat, mostly open fields broken up by a few bayous, and this area was typical. We exited the interstate and headed north toward the woods. After a few miles Alcide took a right onto a road that had needed repaving for years. The trees grew up on either side of the much-patched strip of gray. The bleak winter sky didn't stand a chance of giving much light with this kind of competition, and I shivered in the cab of the truck.

"Not too much longer," Alcide said. I nodded jerkily.

A tiny thread of a road led off to the left, and I pointed. Alcide braked, and we examined the prospect. We gave each other a sharp nod of approval. Alcide backed in, which surprised me; but I decided that it was a good idea. The farther we went into the woods, the more I liked our choice of venue. The road had been graveled not too long ago, so we wouldn't leave tire tracks, for one thing. And I thought the chances were good that this rudimentary road led to a hunting camp, which wouldn't be in much use now that deer season was over.

Sure enough, after we'd crunched a few yards down the track, I spotted a sign nailed to a tree. It proclaimed, "Kiley-Odum Hunt Club private property—KEEP OUT."

We proceeded down the track, Alcide backing slowly and carefully.

"Here," he said, when we'd gone far enough into the woods that it was almost certain we couldn't be seen from the road. He put the truck into Park. "Listen, Sookie, you don't have to get out."

"It'll be quicker if we work together."

He tried to give me a menacing glare, but I gave him a stone face right back, and finally, he sighed. "Okay, let's get this over with," he said.

The air was cold and wet, and if you stood still for a moment the chilling damp would creep into your bones. I could tell the temperature was taking a dive, and the bright sky of the morning was a fond memory. It was an appropriate day to dump a body. Alcide opened the back of the truck, we both pulled on gloves, and we grasped the bright blue-and-green bundle. The cheerful yellow fish looked almost obscene out here in the freezing woods.

"Give it everything you got," Alcide advised me, and on a count of three, we yanked with all our might. That got the bundle half out, and the end of it protruded over the tailgate in a nasty way. "Ready? Let's go again. One, two, three!" Again I yanked, and the body's own gravity shot it out of the truck and onto the road.

If we could have driven off then and there, I would have been much happier; but we had decided we had to take the shower curtain with us. Who was to say what fingerprints might be found somewhere on the duct tape or the curtain itself? There was sure to be other, microscopic evidence that I couldn't even imagine.

I don't watch the Discovery Channel for nothing.

Alcide had a utility knife, and I did let him have the honor of this particular task. I held open a garbage bag while he cut the plastic away and stuffed it into the opening. I tried not to look, but of course I did.

The body's appearance had not improved.

That job, too, was finished sooner than I expected. I half turned to get back in the truck, but Alcide stood, his face raised to the sky. He looked as if he was smelling the forest.

"Tonight's the full moon," he said. His whole body seemed to quiver. When he looked at me, his eyes looked alien. I couldn't say that they had changed in color or contour, but it was as if a different person was looking out of them.

I was very alone in the woods with a comrade who had suddenly taken on a whole new dimension. I fought conflicting impulses to scream, burst into tears, or run. I smiled brightly at him and waited. After a long, fraught pause, Alcide said, "Let's get back in the truck."

I was only too glad to scramble up into the seat.

"What do you think killed him?" I asked, when it seemed to me Alcide had had time to return to normal.

"I think someone gave his neck a big twist," Alcide said. "I can't figure out how he got into the apartment. I know I locked the door last night. I'm sure of it. And this morning it was locked again."

I tried to figure that out for a while, but I couldn't. Then I wondered what actually killed you if your neck was broken. But I decided that wasn't really a great thing to think about.

En route to the apartment, we made a stop at Wal-Mart. On a weekend this close to Christmas, it was swarming with shoppers. Once again, I thought, *I haven't gotten anything for Bill.*

And I felt a sharp pain in my heart as I realized that I might never buy Bill a Christmas present, not now, not ever.

We needed air fresheners, Resolve (to clean the carpet), and a new shower curtain. I packed my misery away and walked a little more briskly. Alcide let me pick out the shower curtain, which I actually enjoyed. He paid cash, so there wouldn't be any record of our visit.

I checked out my nails after we had climbed back in the truck. They were fine. Then I thought of how callous I must be, worrying about my fingernails. I'd just finished disposing of a dead man. For several minutes, I sat there feeling mighty unhappy about myself.

I relayed this to Alcide, who seemed more approachable now that we were back in civilization minus our silent passenger.

"Well, you didn't kill him," he pointed out. "Ah—did you?"

I met his green eyes, feeling only a little surprise. "No, I certainly did not. Did you?"

"No," he said, and from his expression I could tell he'd been waiting for me to ask him. It had never occurred to me to do so.

While I'd never suspected Alcide, of course someone had made the Were into a body. For the first time I tried to figure who could have stuffed the body in the closet. Up until this point, I'd just been busy trying to make the body go away.

"Who has keys?" I asked.

"Just Dad and me, and the cleaning woman who does most of the apartments in the building. She doesn't keep a key of her own. The building manager gives her one." We pulled around behind the row of stores, and Alcide tossed in the garbage bag containing the old shower curtain.

"That's a pretty short list."

"Yes," Alcide said slowly. "Yes, it is. But I know my dad's in Jackson. I talked to him on the phone this morning, right after I got up. The cleaning woman only comes in when we leave a message with the building manager. He keeps a copy of our key, hands it to her when she needs it, and she returns it to him."

"What about the security guard in the garage? Is he on duty all night?"

"Yes, because he's the only line of defense between people sneaking into the garage and taking the elevator. You've always come in that way, but there are actually front doors to the building that face onto the major street. Those front doors are locked all the time. There's no guard there, but you do have to have a key to get in."

"So if someone could sneak past the guard, they could ride up in the elevator to your floor, without being stopped."

"Oh, sure."

"And that someone would have to pick the lock to the door."

"Yes, and carry in a body, and stuff it in the closet. That sounds pretty unlikely," said Alcide.

"But that's apparently what happened. Oh, um . . . did you ever give Debbie a key? Maybe someone borrowed hers?" I tried hard to sound totally neutral. That probably didn't work too well.

Long pause.

"Yes, she had a key," Alcide said stiffly.

I bit down on my lips so I wouldn't ask the next question.

"No, I didn't get it back from her."

I hadn't even needed to ask.

Breaking a somewhat charged silence, Alcide suggested we eat a late lunch. Oddly enough, I found I was really hungry.

We ate at Hal and Mal's, a restaurant close to downtown. It was in an old warehouse, and the tables were just far enough apart to make our conversation possible without anyone calling the police.

"I don't think," I murmured, "that anyone could walk around your building with a body over his shoulder, no matter what the hour."

"We just did," he said, unanswerably. "I figure it had to have happened between, say, two a.m. and seven. We were asleep by two, right?"

"More like three, considering Eric's little visit."

Our eyes met. Eric. Eureka!

"But why would he have done that? Is he nuts about you?" Alcide asked bluntly.

"Not so much nuts," I muttered, embarrassed.

"Oh, wants to get in your pants."

I nodded, not meeting his eyes.

"Lot of that going around," Alcide said, under his breath.

"Huh," I said dismissively. "You're still hung up on that Debbie, and you know it."

We looked right at each other. Better to haul this out of the shadows now, and put it to rest.

"You can read my mind better than I thought," Alcide said. His broad face looked unhappy. "But she's not . . . Why do I care about her? I'm not sure I even like her. I like the hell out of you."

"Thanks," I said, smiling from my heart. "I like the hell out of you, too."

"We're obviously better for each other than either of the people we're dating are for us," he said.

Undeniably true. "Yes, and I would be happy with you."

"And I'd enjoy sharing my day with you."

"But it looks like we're not going to get there."

"No." He sighed heavily. "I guess not."

The young waitress beamed at us as we left, making sure Alcide noticed how well packed into her jeans she was.

"What I think I'll do," Alcide said, "is I'll do my best to yank Debbie out of me by the roots. And then I'll turn up on your doorstep, one day when you least expect it, and I'll hope by then you will have given up on your vampire."

"And then we'll be happy ever after?" I smiled.

He nodded.

"Well, that'll be something to look forward to," I told him.

# Chapter Eight

I WAS SO tired by the time we entered Alcide's apartment that I was sure all I was good for was a nap. It had been one of the longest days of my life, and it was only the middle of the afternoon.

But we had some housekeeping chores to do first. While Alcide hung the new shower curtain, I cleaned the carpet in the closet with Resolve, and opened one of the air fresheners and placed it on the shelf. We closed all the windows, turned on the heat, and breathed experimentally, our eyes locked on each other's.

The apartment smelled okay. We simultaneously breathed out a sigh of relief.

"We just did something really illegal," I said, still uneasy about my own immorality. "But all I really feel is happy we got away with it."

"Don't worry about not feeling guilty," Alcide said. "Something'll come along pretty soon that you'll feel guilty about. Save it up."

This was such good advice that I decided to try it. "I'm going to take a nap," I said, "so I'll be at least a little alert tonight." You didn't want to be slow on the uptake around vampires.

"Good idea," Alcide said. He cocked an eyebrow at me, and I laughed, shaking my head. I went in the smaller bedroom and shut the door, taking off my shoes and falling onto the bed with a feeling of quiet delight. I reached over the side of the bed after a moment, grabbed the fringe of the chenille bedspread, and wrapped it around me. In the quiet apartment, with the heating system blowing a steady stream of warm air into the bedroom, it took only a few minutes to fall asleep.

I woke all of a sudden, and I was completely awake. I knew there was someone else in the apartment. Maybe on some level I'd heard a knock on the front door; or maybe I'd registered the rumble of voices in the living room. I swung silently off the bed and padded to the door, my socks making no noise at all on the beige carpet. I had pushed my door to, but not latched it, and now I turned my head to position my ear at the crack.

A deep, gravelly voice said, "Jerry Falcon came to my apartment last night."

"I don't know him," Alcide replied. He sounded calm, but wary.

"He says you got him into trouble at Josephine's last night."

"I got him into trouble? If he's the guy who grabbed my date, he got himself into trouble!"

"Tell me what happened."

"He made a pass at my date while I was in the men's room. When she protested, he started manhandling her, and she drew attention to the situation."

"He hurt her?"

"Shook her up. And he drew some blood on her shoulder."

"A blood offense." The voice had become deadly serious.

"Yes."

So the fingernail gouges on my shoulder constituted a blood offense, whatever that was.

"And then?"

"I came out of the men's room, hauled him off of her. Then Mr. Hob stepped in."

"That explains the burns."

"Yes. Hob threw him out the back door. And that was the last I saw of him. You say his name is Jerry Falcon?"

"Yeah. He came right to my house then, after the rest of the boys left the bar."

"Edgington intervened. They were about to jump us."

"Edgington was there?" The deep voice sounded very unhappy.

"Oh, yes, with his boyfriend."

"How did Edgington get involved?"

"He told them to leave. Since he's the king, and they work for him from time to time, he expected obedience. But a pup gave him some trouble, so Edgington broke his knee, made the others carry the guy out. I'm sorry there was trouble in your city, Terence. But it was none of our doing."

"You've got guest privileges with our pack, Alcide. We respect you. And those of us who work for the vampires, well, what can I say? Not the best element. But Jerry is their leader, and he was shamed in front of his people last night. How much longer you going to be in our city?"

"Just one more night."

"And it's a full moon."

"Yeah, I know, I'll try to keep a low profile."

"What are you going to do tonight? Try to avoid the change, or come out to my hunting land with me?"

"I'll try to stay out of the moon, try to avoid stress."

"Then you'll keep out of Josephine's."

"Unfortunately, Russell pretty much demanded that we come back tonight. He felt apologetic that my date went through so much aggravation. He made a point of insisting she come back."

"Club Dead on a full-moon night, Alcide. This isn't wise."

"What am I gonna do? Russell calls the shots in Mississippi."

"I can understand. But watch out, and if you see Jerry Falcon there, you turn the other way. This is my city." The deep voice was heavy with authority.

"I understand, Packmaster."

"Good. Now that you and Debbie Pelt have broken up, I hope it's a while before we see you back here, Alcide. Give things a chance to settle down. Jerry's a vindictive son of a bitch. He'll do you an injury if he can, without starting a feud."

"He was the one who caused a blood offense."

"I know, but because of his long association with the vampires, Jerry has too good an opinion of himself. He doesn't always follow the pack traditions. He only came to me, as he should, because Edgington backed the other side."

Jerry wasn't going to be following any tradition anymore. Jerry was lying in the woods to the west.

While I'd napped, it had gotten dark outside. I heard a tap on the glass of the window. I jumped, of course, but then I padded across as quietly as I could. I opened the curtain and held a finger across my lips. It was Eric. I hoped no one on the street outside looked up. He smiled at me and motioned me to open the window. I shook my head vehemently and held my finger across my lips again. If I let Eric in now, Terence would hear, and my presence would be discovered. Terence, I knew instinctively, would not like to find he had been overheard. I tiptoed back to the door and listened. Goodbyes were being said. I glanced back at the window, to see that Eric was watching me with great interest. I held up one finger to indicate it would just be a minute.

I heard the apartment door close. Moments later, there was a knock at my door. As I let Alcide in, I hoped I didn't have those funny creases on my face.

"Alcide, I heard most of that," I said. "I'm sorry I eavesdropped, but it did seem like it concerned me. Um, Eric is here."

"So I see," Alcide said unenthusiastically. "I guess I'd better let him in. Enter, Eric," he said, as he slid open the window.

Eric entered as smoothly as a tall man can enter a small window. He was wearing a suit, complete with vest and tie. His hair was slicked back into a ponytail. He was also wearing glasses.

"Are you in disguise?" I asked. I could hardly believe it.

"Yes, I am." He looked down at himself proudly. "Don't I look different?"

"Yes," I admitted. "You look just like Eric, dressed up for once."

"Do you like the suit?"

"Sure," I said. I have limited knowledge of men's clothes, but I was willing to bet this sort of olive-brown three-piece ensemble had cost more than I made in two weeks. Or four. I might not have picked this out for a guy with blue eyes, but I had to admit he looked spectacular. If they put out a vampire issue of *GQ,* he'd definitely be in the running for a photo shoot. "Who did your hair?" I asked, noticing for the first time that it had been braided in an intricate pattern.

"Oooh, jealous?"

"No, I thought maybe they could teach me how to do that to mine."

Alcide had had enough of fashion commentary. He said belligerently, "What do you mean by leaving the dead man in my closet?"

I have seldom seen Eric at a loss for words, but he was definitely speechless—for all of thirty seconds.

"It wasn't Bubba in the closet, was it?" he asked.

It was our turn to stand with mouths open, Alcide because he didn't know who the hell Bubba was, and me because I couldn't imagine what could have happened to the dazed vampire.

I hastily filled Alcide in on Bubba.

"So that explains all the sightings," he said, shaking his head from side to side. "Damn—they were all for real!"

"The Memphis group wanted to keep him, but it was just impossible," Eric explained. "He kept wanting to go home, and then there'd be incidents. So we started passing him around."

"And now you've lost him," Alcide observed, not too chagrined by Eric's problem.

"It's possible that the people who were trying to get to Sookie in Bon Temps got Bubba instead," Eric said. He tugged on his vest and looked down with some satisfaction. "So, who was in the closet?"

"The biker who marked Sookie last night," Alcide said. "He made a pretty rough pass at her while I was in the men's room."

"Marked her?"

"Yes, blood offense," Alcide said significantly.

"You didn't say anything about this last night." Eric raised an eyebrow at me.

"I didn't want to talk about it," I said. I didn't like the way that came out, kind of forlorn. "Besides, it wasn't much blood."

"Let me see."

I rolled my eyes, but I knew darn good and well that Eric wouldn't give up. I pulled my sweatshirt off my shoulder, along with my bra strap. Luckily, the sweatshirt was so old, the neck had lost its elasticity, and it afforded enough room. The fingernail gouges on my shoulder were crusted half-moons, puffy and red, though I'd scrubbed the area carefully the night before. I know how many germs are under fingernails. "See," I said. "No big deal. I was more mad than scared or hurt."

Eric kept his eyes on the little nasty wounds until I shrugged my clothes back into order. Then he switched his eyes to Alcide. "And he was dead in the closet?"

"Yes," Alcide said. "Had been dead for hours."

"What killed him?"

"He hadn't been bitten," I said. "He looked as though his neck might have been broken. We didn't feel like looking that closely. You're saying you aren't the guilty party?"

"No, though it would have been a pleasure to have done it."

I shrugged, not willing to explore that dark thought. "So, who put him there?" I asked, to get the discussion going again.

"And why?" Alcide asked.

"Would it be too much to ask where he is now?" Eric managed to look as if he were indulging two rowdy children.

Alcide and I shot each other glances. "Um, well, he's . . ." My voice trailed away.

Eric inhaled, sampling the apartment's atmosphere. "The body's not here. You called the police?"

"Well, no," I muttered. "Actually, we, ah . . ."

"We dumped him out in the country," Alcide said. There just wasn't a nice way to say it.

We had surprised Eric a second time. "Well," he said blankly. "Aren't you two enterprising?"

"We worked it all out," I said, maybe sounding a tad defensive.

Eric smiled. It was not a happy sight. "Yes, I'll bet you did."

"The packmaster came to see me today," Alcide said. "Just now, in fact. And he didn't know that Jerry was missing. In fact, Jerry went complaining to Terence after he left the bar last night, telling Terence he had a grievance against me. So he was seen and heard after the incident at Josephine's."

"So you may have gotten away with it."

"I think we did."

"You should have burned him," Eric said. "It would have killed any trace of your smell on him."

"I don't think anyone could pick out our smell," I told him. "Really and truly. I don't think we ever touched him with our bare skin."

Eric looked at Alcide, and Alcide nodded. "I agree," he said. "And I'm one of the two-natured."

Eric shrugged. "I have no idea who would have killed him and put him in the apartment. Obviously, someone wanted his death blamed on you."

"Then why not call the police from a pay phone and tell them there's a dead body in 504?"

"A good question, Sookie, and one I can't answer right now." Eric seemed to lose interest all of a sudden. "I will be at the club tonight. If I need to talk to you, Alcide, tell Russell that I am your friend from out of town, and I've been invited to meet Sookie, your new girlfriend."

"Okay," said Alcide. "But I don't understand why you want to be there. It's asking for trouble. What if one of the vamps recognizes you?"

"I don't know any of them."

"Why are you taking this chance?" I asked. "Why go there at all?"

"There may be something I can pick up on that you won't hear of, or that Alcide won't know because he is not a vampire," Eric said reasonably. "Excuse us for a minute, Alcide. Sookie and I have some business to discuss."

Alcide looked at me to make sure I was okay with this, before he nodded grudgingly and went out to the living room.

Eric said abruptly, "Do you want me to heal the marks on your shoulder?"

I thought of the ugly, crusty crescents, and I thought about the thin shoulder straps on the dress I'd brought to wear. I almost said yes, but then I had a second thought. "How would I explain that, Eric? The whole bar saw him grab me."

"You're right." Eric shook his head, his eyes closed, as if he were angry with himself. "Of course. You're not Were, you're not undead. How would you have healed so quickly?"

Then he did something else unexpected. Eric took my right hand with both of his and gripped it. He looked directly into my face. "I have searched Jackson. I have looked in warehouses, cemeteries, farmhouses, and any-place that had a trace of vampire scent about it: every property Edgington owns, and some his followers own. I haven't found a trace of Bill. I am very afraid, Sookie, that it is becoming most likely that Bill is dead. Finally dead."

I felt like he'd smacked me in the middle of the forehead with a sledgehammer. My knees just folded, and if he hadn't moved quick as lightning, I'd have been on the floor. Eric sat on a chair that was in the corner of the room, and he gathered me up into a bundle in his lap. He said, "I've upset you too much. I was trying to be practical, and instead I was . . ."

"Brutal." I felt a tear trickle out of each eye.

Eric's tongue darted out, and I felt a tiny trace of moisture as he licked up my tears. Vampires just seem to like any body fluid, if they can't get blood, and that didn't particularly bother me. I felt glad someone was holding me in a comforting way, even if it was Eric. I sunk deeper into misery while Eric spent a few moments thinking.

"The only place I haven't checked is Russell Edgington's compound—his mansion, with its outbuildings. It would be amazing if Russell were rash enough to keep another vampire prisoner in his own home. But he's been king for a hundred years. It could be that he is that confident. Maybe I could sneak in over the wall, but I wouldn't come out again. The grounds are patrolled by Weres. It's very unlikely we'll get access to such a secure place, and he won't invite us in except in very unusual circumstances." Eric let all this sink in. "I think you must tell me what you know about Bill's project."

"Is that what all this holding and niceness is about?" I was furious. "You want to get some information out of me?" I leaped up, revitalized with wrath.

Eric jumped up himself and did his best to loom over me. "I think Bill is dead," he said. "And I'm trying to save my own life, and yours, you stupid woman." Eric sounded just as angry as I was.

"I will find Bill," I said, enunciating each world carefully. I wasn't sure how I was going to accomplish this, but I'd just do some very good spying tonight, and something would turn up. I am no Pollyanna, but I have always been optimistic.

"You can't make eyes at Edgington, Sookie. He's not interested in women. And if I flirted with him, he would be suspicious. A vampire mating with another—that's unusual. Edgington hasn't gotten where he is by being gullible. Maybe his second, Betty Joe, would be interested in me, but she is a vampire, too, and the same rule applies. I can't tell you how unusual Bill's fascination with Lorena is. In fact, we disapprove of vampires loving others of our kind."

I ignored his last two sentences. "How'd you find all this out?"

"I met up with a young female vampire last night, and her boyfriend also went to parties at Edgington's place."

"Oh, he's bi?"

Eric shrugged. "He's a werewolf, so I guess he's two-natured in more ways than one."

"I thought vamps didn't date werewolves, either."

"She is being perverse. The young ones like to experiment."

I rolled my eyes. "So, what you're saying is that I need to concentrate on getting an invitation into Edgington's compound, since there's nowhere else in Jackson that Bill can be hidden?"

"He could be somewhere else in the city," Eric said cautiously. "But I don't think so. The possibility is faint. Remember, Sookie, they've had him for days now." When Eric looked at me, what I saw in his face was pity.

That frightened me more than anything.

# *Chapter Nine*

•

I HAD THE shivery, shaky feeling that precedes walking into danger. This was the last night that Alcide could go to Club Dead: Terence had warned him away, very definitely. After this, I would be on my own, if I were even allowed into the club when Alcide did not escort me.

As I dressed, I found myself wishing I were going to an ordinary vampire bar, the kind where regular humans came to gape at the undead. Fangtasia, Eric's bar in Shreveport, was such a place. People would actually come through on tours, make an evening of wearing all black, maybe pouring on a little fake blood or inserting some cheesy fake fangs. They'd stare at the vampires carefully planted throughout the bar, and they'd thrill at their own daring. Every now and then, one of these tourists would step across the line that kept them safe. Maybe he'd make a pass at one of the vamps, or maybe he'd disrespect Chow, the bartender. Then, perhaps, that tourist would find out what he'd been messing with.

At a bar like Club Dead, all the cards were out on the table. Humans were the adornments, the frills. The supernaturals were the necessity.

I'd been excited this time the night before. Now I just felt a detached sort of determination, like I was on a powerful drug that divorced me from all my more ordinary emotions. I pulled on my hose and some pretty black garters that Arlene had given me for my birthday. I smiled as I thought of my red-haired friend and her incredible optimism about men, even after four marriages. Arlene would tell me to enjoy the minute, the second, with every bit of zest I could summon up. She would tell me I never knew what man I might meet, maybe tonight would be the magic night. Maybe wearing garters would change the course of my life, Arlene would tell me.

I can't say I exactly summoned up a smile, but I felt a little less grim as I pulled my dress over my head. It was the color of champagne. There wasn't much of it. I had on black heels and jet earrings, and I was trying to decide if my old coat would look too horrible, or if I should just freeze my butt off out of vanity. Looking at the very worn blue cloth coat, I sighed. I carried it into the living room over my arm. Alcide was ready, and he was standing in the middle of the room waiting for me. Just as I registered the fact that he was looking distinctly nervous, Alcide pulled one of the wrapped boxes out of the pile he'd collected during his morning shopping. He got that self-conscious look on his face, the one he'd been wearing when I'd returned to the apartment.

"I think I owe you this," he said. And handed me the large box.

"Oh, Alcide! You got me a present?" I know, I know, I was standing there holding the box. But you have to understand, this is not something that happens to me very often.

"Open it," he said gruffly.

I tossed the coat onto the nearest chair and I unwrapped the gift awkwardly—I wasn't used to my fake nails. After a little maneuvering, I opened the white cardboard box to find that Alcide had replaced my evening wrap. I pulled out the long rectangle slowly, savoring every moment. It was beautiful; a black velvet wrap with beading on the ends. I couldn't help but realize that it cost five times what I'd spent on the one that had been damaged.

I was speechless. That hardly ever happens to me. But I don't get too many presents, and I don't take them lightly. I wrapped the velvet around me, luxuriating in the feel of it. I rubbed my cheek against it.

"Thank you," I said, my voice wobbling.

"You're welcome," he said. "God, don't cry, Sookie. I meant you to be happy."

"I'm real happy," I said. "I'm not going to cry." I choked back the tears, and went to look at myself in the mirror in my bathroom. "Oh, it's beautiful," I said, my heart in my voice.

"Good, glad you like it," Alcide said brusquely. "I thought it was the least I could do." He arranged the wrap so that the material covered the red, scabbed marks on my left shoulder.

"You didn't owe me a thing," I said. "It's me that owes you." I could tell that my being serious worried Alcide just as much as my crying. "Come on," I said. "Let's go to Club Dead. We'll learn everything, tonight, and no one will get hurt."

Which just goes to prove I don't have second sight.

ALCIDE WAS WEARING a different suit and I a different dress, but Josephine's seemed just the same. Deserted sidewalk, atmosphere of doom. It was even colder tonight, cold enough for me to see my breath on the air, cold enough to makc mc pathetically grateful for the warmth of the velvet wrap. Tonight, Alcide practically leaped from the truck to the cover of the awning, not even helping me down, and then stood under it waiting for me.

"Full moon," he explained tersely. "It'll be a tense night."

"I'm sorry," I said, feeling helpless. "This must be awfully hard on you." If he hadn't been obliged to accompany me, he could have been off bounding through the woods after deer and bunnies. He shrugged my apology off. "There'll always be tomorrow night," he said. "That's almost as good." But he was humming with tension.

Tonight I didn't jump quite so much when the truck rolled away, apparently on its own, and I didn't even quiver when Mr. Hob opened the door. I can't say the goblin looked pleased to see us, but I couldn't tell you what his ordinary facial expression really meant. So he could have been doing emotional cartwheels of joy, and I wouldn't have known it.

Somehow, I doubted he was that excited about my second appearance in his club. Or was he the owner? It was hard to imagine Mr. Hob naming a club "Josephine's." "Dead Rotten Dog," maybe, or "Flaming Maggots," but not "Josephine's."

"We won't have trouble tonight," Mr. Hob told us grimly. His voice was bumpy and rusty, as if he didn't talk much, and didn't enjoy it when he did.

"It wasn't her fault," Alcide said.

"Nonetheless," Hob said, and left it at that. He probably felt he didn't need to say anything else, and he was right. The short, lumpy goblin jerked his head at a group of tables that had been pushed together. "The king is waiting for you."

The men stood as I reached the table. Russell Edgington and his special friend Talbot were facing the dance floor; and across from them were an older (well, he'd become undead when he was older) vampire, and a woman, who of course stayed seated. My gaze trailed over her, came back, and I shrieked with delight.

"Tara!"

My high school friend shrieked right back and jumped up. We gave each other a full frontal hug, rather than the slightly less enthusiastic half-hug that was our norm. We were both strangers in a strange land, here at Club Dead.

Tara, who is several inches taller than I am, has dark hair and eyes and olive skin. She was wearing a long-sleeved gold-and-bronze dress that shimmered as she moved, and she had on high, high heels. She had attained the height of her date.

Just as I was disengaging from the embrace and giving her a happy pat on the back, I realized that seeing Tara was the worst thing that could have happened. I went into her mind, and I saw that, sure enough, she was about to ask me why I was with someone who wasn't Bill.

"Come on, girlfriend, come to the ladies' with me for a second!" I said cheerfully, and she grabbed her purse, while giving her date a perfect smile, both promising and rueful. I gave Alcide a little wave, asked the other gentlemen to excuse us, and we walked briskly to the rest rooms, which were off the passage leading to the back door. The ladies' room was empty. I pressed my back against the door to keep other females out. Tara was facing me, her face lit up with questions.

"Tara, please, don't say anything about Bill or anything about Bon Temps."

"You want to tell me why?"

"Just . . ." I tried to think of something reasonable, couldn't. "Tara, it'll cost me my life if you do."

She twitched, and gave me a steady stare. Who wouldn't? But Tara had been through a lot in her life, and she was a tough, if wounded, bird. "I'm so happy to see you here," she said. "It was lonely being in this crowd by myself. Who's your friend? What is he?"

I always forgot that other people couldn't tell. And sometimes I nearly forgot that other people didn't know about Weres and shifters. "He's a surveyor," I said. "Come on, I'll introduce you."

"Sorry we left so quickly," I said, smiling brightly at all the men. "I forgot my manners." I introduced Tara to Alcide, who looked appropriately appreciative. Then it was Tara's turn. "Sook, this is Franklin Mott."

"A pleasure to meet you," I said, and extended my hand before I realized my faux pas. Vampires don't shake hands. "I beg your pardon," I said hastily, and gave him a little wave instead. "Do you live here in Jackson, Mr. Mott?" I was determined not to embarrass Tara.

"Please call me Franklin," he said. He had a wonderful mellow voice with a light Italion accent. When he had died, he had probably been in his late fifties or early sixties; his hair and mustache were iron gray, and his face was lined. He looked vigorous and very masculine. "Yes, I do, but I own a business that has a franchise in Jackson, one in Ruston, and one in Vicksburg. I met Tara at a gathering in Ruston."

Gradually we progressed through the social do-si-do of getting seated, explaining to the men how Tara and I had attended high school together, and ordering drinks. All the vampires, of course, ordered synthetic blood, and Talbot, Tara, Alcide, and I got mixed drinks. I decided another champagne cocktail would be good. The waitress, a shifter, was moving in an odd, almost slinking manner, and she didn't seem inclined to talk much. The night of the full moon was making itself felt in all kinds of ways.

There were far fewer of the two-natured in the bar

this night of the moon cycle. I was glad to see Debbie and her fiancé were missing, and there were only a couple of the Were bikers. There were more vampires, and more humans. I wondered how the vampires of Jackson kept this bar a secret. Among the humans who came in with Supe dates, surely one or two were inclined to talk to a reporter or just tell a group of friends about the bar's existence?

I asked Alcide, and he said quietly, "The bar's spell-bound. You wouldn't be able to tell anyone how to get here if you tried."

I'd have to experiment with that later, see if it worked. I wonder who did the spell casting, or whatever it was called. If I could believe in vampires and werewolves and shape-shifters, it was not too far a stretch to believe in witches.

I was sandwiched between Talbot and Alcide, so by way of making conversation I asked Talbot about secrecy. Talbot didn't seem averse to chatting with me, and Alcide and Franklin Mott had found they had acquaintances in common. Talbot had on too much cologne, but I didn't hold that against him. Talbot was a man in love, and furthermore, he was a man addicted to vampiric sex . . . the two states are not always combined. He was a ruthless, intelligent man who could not understand how his life had taken such an exotic turn. (He was a big broadcaster, too, which was why I could pick up so much of his life.)

He repeated Alcide's story about the spell on the bar. "But the way what happens here is kept a secret, that's different," Talbot said, as if he was considering a long answer and a short answer. I looked at his pleasant, handsome face and reminded myself that he knew Bill was being tortured, and he didn't care. I wished he would think about Bill again, so I could learn more; at least I would know if Bill was dead or alive. "Well, Miss

Sookie, what goes on here is kept secret by terror and punishment."

Talbot said that with relish. He liked that. He liked that he had won the heart of Russell Edgington, a being who could kill easily, who deserved to be feared. "Any vampire or Were—in fact, any sort of supernatural creature, and you haven't seen quite a few of them, believe me—who brings in a human is responsible for that human's behavior. For example, if you were to leave here tonight and call a tabloid, it would be Alcide's bounden duty to track and kill you."

"I see." And indeed, I did. "What if Alcide couldn't bring himself to do that?"

"Then his life would be forfeit, and one of the bounty hunters would be commissioned to do the job."

Jesus Christ, Shepherd of Judea. "There are bounty hunters?" Alcide could have told me a lot more than he had; that was an unpleasant discovery. My voice may have been a little on the croaky side.

"Sure. The Weres who wear the motorcycle gear, in this area. In fact, they're asking questions around the bar tonight because . . ." His expression sharpened, became suspicious. "The man who was bothering you . . . did you see him again last night? After you left the bar?"

"No," I said, speaking the technical truth. I hadn't seen him again—last night. I knew what God thought about technical truths, but I also figured he expected me to save my own life. "Alcide and I, we went right back to the apartment. I was pretty upset." I cast my eyes down like a modest girl unused to approaches in bars, which was also a few steps away from the truth. (Though Sam keeps such incidents down to a minimum, and it was widely known I was crazy and therefore undesirable, I certainly had to put up with the occasional aggressive advance, as well as a certain amount of half-hearted passes from guys who got too drunk to care that I was supposed to be crazy.)

"You were sure plucky when it looked like there was going to be a fight," Talbot observed. Talbot was thinking that my courage last night didn't jibe with my demure demeanor this evening. Darn it, I'd overplayed my role.

"Plucky is the word for Sookie," Tara said. It was a welcome interruption. "When we danced together on stage, about a million years ago, she was the one who was brave, not me! I was shaking in my shoes."

Thank you, Tara.

"You danced?" asked Franklin Mott, his attention caught by the conversation.

"Oh, yes, and we won the talent contest," Tara told him. "What we didn't realize, until we graduated and had some experience in the world, was that our little routine was really, ah—"

"Suggestive," I said, calling a spade a spade. "We were the most innocent girls in our little high school, and there we were, with this dance routine we lifted straight off MTV."

"It took us years to understand why the principal was sweating so hard," Tara said, her smile just rascally enough to be charming. "As a matter of fact, let me go talk to the deejay right now." She sprang up and worked her way over to the vampire who'd set up his gear on the small stage. He bent over and listened intently, and then he nodded.

"Oh, no." I was going to be horribly embarrassed.

"What?" Alcide was amused.

"She's going to make us do it all over again."

Sure enough, Tara wiggled her way through the crowd to get back to me, and she was beaming. I had thought of twenty-five good reasons not to do what she wanted by the time she seized my hands and pulled me to my feet. But it was evident that the only way I could get out of this was to go forward. Tara had her heart set on this exhibition, and Tara was my friend. The crowd made a space as Pat Benatar's "Love Is a Battlefield" began to play.

Unfortunately, I remembered every bump and grind, every hip thrust.

In our innocence, Tara and I had planned our routine almost like pairs figure skating, so we were touching (or very near) during the whole thing. Could it have looked more like some lesbian tease act performed in a stripper bar? Not much. Not that I'd ever been to a stripper bar, or a porno movie house; but I assume the rise of communal lust I felt in Josephine's that night was similar. I didn't like being the object of it—but yet, I discovered I felt a certain flood of power.

Bill had informed my body about good sex, and I was sure that now I danced like I knew about enjoying sex—and so did Tara. In a perverse way, we were having an "I am woman, hear me roar" moment. And, by golly, love sure *was* a battlefield. Benatar was right about that.

We had our sides to the audience, Tara gripping my waist, for the last few bars, and we pumped our hips in unison, and brought our hands sweeping to the floor. The music stopped. There was a tiny second of silence, and then a lot of applause and whistling.

The vampires thought of the blood flowing in our veins, I was sure from the hungry looks on their faces—especially those lower main lines on our inner thighs. And I could hear that the werewolves were imagining how good we would taste. So I was feeling quite edible as I made my way back to our table. Tara and I were patted and complimented along the way, and we received many invitations. I was halfway tempted to accept the dance offer of a curly-haired brunette vamp who was just about my size and cute as a bunny. But I just smiled and kept on going.

Franklin Mott was delighted. "Oh, you were so right," he said as he held Tara's chair for her. Alcide, I observed, remained seated and glowered at me, forcing Talbot to lean over and pull my chair out for me, an awkward and makeshift courtesy. (He did get a caress on the shoulder from Russell for his gesture.) "I can't believe you girls didn't get expelled," Talbot said, covering the awkward moment. I never would have pegged Alcide for a possessive jerk.

"We had no clue," Tara protested, laughing. "None. We couldn't understand what all the fuss was about."

"What bit your ass?" I asked Alcide, very quietly. But when I listened carefully, I could pick out the source of his dissatisfaction. He was resenting the fact that he had acknowledged to me that he still had Debbie in his heart, because otherwise he'd make a determined effort to share my bed tonight. He felt both guilty and angry about that, since it was the full moon—come to think of it, his time of the month. In a way.

"Not looking for your boyfriend too hard, are you?" he said coldly, in a nasty undertone.

It was like he'd thrown a bucket of cold water in my face. It was a shock, and it hurt terribly. Tears welled up in my eyes. It was also completely obvious to everyone at the table that he had said something to upset me.

Talbot, Russell, and Franklin all gave Alcide level looks practically laden with threat. Talbot's look was a weak echo of his lover's, so it could be disregarded, but Russell was the king, after all, and Franklin was apparently an influential vampire. Alcide recalled where he was, and with whom.

"Excuse me, Sookie, I was just feeling jealous," he said, loud enough for all at the table to hear. "That was really interesting."

"Interesting?" I said, as lightly as I could. I was pretty damn mad, myself. I ran my fingers through his hair as I leaned over to his chair. "Just interesting?" We smiled at each other quite falsely, but the others bought it. I felt like taking a handful of that black hair and giving it a good hard yank. He might not be a mind reader like me, but he could read that impulse loud and clear. Alcide had to force himself not to flinch.

Tara stepped in once again to ask Alcide what his occupation was—God bless her—and yet another awkward moment passed harmlessly by. I pushed my chair a little farther back from the circle around the table and let my mind roam. Alcide had been right about the fact that I needed to be at work, rather than amusing myself; but I didn't see how I could have refused Tara something she enjoyed so much.

A parting of the bodies crowding the little dance floor gave me a glimpse of Eric, leaning against the wall behind the small stage. His eyes were on me, and they were full of heat. *There* was someone who wasn't pissed off at me, someone who had taken our little routine in the spirit in which it was offered.

Eric looked quite nice in the suit and glasses. The glasses made him seem somehow less threatening, I decided, and turned my mind to business. Fewer Weres and humans made it easier to listen in to each one, easier to track the thread of thought back to its owner. I closed my eyes to help me concentrate, and almost immediately I caught a snatch of inner monologue that shook me up.

"Martyrdom," the man was thinking. I knew the thinker was a man, and that his thoughts were coming from the area behind me, the area right around the bar. My head began to turn, and I stopped myself. Looking wouldn't help, but it was an almost irresistible impulse. I looked down instead, so the movements of the other patrons wouldn't distract me.

People don't really think in complete sentences, of course. What I'm doing, when I spell out their thoughts, is translating.

"When I die, my name will be famous," he thought. "It's almost here. God, please let it not hurt. At least he's here with me . . . I hope the stake's sharp enough."

Oh, *dammit*. The next thing I knew I was on my feet, walking away from the table.

I WAS INCHING along, blocking the noise of the music and the voices so I could listen sharply to what was being said silently. It was like walking underwater. At the bar, slugging back a glass of synthetic blood, was a woman with a poof of teased hair. She was dressed in a tight-bodiced dress with a full skirt fluffing out around it. Her muscular arms and broad shoulders looked pretty strange with the outfit; but I'd never tell her so, nor would any sane person. This had to be Betty Joe Pickard, Russell Edgington's second in command. She had on white gloves and pumps, too. All she needed was a little hat with a half-veil, I decided. I was willing to bet Betty Joe had been a big fan of Mamie Eisenhower's.

And standing behind this formidable vampire, also facing the bar, were two male humans. One was tall, and oddly familiar. His gray-threaded brown hair was long, but neatly combed. It looked like a regular men's haircut, allowed to grow however it wanted to grow. The hairstyle looked odd with his suit. His shorter companion had rough black hair, tousled and flecked with gray. This second man wore a sports coat that maybe came off the rack from JCPenney on a sale day.

And inside that cheap coat, in a specially sewn pocket, he carried a stake.

Horribly enough, I hesitated. If I stopped him, I would be revealing my hidden talent, and to reveal that would

be to unmask my identity. The consequences of this rev-
elation would depend on what Edgington knew about
me; he apparently knew Bill's girlfriend was a barmaid
at Merlotte's in Bon Temps, but not her name. That's
why I'd been free to introduce myself as Sookie Stackhouse. If Russell knew Bill's girlfriend was a telepath,
and he discovered I was a telepath, who knew what
would happen then?

Actually, I could make a good guess.

As I dithered, ashamed and frightened, the decision
was made for me. The man with the black hair reached
inside his coat and the fanaticism roiling in his head
reached fever pitch. He pulled out the long sharpened
piece of ash, and then a lot happened.

I yelled, *"STAKE!"* and lunged for the fanatic's arm,
gripping it desperately with both my hands. The vampires and their humans whirled around looking for the
threat, and the shifters and Weres wisely scattered to the
walls to leave the floor free for the vampires. The tall
man beat at me, his big hands pounding at my head and
shoulders, and his dark-haired companion kept twisting
his arm, trying to free it from my grasp. He heaved from
side to side to throw me off.

Somehow, in the melee, my eyes met those of the
taller man, and we recognized each other. He was G.
Steve Newlin, former leader of the Brotherhood of the
Sun, a militant anti-vampire organization whose Dallas
branch had more or less bit the dust after I'd paid it a
visit. He was going to tell them who I was, I just knew
it, but I had to pay attention to what the man with the
stake was doing. I was staggering around on my heels,
trying to keep my feet, when the assassin finally had a
stroke of brilliance and transferred the stake from his
pinned right hand to his free left.

With a final punch to my back, Steve Newlin dashed
for the exit, and I caught a flash of creatures bounding

in pursuit. I heard lots of yowling and tweeting, and then the black-haired man threw back his left arm and plunged the stake into my waist on my right side.

I let go of his arm then, and stared down at what he'd done to me. I looked back up into his eyes for a long moment, reading nothing there but a horror to mirror my own. Then Betty Joe Pickard swung back her gloved fist and hit him twice—boom-boom. The first blow snapped his neck. The second shattered his skull. I could hear the bones break.

And then he went down to the floor, and since my legs were tangled with his, I went down, too. I landed flat on my back.

I lay looking up at the ceiling of the bar, at the fan that was rotating solemnly above my head. I wondered why the fan was on in the middle of winter. I saw a hawk fly across the ceiling, narrowly avoiding the fan blades. A wolf came to my side and licked my face and whined, but turned and dashed away. Tara was screaming. I was not. I was so cold.

With my right hand, I covered the spot where the stake entered my body. I didn't want to see it, and I was scared I'd look down. I could feel the growing wetness around the wound.

"Call nine-one-one!" Tara yelled as she landed on her knees beside me. The bartender and Betty Joe exchanged a look over her head. I understood.

"Tara," I said, and it came out like a croak. "Honey, all the shifters are changing. It's full moon. The police can't come in here, and they'll come if anyone calls nine-one-one."

The shifter part just didn't seem to register with Tara, who didn't know such things were possible. "The vampires are not gonna let you die," Tara said confidently. "You just saved one of them!"

I wasn't so sure about that. I saw Franklin Mott's face

above Tara. He was looking at me, and I could read his expression.

"Tara," I whispered, "you have to get out of here. This is getting crazy, and if there's any chance the police are coming, you can't be here."

Franklin Mott nodded in approval.

"I'm not going to leave you until you have help," Tara said, her voice full of determination. Bless her heart.

The crowd around me consisted of vampires. One of them was Eric. I could not decipher his face.

"The tall blond will help me," I told Tara, my voice barely a rasp. I pointed a finger at Eric. I didn't look at him for fear I'd read rejection in his eyes. If Eric wouldn't help me, I suspected I would lie here and die on this polished wood floor in a vampire bar in Jackson, Mississippi.

My brother, Jason, would be so pissed off.

Tara had met Eric in Bon Temps, but their introduction had been on a very stressful night. She didn't seem to identify the tall blond she'd met that night with the tall blond she saw tonight, wearing glasses and a suit and with his hair pulled back strictly into a braid.

"Please help Sookie," she said to him directly, as Franklin Mott almost yanked her to her feet.

"This young man will be *glad* to help your friend," Mott said. He gave Eric a sharp look that told Eric he damn well better agree.

"Of course. I'm a good friend of Alcide's," Eric said, lying without a blink.

He took Tara's place by my side, and I could tell after he was on his knees that he caught the smell of my blood. His face went even whiter, and his bones stood out starkly under his skin. His eyes blazed.

"You don't know how hard it is," he whispered to me, "not to bend over and lick."

"If you do, everyone else will," I said. "And they

won't just lick, they'll bite." There was a German shepherd staring at me with luminous yellow eyes, just past my feet.

"That's the only thing stopping me."

"Who are you?" asked Russell Edgington. He was giving Eric a careful once-over. Russell was standing to my other side, and he bent over both of us. I had been loomed over enough, I can tell you that, but I was in no position to do a damn thing about it.

"I'm a friend of Alcide's," Eric repeated. "He invited me here tonight to meet his new girlfriend. My name is Leif."

Russell could look down at Eric, since Eric was kneeling, and his golden brown eyes bored into Eric's blue ones. "Alcide doesn't hang with many vampires," Russell said.

"I'm one of the few."

"We have to get this young lady out of here," Russell said.

The snarling a few feet away increased in intensity. There appeared to be a knot of animals gathered around something on the floor.

"Take that out of here!" roared Mr. Hob. "Out the back door! You know the rules!"

Two of the vampires lifted the corpse, for that was what the Weres and shifters were squabbling over, and carried it out the back door, followed by all the animals. So much for the black-haired fanatic.

Just this afternoon Alcide and I had disposed of a corpse. We'd never thought of just bringing it down to the club, laying it in the alley. Of course, this one was fresh.

". . . maybe has nicked a kidney," Eric was saying. I had been unconscious, or at least somewhere else, for a few moments.

I was sweating heavily, and the pain was excruciating.

I felt a flash of chagrin when I realized I was sweating all over my dress. But possibly the big bloody hole had already ruined the dress anyway, huh?

"We'll take her to my place," Russell said, and if I hadn't been sure I was very badly hurt, I might have laughed. "The limo's on its way. I'm sure a familiar face would make her more comfortable, don't you agree?"

What I thought was, Russell didn't want to get his suit nasty picking me up. And Talbot probably couldn't lug me. Though the small vampire with curly black hair was still there, and still smiling, I would be awful bulky for him . . .

And I lost some more time.

"Alcide turned into a wolf and chased after the assassin's companion," Eric was telling me, though I didn't remember asking. I started to tell Eric who the companion was, and then I realized that I'd better not. "Leif," I muttered, trying to commit the name to memory. "Leif. I guess my garters are showing. Does that mean . . . ?"

"Yes, Sookie?"

. . . and I was out again. Then I was aware I was moving, and I realized that Eric was carrying me. Nothing had ever hurt so badly in my life, and I reflected, not for the first time, that I'd never even been in a hospital until I'd met Bill, and now I seemed to spend half my time battered or recovering from being battered. This was very significant and important.

A lynx padded out of the bar beside us. I looked down into the golden eyes. What a night this was turning out to be for Jackson. I hoped all the good people had decided to stay home tonight.

And then we were in the limo. My head was resting on Eric's thigh, and in the seat across from us sat Talbot, Russell, and the small curly-haired vampire. As we stopped at a light, a bison lumbered by.

"Lucky no one's out in downtown Jackson on a weekend night in December," Talbot was remarking, and Eric laughed.

We drove for what seemed like some time. Eric smoothed my skirt over my legs, and brushed my hair out of my face. I looked up at him, and . . .

". . . did she know what he was going to do?" Talbot was asking.

"She saw him pull the stake out, she said," Eric said mendaciously. "She was going to the bar to get another drink."

"Lucky for Betty Joe," Russell said in his smooth Southern drawl. "I guess she's still hunting the one that got away."

Then we pulled up into a driveway and stopped at a gate. A bearded vampire came up and peered in the window, looking at all the occupants carefully. He was far more alert than the indifferent guard at Alcide's apartment building. I heard an electronic hum, and the gate opened. We went up a driveway (I could hear the gravel crunching) and then we swung around in front of a mansion. It was lit up like a birthday cake, and as Eric carefully extracted me from the limo, I could see we were under a porte cochere that was as fancy as all get-out. Even the carport had columns. I expected to see Vivian Leigh come down the steps.

I had a blank moment again, and then we were in the foyer. The pain seemed to be fading away, and its absence left me giddy.

As the master of this mansion, Russell's return was a big event, and when the inhabitants smelled fresh blood, they were doubly quick to come thronging. I felt like I'd landed in the middle of romance cover model contest. I had never seen so many cute men in one place in my life. But I could tell they were not for me. Russell was like the gay vampire Hugh Hefner, and this was the Playboy Mansion, with an emphasis on the "boy."

"Water, water, everywhere, nor any drop to drink," I said, and Eric laughed out loud. That was why I liked him, I thought rosily; he "got" me.

"Good, the shot's taking effect," said a white-haired man in a sports shirt and pleated trousers. He was human, and he might as well have had a stethoscope tattooed around his neck, he was so clearly a doctor. "Will you be needing me?"

"Why don't you stay for a while?" Russell suggested. "Josh will keep you company, I'm sure."

I didn't get to see what Josh looked like, because Eric was carrying me upstairs then.

"Rhett and Scarlet," I said.

"I don't understand," Eric told me.

"You haven't seen *Gone with the Wind*?" I was horrified. But then, why should a vampire Viking have seen that staple of the Southern mystique? But he'd read *The Rhyme of the Ancient Mariner*, which I had worked my way through in high school. "You'll have to watch it on video. Why am I acting so stupid? Why am I not scared?"

"That human doctor gave you a big dose of drugs," Eric said, smiling down at me. "Now I am carrying you to a bedroom so you can be healed."

"He's here," I told Eric.

His eyes flashed caution at me. "Russell, yes. But I'm afraid that Alcide made less than a stellar choice, Sookie. He raced off into the night after the other attacker. He should have stayed with you."

"Screw him," I said expansively.

"He wishes, especially after seeing you dance."

I wasn't feeling quite good enough to laugh, but it did cross my mind. "Giving me drugs maybe wasn't such a great idea," I told Eric. I had too many secrets to keep.

"I agree, but I am glad you're out of pain."

Then we were in a bedroom, and Eric was laying me

on a gosh-to-goodness canopied four-poster. He took the opportunity to whisper, "Be careful," in my ear. And I tried to bore that thought into my drug-addled brain. I might blurt out the fact that I knew, beyond a doubt, that Bill was somewhere close to me.

# Chapter Ten

THERE WAS QUITE a crowd in the bedroom, I noticed. Eric had gotten me situated on the bed, which was so high, I might need a stepstool to get down. But it would be convenient for the healing, I had heard Russell comment, and I was beginning to worry about what constituted "the healing." The last time I'd been involved in a vampire "healing," the treatment had been what you might call nontraditional.

"What's gonna happen?" I asked Eric, who was standing at the side of the bed on my left, non-wounded, side.

But it was the vampire who had taken his place to my right who answered. He had a long, horsy face, and his blond eyebrows and eyelashes were almost invisible against his pallor. His bare chest was hairless, too. He was wearing a pair of pants, which I suspected were vinyl. Even in the winter, they must be, um, unbreathing. I wouldn't like to peel those suckers off. This vamp's saving grace was his lovely straight pale hair, the color of white corn.

"Miss Stackhouse, this is Ray Don," Russell said.

"How de do." Good manners would make you welcome anywhere, my gran had always told me.

"Pleased to meet you," he responded correctly. He had been raised right, too, though no telling when that had been. "I'm not going to ask you how you're doing, cause I can see you got a great big hole in your side."

"Kind of ironic, isn't it, that it was the human that got staked," I said socially. I hoped I would see that doctor again, because I sure wanted to ask him what he'd given me. It was worth its weight in gold.

Ray Don gave me a dubious look, and I realized I'd just shot out of his comfort zone, conversationally. Maybe I could give Ray Don a Word of the Day calendar, like Arlene gave me every Christmas.

"I'll tell you what's going to happen, Sookie," Eric said. "You know, when we start to feed and our fangs come out, they release a little anticoagulant?"

"Um-hum."

"And when we are ready to finish feeding, the fangs release a little coagulant and a little trace of the, the—"

"Stuff that helps you all heal so fast?"

"Yes, exactly."

"So, Ray Don is going to what?"

"Ray Don, his nest mates say, has an extra supply of all these chemicals in his body. This is his talent."

Ray Don beamed at me. He was proud of that.

"So he will start the process on a volunteer, and when he has fed, he will begin cleaning your wound and healing it."

What Eric had left out of this narrative was that at some point during this process, the stake was going to have to come out, and that no drug in the world could keep that from hurting like a son of a bitch. I realized that in one of my few moments of clarity.

"Okay," I said. "Let's get the show on the road."

The volunteer turned out to be a thin blond human

teenager, who was no taller than me and probably no wider in the shoulders. He seemed to be quite willing. Ray Don gave him a big kiss before he bit him, which I could have done without, since I'm not into public displays of carnal affection. (When I say "big," I don't mean a loud smack, but the intense, moaning, tonsil-sucking kind.) When that was done, to both their satis-factions, Blondie inclined his head to one side, and the taller Ray Don sank his fangs in. There was much cleav-ing, and much panting—and even to drug-addled me, Ray Don's vinyl pants didn't leave enough to the imag-ination.

Eric watched without apparent reaction. Vampires seem, as a whole, to be extremely tolerant of any sexual preference; I guess there aren't that many taboos when you've been alive a few hundred years.

When Ray Don drew back from Blondie and turned to face the bed, he had a bloody mouth. My euphoria evaporated as Eric instantly sat on the bed and pinned my shoulders. The Big Bad Thing was coming.

"Look at me," he demanded. "Look at me, Sookie."

I felt the bed indent, and I assumed Ray Don was kneeling beside it and leaning over to my wound.

There was a jar in the torn flesh of my side that jolted me down to the marrow of my bones. I felt the blood leave my face and felt hysteria bubbling up my throat like my blood was leaving the wound.

"Don't, Sookie! Look at me!" Eric said urgently.

I looked down to see that Ray Don had grabbed the stake.

Next he would . . .

I screamed over and over, until I didn't have the en-ergy. I met Eric's eyes as I felt Ray Don's mouth suck-ing at the wound. Eric was holding my hands, and I was digging my nails into him like we were doing something else. He won't mind, I thought, as I realized I'd drawn blood.

And sure enough, he didn't. "Let go," he advised me, and I loosened my grip on his hands. "No, not of me," he said, smiling. "You can hold on to me as long as you want. Let go of the pain, Sookie. Let go. You need to drift away."

It was the first time I had relinquished my will to someone else. As I looked at him, it became easy, and I retreated from the suffering and uncertainty of this strange place.

The next thing I knew, I was awake. I was tucked in the bed, lying on my back, my formerly beautiful dress removed. I was still wearing my beige lace underwear, which was good. Eric was in the bed with me, which was not. He was really making a habit of this. He was lying on his side, his arm draped over me, one leg thrown over mine. His hair was tangled with my hair, and the strands were almost indistinguishable, the color was so similar. I contemplated that for a while, in a sort of misty, drifting state.

Eric was having downtime. He was in that absolutely immobile state into which vampires retreat when they have nothing else to do. It refreshes them, I think, reduces the wear and tear of the world that ceaselessly passes them by, year after year, full of war and famine and inventions that they must learn how to master, changing mores and conventions and styles that they must adopt in order to fit in. I pulled down the covers to check out my side. I was still in pain, but it was greatly reduced. There was a large circle of scar tissue on the site of the wound. It was hot and shiny and red and somehow glossy.

"It's much better," Eric said, and I gasped. I hadn't felt him rouse from his suspended animation.

Eric was wearing silk boxers. I would have figured him for a Jockey man.

"Thank you, Eric." I didn't care for how shaky I sounded, but an obligation is an obligation.

"For what?" His hand gently stroked my stomach.

"For standing by me in the club. For coming here with me. For not leaving me alone with all these people."

"How grateful are you?" he whispered, his mouth hovering over mine. His eyes were very alert now, and his gaze was boring into mine.

"That kind of ruins it, when you say something like that," I said, trying to keep my voice gentle. "You shouldn't want me to have sex with you just because I owe you."

"I don't really care why you have sex with me, as long as you do it," he said, equally gently. His mouth was on mine then. Try as I might to stay detached, I wasn't too successful. For one thing, Eric had had hundreds of years to practice his kissing technique, and he'd used them to good advantage. I snuck my hands up to his shoulders, and I am ashamed to say I responded. As sore and tired as my body was, it wanted what it wanted, and my mind and will were running far behind. Eric seemed to have six hands, and they were everywhere, encouraging my body to have its way. A finger slid under the elastic of my (minimal) panties, and glided right into me.

I made a noise, and it was not a noise of rejection. The finger began moving in a wonderful rhythm. Eric's mouth seemed bent on sucking my tongue down his throat. My hands were enjoying the smooth skin and the muscles that worked underneath it.

Then the window flew open, and Bubba crawled in.

"Miss Sookie! Mr. Eric! I tracked you down!" Bubba was proud.

"Oh, good for you, Bubba," Eric said, ending the kiss.

I clamped my hand on his wrist, and pulled his hand away. He allowed me to do it. I am nowhere near as strong as the weakest vampire.

"Bubba, have you been here the whole time? Here in Jackson?" I asked, once I had some wits in my head. It was a good thing Bubba had come in, though Eric didn't think so.

"Mr. Eric told me to stick with you," Bubba said simply. He settled into a low chair tastefully upholstered in flowered material. He had a dark lock of hair falling over his forehead, and he was wearing a gold ring on every finger. "You get hurt bad at that club, Miss Sookie?"

"It's a lot better now," I said.

"I'm sorry I didn't do my job, but that little critter guarding the door wouldn't let me in. He didn't seem to know who I was, if you can believe that."

Since Bubba himself hardly remembered who he was, and had a real fit when he did, maybe it wasn't too surprising that a goblin wouldn't be current on American popular music.

"But I saw Mr. Eric carrying you out, so I followed you."

"Thank you, Bubba. That was real smart."

He smiled, in a slack and dim sort of way. "Miss Sookie, what you doing in bed with Mr. Eric if Bill is your boyfriend?"

"That's a real good question, Bubba," I said. I tried to sit up, but I couldn't do it. I made a little pain sound, and Eric cursed in another language.

"I am going to give her blood, Bubba," Eric said. "Let me tell you what I need you to do."

"Sure," Bubba said agreeably.

"Since you got over the wall and into the house without being caught, I need you to search this estate. We think Bill is here somewhere. They are keeping him prisoner. Don't try to free him. This is an order. Come back here and tell us when you have found him. If they see you, don't run. Just don't say anything. Nothing. Not about me, or Sookie, or Bill. Nothing more than, 'Hi, my name is Bubba.' "

"Hi, my name is Bubba."

"Right."

"Hi, my name is Bubba."

"Yes. That's fine. Now, you sneak, and you be quiet and invisible."

Bubba smiled at us. "Yes, Mr. Eric. But after that, I gotta go find me some food. I'm mighty hungry."

"Okay, Bubba. Go search now."

Bubba scrambled back out the window, which was on the second story. I wondered how he was going to get to the ground, but if he'd gotten into the window, I was sure he could get out of it.

"Sookie," Eric said, right in my ear. "We could have a long argument about you taking my blood, and I know everything you would say. But the fact is, dawn is coming. I don't know if you will be allowed to stay the day here or not. I will have to find shelter, here or elsewhere. I want you strong and able to defend yourself; at least able to move quickly."

"I know Bill is here," I said, after I'd thought this over for a moment. "And no matter what we almost just did—thank God for Bubba—I need to find Bill. The best time to get him out of here would be while all you vampires are asleep. Can he move at all during the daytime?"

"If he knows he is in great danger, he may be able to stagger," Eric said, slowly and thoughtfully. "Now I am even more sure you will need my blood, because you need strength. He will need to be covered thoroughly. You will need to take the blanket off this bed; it's thick. How will you get him out of here?"

"That's where you come in," I said. "After we do this blood thing, you need to go get me a car—a car with a great big trunk, like a Lincoln or a Caddy. And you need to get the keys to me. And you'll need to sleep somewhere else. You don't want to be here when they wake up and find their prisoner is gone." Eric's hand was resting quietly on my stomach, and we were still wrapped up together in the bedding. But the situation felt completely different.

"Sookie, where will you take him?"

"An underground place," I said uncertainly. "Hey, maybe Alcide's parking garage! That's better than being out in the open."

Eric sat up against the headboard. The silk boxers were royal blue. He spread his legs and I could see up the leg hole. Oh, Lord. I had to close my eyes. He laughed.

"Sit up with your back against my chest, Sookie. That will make you more comfortable."

He carefully eased me up against him, my back to his chest, and wrapped his arms around me. It was like leaning against a firm, cool, pillow. His right arm vanished, and I heard a little crunch sound. Then his wrist appeared in front of my face, blood running from the two wounds in his skin.

"This will cure you of everything," Eric said.

I hesitated, then derided myself for my foolish hesitation. I knew that the more of Eric's blood I had in me, the more he would know me. I knew that it would give him some kind of power over me. I knew that I would be stronger for a long time, and given how old Eric was, I would be very strong. I would heal, and I would feel wonderful. I would be more attractive. This was why vampires were preyed upon by Drainers, humans who worked in teams to capture vamps, chain them with silver, and drain their blood into vials, which sold for varying sums on the black market. Two hundred dollars had been the going price for one vial last year; God knows what Eric's blood would bring, since he was so old. Proving that provenance would definitely be a problem for the Drainer. Draining was an extremely hazardous occupation, and it was also extremely illegal.

Eric was giving me a great gift.

I have never been what you would call squeamish, thank goodness. I closed my mouth over the little wounds, and I sucked.

Eric moaned, and I could tell quickly that he was once again pleased to be in such close contact. He began to move a little, and there wasn't a lot I could do about it. His left arm was keeping me firmly clamped against him, and his right arm was, after all, feeding me. It was still hard not to be icked out by the process. But Eric was definitely having a good time, and since with every pull I felt better, it was hard to argue with myself that this was a bad thing to be doing. I tried not to think, and I tried not to move myself in response. I remembered the time I'd taken Bill's blood because I needed extra strength, and I remembered Bill's reaction.

Eric pressed against me even harder, and suddenly he said, "Ohhhhh," and relaxed all over. I felt wetness against my back, and I took one deep, last draw. Eric groaned again, a deep and guttural sound, and his mouth trailed down the side of my neck.

"Don't bite me," I said. I was holding on to the remnants of my sanity with difficulty. What had excited me, I told myself, was my memory of Bill; his reaction when I'd bitten him, his intense arousal. Eric just happened to be here. I couldn't have sex with a vampire, especially Eric, just because I found him attractive—not when there would be such dire consequences. I was just too strung out to enumerate those consequences to myself. I was an adult, I told myself sternly; true adults don't have sex just because the other person is skilled and pretty.

Eric's fangs scraped my shoulder.

I launched myself out of that bed like a rocket. Intending to locate a bathroom, I flung open the door to find the short brunette vampire, the one with the curly hair, standing just outside, his left arm draped with clothes, his right raised to knock.

"Well, look at you," he said, smiling. And he certainly was looking. He burned his candle at both ends, apparently.

"You needed to talk to me?" I leaned against the door frame, doing my best to look wan and frail.

"Yes, after we cut your beautiful dress off, Russell figured you'd need some clothes. I happened to have these in my closet, and since we're the same height . . ."

"Oh," I said faintly. I'd never shared clothes with a guy. "Well, thank you so much. This is very kind of you." And it was. He'd brought some sweats (powder blue) and socks, and a silk bathrobe, and even some fresh panties. I didn't want to think about that too closely.

"You seem better," the small man said. His eyes were admiring, but not in any real personal way. Maybe I'd overestimated my charms.

"I am very shaky," I said quietly. "I was up because I was on my way to the bathroom."

Curly's brown eyes flared, and I could tell he was looking at Eric over my shoulder. This view definitely was more to his taste, and his smile became frankly inviting. "Leif, would you like to share my coffin today?" he asked, practically batting his eyelashes.

I didn't dare turn to look at Eric. There was a patch on my back that was still wet. I was suddenly disgusted with myself. I'd had thoughts about Alcide, and more than had thoughts about Eric. I was not pleased with my moral fiber. It was no excuse that I knew Bill had been unfaithful to me, or at least it wasn't much of an excuse.

It was probably also not an excuse that being with Bill had accustomed me to regular, spectacular sex. Or not much of an excuse.

It was time to pull my moral socks up and behave myself. Just deciding that made me feel better.

"I have to run an errand for Sookie," Eric was telling the curly-haired vamp. "I am not sure I'll return before daybreak, but if I do, you can be sure I'll seek you out." Eric was flirting back. While all this repartee was flying around me, I pulled on the silk robe, which was black and pink and white, all flowers. It was really outstanding. Curly spared me a glance, and seemed more interested than he had when I'd just appeared in my undies.

"Yum," he said simply.

"Again, thanks," I said. "Could you tell me where the nearest bathroom is?"

He pointed down the hall to a half-open door.

"Excuse me," I said to both of them, and reminded myself to walk slowly and carefully, as if I was still in pain, as I made my way down the hall. Past the bathroom, by maybe two doors, I could see the head of the staircase. Okay, I knew the way out now. That was actually a comfort.

The bathroom was just a regular old bathroom. It was full of the stuff that usually clutters bathrooms: hair dryers, hot curlers, deodorant, shampoo, styling gel. Some makeup. Brushes and combs and razors.

Though the counter was clean and orderly, it was apparent several people shared the room. I was willing to bet Russell Edgington's personal bathroom looked nothing like this one. I found some bobby pins and secured my hair on top of my head, and I took the quickest shower on record. Since my hair had just been washed that morning, which now seemed years ago and took forever to dry besides, I was glad to skip it in favor of scrubbing my skin vigorously with the scented soap in the built-in dish. There were clean towels in the closet, which was a relief.

I was back in the bedroom within fifteen minutes. Curly was gone, Eric was dressed, and Bubba was back.

Eric did not say one word about the embarrassing incident that had taken place between us. He eyed the robe appreciatively but silently.

"Bubba has scoped out the territory, Sookie," Eric said, clearly quoting.

Bubba was smiling his slightly lopsided smile. He was pleased with himself. "Miss Sookie, I found Bill," he said triumphantly. "He ain't in such good shape, but he's alive."

I sank into a chair with no forewarning. I was just lucky it was behind me. My back was still straight—but all of a sudden, I was sitting instead of standing. It was one more strange sensation in a night full of them.

When I was able to think of anything else, I noticed vaguely that Eric's expression was a bewildering blend of things: pleasure, regret, anger, satisfaction. Bubba just looked happy.

"Where is he?" My voice didn't even sound like my own.

"There's a big building in back of here, like a four-car garage, but it's got apartments on top of it and a room to the side."

Russell liked to keep his help handy.

"Are there other buildings? Could I get confused?"

"There's a swimming pool, Miss Sookie, and it's got a little building right by it for people to change into their bathing suits. And there's a great big toolshed, I think that's what it's for, but it's separate from the garage."

Eric said, "What part of the garage is he being kept in?"

Bubba said, "The room to the right side. I think maybe the garage used to be stables, and the room is where they kept the saddles and stuff. It isn't too big."

"How many are in there with him?" Eric was asking some good questions. I could not get over Bubba's assurance that Bill was still alive and that I was very close to him.

"They got three in there right now, Mr. Eric, two men and one woman. All three are vamps. She's the one with the knife."

I shrank inside myself. "Knife," I said.

"Yes'm, she's cut him up pretty bad."

This was no time to falter. I'd been priding myself on my lack of squeamishness earlier. This was the moment to prove I'd been telling the truth to myself.

"He's held out this long," I said.

"He has," Eric agreed. "Sookie, I will go to get a car. I'll try to park it back there by the stables."

"Do you think they'll let you back in?"

"If I take Bernard with me."

"Bernard?"

"The little one." Eric smiled at me, and his own smile was a little lopsided.

"You mean . . . Oh, if you take Curly with you, they'll let you back in because he lives here?"

"Yes. But I may have to stay here. With him."

"You couldn't, ah, get out of it?"

"Maybe, maybe not. I don't want to be caught here, rising, when they discover Bill is gone, and you with him."

"Miss Sookie, they'll put werewolves to guarding him during the day."

We both looked at Bubba simultaneously.

"Those werewolves that have been on your trail? They'll be guarding Bill when the vamps go to sleep."

"But tonight is the full moon," I said. "They'll be worn out when it's their turn to take over. If they show up at all."

Eric looked at me with some surprise. "You're right, Sookie. This is the best opportunity we're going to get."

We talked it over some more; perhaps I could act very weak and hole up in the house, waiting for a human ally of Eric's to arrive from Shreveport. Eric said he would call the minute he got out of the immediate area, on his cell phone.

Eric said, "Maybe Alcide could lend a hand tomorrow morning."

I have to admit, I was tempted by the idea of calling him in again. Alcide was big and tough and competent, and something hidden and weak in me suggested that surely Alcide would be able to manage everything better than I would. But my conscience gave an enormous twinge. Alcide, I argued, could not be involved further. He'd done his job. He had to deal with these people in a business way, and it would ruin him if Russell figured out his part in the escape of Bill Compton.

We couldn't spend any more time in discussion, because it lacked only two hours until dawn. With a lot of details still loose, Eric went to find Curly—Bernard— and coyly request his company on an errand to obtain a car I assumed he intended to rent, and what car rental place would be open at this hour was a mystery to me, but Eric didn't seem to anticipate any trouble. I tried to dismiss my doubts from my mind. Bubba agreed to go over Russell's wall again, as he'd entered, and find a place to go to ground for the day. Only the fact that this was the night of the full moon had saved Bubba's life, Eric said, and I was willing to believe it. The vampire guarding the gate might be good, but he couldn't be everywhere.

My job was to play weak until day, when the vampires would retire, and then somehow get Bill out of the stable and into the trunk of the car Eric would provide. They'd have no reason to stop me from leaving.

"This is maybe the worst plan I have ever heard," Eric said.

"You got that right, but it's all we have."

"You'll do great, Miss Sookie," Bubba told me encouragingly.

That's what I needed, a positive attitude. "Thank you, Bubba," I said, trying to sound as grateful as I felt. I was energized by Eric's blood. I felt like my eyes were shooting sparks and my hair was floating around my head in a electric halo.

"Don't get too carried away," Eric advised. He reminded me that this was a common problem with people who ingested black-market vampire blood. They attempted crazy things since they felt so strong, so invincible, and sometimes they just weren't up to the attempted feat—like the guy who tried to fight a whole gang at once, or the woman who took on an oncoming train. I took a deep breath, trying to impress his warning on my brain. What I wanted to do was lean out the window and see if I could crawl up the wall to the roof. Wow, Eric's blood was *awesome*. That was a word I'd never used before, but it was accurate. I'd never realized what a difference there would be between taking Bill's blood and taking Eric's.

There was a knock at the door, and we all looked at it as if we could see through it.

In an amazingly short time, Bubba was out the window, Eric was sitting in the chair by the bed, and I was in the bed trying to look weak and shaky.

"Come in," Eric called in a hushed voice, as befitted the companion of someone recuperating from a terrible wound.

It was Curly—that is, Bernard. Bernard was wearing jeans and a dark red sweater, and he looked good enough to eat. I closed my eyes and gave myself a stern lecture. The blood infusion had made me very lively.

"How is she doing?" Bernard asked, almost whispering. "Her color is better."

"Still in pain, but healing, thanks to the generosity of your king."

"He was glad to do it," Bernard said courteously. "But he will be, ah, best pleased if she can leave on her own tomorrow morning. He is sure by then her boyfriend will be back at his apartment after he has enjoyed the moon tonight. I hope this doesn't seem too brusque?"

"No, I can understand his concern," Eric said, being polite right back.

Apparently, Russell was afraid that I would stay for several days, cashing in on my act of heroism. Russell, unused to having human female houseguests, wanted me to go back to Alcide, when he was sure Alcide would be able to see after me. Russell was a little uneasy about an unknown woman wandering around his compound during the day, when he and all his retinue would be in their deep sleep.

Russell was quite right to worry about this.

"Then I'll go get her a car and park it in the area to the rear of the house, and she can drive herself out tomorrow. If you can arrange that she'll have safe passage through the front gates—I assume they are guarded during the day?—I will have fulfilled my obligation to my friend Alcide."

"That sounds very reasonable," Bernard said, giving me a fraction of the smile he was aiming at Eric. I didn't return it. I closed my eyes wearily. "I'll leave word at the gate when we go. My car okay? It's just a little old egg-beater, but it'll get us to . . . where did you want to go?"

"I'll tell you when we're on the road. It's close to the home of a friend of mine. He knows a man who'll loan me the car for a day or two."

Well, he'd found a way to obtain a car without a paper trail. Good.

I felt movement to my left. Eric bent over me. I knew it was Eric, because his blood inside me informed me so. This was really scary, and this was why Bill had warned me against taking blood from any vampire other than him. Too late. Rock and a hard place.

He kissed my cheek in a chaste, friend-of-the-boyfriend way. "Sookie," he said very quietly. "Can you hear me?"

I nodded just a trifle.

"Good. Listen, I am going to get you a car. I'll leave the keys up here by the bed when I get back. In the morning, you need to drive out of here and back to Alcide's. Do you understand?"

I nodded again. "Bye," I said, trying to make my voice drowsy. "Thank you."

"My pleasure," he said, and I heard the edge in his voice. With an effort, I kept my face straight.

It's hard to credit, but I actually fell asleep after they left. Bubba had evidently obeyed, and gone over the fence to arrange shelter for the day. The mansion became very quiet as the night's revelries drew to a close. I supposed the werewolves were off having their last howl somewhere. As I was drifting off, I wondered how the other shape-shifters had fared. What did they do with their clothes? Tonight's drama at Club Dead had been a fluke; I was sure they had a normal procedure. I wondered where Alcide was. Maybe he had caught that son of a bitch Newlin.

I woke up when I heard the chink of keys.

"I'm back," Eric said. His voice was very quiet, and I had to open my eyes a little to make sure he was actually there. "It's a white Lincoln. I parked out by the garage; there wasn't room inside, which is a real pity.

They wouldn't let me get any closer to confirm what Bubba said. Are you hearing me?"

I nodded.

"Good luck." Eric hesitated. "If I can disentangle myself, I'll meet you in the parking garage at first dark tonight. If you aren't there, I'll go back to Shreveport."

I opened my eyes. The room was dark, still; I could see Eric's skin glowing. Mine was, too. That scared the tar out of me. I had just stopped glowing from taking Bill's blood (in an emergency situation), when here came another crisis, and now I was shining like a disco ball. Life around vampires was just one continuous emergency, I decided.

"We'll talk later," Eric said ominously.

"Thanks for the car," I said.

Eric looked down at me. He seemed to have a hickey on his neck. I opened my mouth, and then shut it again. Better not to comment.

"I don't like having feelings," Eric said coldly, and he left.

That was a tough exit line to top.

# Chapter Eleven

THERE WAS A line of light in the sky when I crept out of the mansion of the king of Mississippi. It was a little warmer this morning, and the sky was dark with not just night, but rain. I had a little roll of my belongings under my arm. Somehow my purse and my black velvet shawl had made it here to the mansion from the nightclub, and I had rolled my high heels in the shawl. The purse did have the key to Alcide's apartment in it, the one he'd loaned me, so I felt reassured that I could find shelter there if need be. I had the blanket from the bed folded neatly under my other arm. I'd made the bed up, so its loss would not be obvious for a little while.

What Bernard had not loaned me was a jacket. When I'd snuck out, I'd snagged a dark blue quilted jacket that had been hanging on the banister. I felt very guilty. I'd never stolen anything before. Now I had taken the blanket and the jacket. My conscience was protesting vigorously.

When I considered what I might have to do to get out of this compound, taking a jacket and a blanket seemed pretty mild. I told my conscience to shut up.

As I crept through the cavernous kitchen and opened the back door, my feet were sliding around in the elastic-sided slippers Bernard had included in the bundle of clothes he'd brought to my room. The socks and slippers were better than teetering in the heels, by a long shot.

I hadn't seen anyone so far. I seemed to have hit the magic time. Almost all the vampires were securely in their coffins, or beds, or in the ground, or whatever the heck they did during the day. Almost all the Were creatures, of whatever persuasion, were not back from their last night's binge or were already sleeping it off. But I was vibrating with tension, because at any moment this luck might run out.

Behind the mansion, there was indeed a smallish swimming pool, covered for the winter by a huge black tarp. It had weighted edges that extended far beyond the actual perimeter of the pool. The tiny pool house was completely dark. I moved silently down a pathway created with uneven flagstones, and after I passed through a gap in a dense hedge, I found myself in a paved area. With my enhanced vision, I was able to see instantly that I had found the courtyard in front of the former stables. It was a large edifice sided with white clapboards, and the second story (where Bubba had spotted apartments) had gable-style windows. Though his was the fanciest garage I had ever seen, the bays for cars did not have doors, but open archways. I could count four vehicles parked inside, from the limo to a Jeep. And there, on the right, instead of a fifth archway, there was a solid wall, and in it, a door.

*Bill,* I thought. *Bill.* My heart was pounding now. With an overwhelming sense of relief, I spotted the Lincoln parked close to the door. I turned the key in the driver's door, and it clicked open. When I opened the door, the dome light came on, but there didn't seem to be anyone here to see it. I tucked my little bundle of belongings on the passenger seat, and I eased the driver's door almost shut. I found a little switch and turned off the dome light. I took a precious minute to look at the dashboard, though I was so excited and terrified, it was hard to focus. Then I went to the rear of the vehicle and unlocked the trunk. It was just huge— but not clean, like the interior. I had the idea that Eric had gathered up all the large contents and tossed them in the trash, leaving the bottom littered with cigarette rolling papers, plastic bags, and spots of white powder on the floor. Hmmm. Well, okay. That couldn't be too important. Eric had stuck in two bottles of blood, and I moved them over to one side. The trunk was dirty, yes, but clear of anything that would cause Bill discomfort.

I took a deep breath, and clutched the blanket to my chest. Wrapped in its folds was the stake that had hurt me so badly. It was the only weapon I had, and despite its grisly appearance (it was still stained with my blood and a little tissue), I had retrieved it from the wastebasket and brought it with me. After all, I knew for sure it could cause damage.

The sky was a shade lighter, but when I felt raindrops on my face, I felt confident the darkness would last a little longer. I skulked my way to the garage. Creeping around surely looked suspicious, but I simply could not make myself stride purposefully over to the door. The gravel made silence almost impossible, but still I tried to step lightly.

I put my ear to the door, listened with all my enhanced ability. I was picking up nothing. At least I knew there was no human inside. Turning the knob slowly, easing it back into position after I pushed, I stepped into the room.

The floor was wooden, and covered with stains. The smell was awful. I knew immediately that Russell had used this room for torture before. Bill was in the center of the room, lashed to a straight-back chair by silver chains.

After the confused emotions and unfamiliar surroundings of the past few days, I felt like the world suddenly came into focus.

Everything was clear. Here was Bill. I would save him.

And after I'd had a good look at him in the light of the naked bulb hanging from the ceiling, I knew I would do *anything* to save him.

I had never imagined anything so bad.

There were burn marks under the silver chains, which were draped all around him. I knew that silver caused unremitting agony to a vampire, and my Bill was suffering that now. He had been burned with other things, and cut, cut more than he could heal. He had been starved, and he had been denied sleep. He was slumped over now, and I knew he was taking what respite he could while his tormenters were gone. His dark hair was matted with blood.

There were two doors leading out of the windowless room. One, to my right, led to a dormitory of sorts. I could see some beds through the open doorway. There was a man passed out on one, just sprawled across the cot fully clothed. One of the werewolves, back after his monthly toot. He was snoring, and there were dark smears around his mouth that I didn't want to look at more closely. I couldn't see the rest of the room, so I couldn't be sure if there were others; it would be smart to assume there were.

The door at the rear of the room led farther back into the garage, perhaps to the stairs going up to the apartments. I couldn't spare the time to investigate. I had a feeling of urgency, impelling me to get Bill out as fast as I could. I was trembly with the need to hurry. So far,

I had encountered enormous luck. I couldn't count on its holding.

I took two steps closer to Bill.

I knew when he smelled me, realized it was me.

His head snapped up and his eyes blazed at me. A terrible hope shone on his filthy face. I held up a finger; I stepped quietly over to the open door to the dormitory, and gently, gently, slid it almost shut. Then I glided behind him, looking down at the chains. There were two small padlocks, like the ones you put on your locker at school, holding the chains together. "Key?" I breathed in Bill's ear. He had an unbroken finger, and that was the one he used to point at the door I'd come in by. Two keys hung on a nail by the door, quite high from the floor, and always in Bill's sight. Of course they'd think of that. I put the blanket and stake on the floor by Bill's feet. I crept across the stained floor, and reached up as far as I could strain. I couldn't reach the keys. A vampire who could float would be able to get them. I reminded myself I was strong, strong from Eric's blood.

There was a shelf on the wall that held interesting things like pokers and pincers. Pincers! I stood on my tiptoes and lifted them off the shelf, trying hard to keep my gorge from rising when I saw they were crusted with—oh, horrible stuff. I held them up, and they were very heavy, but I managed to clamp them on the keys, work them forward off the nail, and lower the pincers until I could take the keys from their pointed ends. I exhaled a giant sigh of relief, as silently as you can exhale. That hadn't been so hard.

In fact, that was the last easy thing I encountered. I began the horrible task of unwrapping Bill, while trying to keep the movement of the chains as silent as I could. It was oddly difficult to unwind the shiny rope of links. In fact, they seemed to be sticking to Bill, whose whole body was rigid with tension.

Then I understood. He was trying not to scream out loud as the chains were pulled out of his charred flesh. My stomach lurched. I had to stop my task for a few precious seconds, and I had to inhale very carefully. If it was this hard for me to witness his agony, how much harder must it be for Bill to endure it?

I braced up my mental fortitude, and I began working again. My grandmother always told me women could do whatever they had to do, and once again, she was right.

There were literally yards of silver chain, and the careful unwinding took more time than I liked. *Any* time was more time than I liked. The danger lurked right over my shoulder. I was breathing disaster, in and out, with every breath. Bill was very weak, and struggling to stay awake now that the sun had risen. It helped that the day was so dark, but he would not be able to move much when the sun was high, no matter how dreary the day.

The last bit of chain slid to the floor.

"You have to stand up," I said in Bill's ear. "You just have to. I know it hurts. But I can't carry you." At least, I didn't think I could. "There's a big Lincoln outside, and the trunk is open. I'm putting you in the trunk, wrapped in this blanket, and we're driving out of here. Understand, babe?"

Bill's dark head moved a fraction of an inch.

Right then our luck ran out.

"Who the hell are you?" asked a heavily accented voice. Someone had come through the door at my back

Bill flinched under my hands. I whirled to face her, dipping to pick up the stake as I did so, and then she was on me.

I had talked myself into believing they were all in their coffins for the day, but this one was doing her best to kill me.

I would have been dead in a minute if she hadn't been as shocked as I was. I twisted my arm from her grasp and pivoted around Bill in his chair. Her fangs were all out, and she was snarling at me over Bill's head. She was a blond, like me, but her eyes were brown and her build was smaller; she was a tiny woman. She had dried blood on her hands, and I knew it was Bill's. A flame started up inside me. I could feel it flicker through my eyes.

"You must be his little human bitch whore," she said. "He was fucking me, all this time, you understand. The minute he saw me, he forgot about you, except for pity."

Well, Lorena wasn't elegant, but she knew where to sink the verbal knife. I batted the words aside, because she wanted to distract me. I shifted my grip on the stake to be ready, and she leaped across Bill to land on top of me.

As she moved, without a conscious decision I whipped up the stake and pointed it at an angle. As she came down on me, the sharp point went in her chest and out the other side. Then we were on the floor. I was still gripping the end of the stake, and she was holding herself off of me with her arms. She looked down at the wood in her chest, astonished. Then she looked in my eyes, her mouth agape, her fangs retracting. "No," she said. Her eyes went dull.

I used the stake to push her to my left side, and I scrambled up off the floor. I was panting, and my hands shook violently. She didn't move. The whole incident had been so swift and so quiet that it hardly felt real.

Bill's eyes went from the thing on the floor to me. His expression was unreadable. "Well," I told him, "I killed *her* ass."

Then I was on my knees beside her, trying not to vomit.

It took me more precious seconds to regain control of myself. I had a goal I had to meet. Her death would not do me a bit of good if I couldn't get Bill out of here

before someone else came in. Since I had done something so horrible, I had to get something, some advantage out of it.

It would be a smart thing to conceal the body—which
was beginning to shrivel—but that had to take second
place to removing Bill. I wrapped the blanket around his
shoulders as he sat slumped in the stained chair. I'd been
afraid to look at his face since I'd done this thing.

"That was Lorena?" I whispered in Bill's ear, plagued
by a sudden doubt. "She did this to you?"

He gave that tiny nod again.

Ding dong, the witch was dead.

After a pause, while I waited to feel something, the
only thing I could think of was asking Bill why someone
named Lorena would have a foreign accent. That was
dumb, so I forgot about it.

"You got to wake up. You got to stay awake till I get
you in the car, Bill." I was trying to keep a mental eye
open for the Weres in the next room. One of them began
snoring behind the closed door, and I felt the mental stir
of another, one I hadn't been able to spot. I froze for
several seconds, before I could feel that mind settle into
a sleep pattern again. I took a deep, deep breath and
pulled a flap of blanket over Bill's head. Then I got his
left arm draped around my neck, and I heaved. He came
up out of the chair, and though he gave a ragged hiss of
pain, he managed to shuffle to the door. I was more than
half carrying him, so I was glad to stop there and grab
the knob and twist it. Then I almost lost hold of him,
since he was literally sleeping on his feet.

Only the danger that we would be caught was stim-
ulating him enough to afford movement.

The door opened, and I checked to make sure the
blanket, which happened to be fuzzy and yellow, completely covered his head. Bill moaned and went almost
completely limp when he felt the sunlight, weak and

watery as it was. I began talking to him under my breath, cursing him and challenging him to move, telling him I could keep him awake if that bitch Lorena could, telling him I would beat him up if he didn't make it to the car.

Finally, with a tremendous effort that left me trembling, I got Bill to the trunk of the car. I pushed it open. "Bill, just sit on the lip here," I told him, tugging at him until he was facing me and sitting on the edge of the trunk. But the life left him completely at that point, and he simply collapsed backward. As he folded into the space, he made a deep pain noise that tore at my heart, and then he was absolutely silent and limp. It was always terrifying to see Bill die like that. I wanted to shake him, scream at him, pound on his chest.

There was no point in any of that.

I made myself shove all the sticking-out bits—a leg, an arm—into the trunk with him, and then I closed it. I allowed myself the luxury of a moment of intense relief.

Standing in the dim daylight in the deserted courtyard, I conducted a brief inner debate. Should I attempt to hide Lorena's body? Would such an effort be worth the time and energy?

I changed my mind about six times in the course of thirty seconds. I finally decided that yeah, it might be worth it. If there was no body to see, the Weres might suppose that Lorena had taken Bill somewhere for a little extra torture session. And Russell and Betty Joe would be dead to the world and unavailable to give instructions. I had no illusions that Betty Joe would be grateful enough to me to spare me, if I should get caught right now. A somewhat quicker death would be the most I could hope for.

My decision reached, back into that awful blood-stained room I went. Misery had soaked into the walls, along with the stains. I wondered how many humans, Weres, and vampires had been held prisoner in this room. Gathering up the chains as silently as I could, I stuffed them in Lorena's blouse, so anyone checking out the room might assume they were still around Bill. I looked around to see if there was any more cleanup I needed to do. There was so much blood in the room already, Lorena's made no difference.

Time to get her out of there.

To keep her heels from dragging and making noise, I had to lift her onto my shoulder. I had never done such a thing, and the procedure was awkward. Lucky for me she was so small, and lucky I'd practiced blocking things out of my mind all these years. Otherwise, the way Lorena dangled, completely limp, and the way she was beginning to flake away, would have freaked me out. I gritted my teeth, to hold back the bubble of hysteria starting up my throat.

It was raining heavily as I carried the body to the pool. Without Eric's blood, I could never have lifted the weighted edge of the pool cover, but I managed it with one hand and pushed what was left of Lorena into the pool with one foot. I was aware at any second that someone could look out the windows at the back of the mansion and see me, realize what I was doing—but if any of the humans living in the house did so, they decided to keep silent.

I was beginning to feel overwhelmingly weary. I trudged back down the flagstone path through the hedge to the car. I leaned on it for a minute, just breathing, gathering myself. Then I got in the driver's seat, and turned the key in the ignition. The Lincoln was the biggest car I'd ever driven, and one of the most luxurious cars I'd ever been in, but just at the moment I could take no interest or pleasure in it. I buckled my seat belt, adjusted the mirror and the seat, and looked at the dashboard carefully. I was going to need the windshield wipers, of course. This car was a new one, and the lights came on automatically, so that was one less worry.

I took a deep breath. This was at least phase three of the rescue of Bill. It was scary how much of this had happened by sheer chance, but the best-laid plans never take every happenstance into account anyway. Not possible. Generally, my plans tended to be what I called roomy.

I swung the car around and drove out of the courtyard. The drive swept in a graceful curve and went across the front of the main building. For the first time, I saw the facade of the mansion. It was as beautiful—white painted siding, huge columns—as I had imagined. Russell had spent a pretty penny renovating the place.

The driveway wound through grounds that still looked manicured even in their winter brown state, but that long driveway was all too short. I could see the wall ahead of me. There was the checkpoint at the gate, and it was manned. I was sweating despite the cold.

I stopped just before the gate. There was a little white cubicle to one side, and it was glass from waist level up. It extended inside and outside the wall, so guards could check both incoming and outgoing vehicles. I hoped it was heated, for the sake of the two Weres on duty. Both of them were wearing their leathers and looking mighty grumpy. They'd had a hard night, no doubt about it. As I pulled to a stop, I resisted an almost overwhelming temptation to plow right through those gates. One of the Weres came out. He was carrying a rifle, so it was a good thing I hadn't acted on that impulse.

"I guess Bernard told you all I'd be leaving this morning?" I said, after I'd rolled down my window. I attempted a smile.

"You the one who got staked last night?" My questioner was surly and stubbly, and he smelled like a wet dog.

"Yeah."

"How you feeling?"

"Better, thank you."

"You coming back for the crucifixion?"

Surely I hadn't heard him right. "Excuse me?" I asked faintly.

His companion, who'd come to stand in the hut's door, said, "Doug, shut up."

Doug glowered at his fellow Were, but he shrugged after the glower didn't have any effect. "Okay, you're cleared to go."

The gates opened, way too slowly to suit me. When they were wide, and the Weres had stepped back, I drove sedately through. I suddenly realized I had no idea which way to go, but it seemed correct to turn left, since I wanted to head back to Jackson. My subconscious was telling me we had turned right to enter the driveway the night before.

My subconscious was a big fat liar.

After five minutes, I was fairly positive I was lost, and the sun continued to rise, naturally, even through the mass of clouds. I couldn't remember how well the blanket covered Bill, and I wasn't sure how light-tight the trunk would be. After all, safe transportation of vampires was not something the carmakers would cover in their list of specs.

On the other hand, I told myself, the trunk would have to be waterproof—that was sure important—so light-proof couldn't be far behind. Nonetheless, it seemed vitally important to find a dark place to park the Lincoln for the remaining hours of the day. Though every impulse told me to drive hard and get as far away from the mansion as I could, just in case someone went checking for Bill and put two and two together, I pulled over to the side of the road and opened the glove compartment. God bless America! There was a map of Mississippi with an inset for Jackson.

Which would have helped if I'd had any idea where I was at the moment.

People making desperate escapes aren't supposed to get lost.

I took a few deep breaths. I pulled back out into the road and drove on until I saw a busy gas station. Though the Lincoln's tank was full (thank you, Eric) I pulled in and parked at one of the pumps. The car on the other side was a black Mercedes, and the woman pumping the gas was an intelligent-looking middle-aged woman dressed in casual, comfortable, nice clothes. As I got the windshield squeegee out of its vat of water, I said, "You wouldn't happen to know how to get back to I-20 from here, would you?"

"Oh, sure," she said. She smiled. She was the kind of person who just loves to help other people, and I was thanking my lucky stars I'd spotted her. "This is Madison, and Jackson is south of here. I-55 is maybe a mile over that way." She pointed west. "You take I-55 south, and you'll run right into I-20. Or, you could take . . ."

I was about to be overloaded with information. "Oh, that sounds perfect. Let me just do that, or I'll lose track."

"Sure, glad I could help."

"Oh, you surely did."

We beamed at each other, just two nice women. I had to fight an impulse to say, "There's a tortured vampire in my trunk," out of sheer giddiness. I had rescued Bill, and I was alive, and tonight we would be on our way back to Bon Temps. Life would be wonderfully trouble-free. Except, of course, for dealing with my unfaithful boyfriend, finding out if the werewolf's body we'd disposed of in Bon Temps had been found, waiting to hear the same about the werewolf who'd been stuffed in Alcide's closet, and waiting for the reaction of the queen of Louisiana to Bill's indiscretion with Lorena. His verbal indiscretion: I didn't think for one minute that she would care about his sexual activities.

Other than that, we were hunky-dory.

"Sufficient unto the day is the evil thereof," I told myself. That had been Gran's favorite Bible quotation. When I was about nine, I'd asked her to explain that to me, and she'd said, "Don't go looking for trouble; it's already looking for you."

Bearing that in mind, I cleared my mental decks. My next goal was simply to get back to Jackson and the shelter of the garage. I followed the instructions the kind woman had given me, and I had the relief of entering Jackson within a half hour.

I knew if I could find the state capitol, I could find Alcide's apartment building. I hadn't allowed for one-way streets, and I hadn't been paying awful close attention to directions when Alcide gave me my little tour of downtown Jackson. But there aren't that many five-story buildings in the whole state of Mississippi, even in the capital. After a tense period of cruising, I spotted it.

*Now*, I thought, *all my troubles will be over*. Isn't it dumb to think that? Ever?

I pulled into the area by the little guard cubicle, where you had to wait to be recognized while the guy flipped the switch, or punched the button, or whatever made the barrier lift up. I was terrified he might deny me entrance because I didn't have a special sticker, like Alcide did on his truck.

The man wasn't there. The cubicle was empty. Surely that was wrong? I frowned, wondering what to do. But here the guard came, in his heavy brown uniform, trudging up the ramp. When he saw I was waiting, he looked stricken, and hurried up to the car. I sighed. I would have to talk to him after all. I pushed the button that would lower my window.

"I'm sorry I was away from my post," he said instantly. "I had to, ah . . . personal needs."

I had a little leverage here.

"I had to go borrow me a car," I said. "Can I get a temporary sticker?" I looked at him in a way that clued him in to my mindset. That look said, "Don't hassle me about getting the sticker, and I won't say a word about you leaving your post."

"Yes, ma'am. That's apartment 504?"

"You have a wonderful memory," I said, and his seamed face flushed.

"Part of the job," he said nonchalantly, and handed me a laminated number that I stuck on the dashboard. "If you'll just hand that in when you leave for good, please? Or if you plan on staying, you'll have to fill out a form we can have on file, and we'll give you a sticker. Actually," he said, stumbling a little, embarrassed, "Mr. Herveaux will have to fill it out, as the property owner."

"Sure," I said. "No problem." I gave him a cheery wave, and he retreated to the cubicle to raise the barrier.

I drove into the dark parking garage, feeling that rush of relief that follows clearing a major hurdle.

Reaction set in. I was shaking all over when I took the keys out of the ignition. I thought I saw Alcide's pickup over a couple of rows, but I had parked as deeply in the garage as I could—in the darkest corner, away from all the other cars, as it happened. This was as far as I had planned. I had no idea what to do next. I hadn't really believed I would get this far. I leaned back in the comfortable seat just for a minute, to relax and stop shaking before I got out. I'd had the heater on full blast during my drive from the mansion, so it was toasty warm inside the car.

When I woke up, I'd been asleep for hours.

The car was cold, and I was colder, despite the stolen quilted jacket. I got out of the driver's seat stiffly, stretching and bending to relieve cramped joints.

Maybe I should check on Bill. He had gotten rolled around in the trunk, I was sure, and I needed to make sure he was covered.

Actually, I just wanted to see him again. My heart actually beat faster at the thought. I was a real idiot.

I checked my distance from the weak sunlight at the entrance; I was well away. And I had parked so the trunk opening was pointed away from that bit of sunlight.

Yielding to temptation, I stepped around to the back of the car. I turned the key in the lock, pulled it out and popped it in my jacket pocket, and watched as the lid rose.

In the dim garage, I couldn't see too well, and it was hard to make out even the fuzzy yellow blanket. Bill appeared to be pretty well concealed. I bent over a little more, so I could arrange a fold further over his head. I had only a second's warning, a scuff of a shoe against the concrete, and then I felt a forceful shove from behind.

I fell into the trunk on top of Bill.

An instant and extra shove brought my legs in, and the trunk slammed shut.

Now Bill and I were locked in the trunk of the Lincoln.

# Chapter Twelve

DEBBIE. I FIGURED it had been Debbie. After I got over my initial flood of panic, which lasted longer than I wanted to admit, I tried to relive the few seconds carefully. I'd caught a trace of brain pattern, enough to inform me that my attacker was a shifter. I figured it must have been Alcide's former girlfriend—his not-so-former girlfriend, apparently, since she was hanging around his garage.

Had she been waiting for me to return to Alcide since the night before? Or had she met up with him at some point during the craziness of the full moon? Debbie had been even more angered by my escorting Alcide than I could have imagined. Either she loved him, or she was extremely possessive.

Not that her motivation was any big concern right now. My big concern was air. For the first time, I felt lucky that Bill didn't breathe.

I made my own breath slow and even. No deep, panicky gasps, no thrashing. I made myself figure things out. Okay, I'd entered the trunk probably about, hmm, one p.m. Bill would wake around five, when it was getting dark. Maybe he'd sleep a little longer, because he'd been so exhausted—but no later than six-thirty, for sure. When he was awake, he'd be able to get us out of here. Or would he? He was very weak. He'd been terribly injured, and his injuries would take a while in healing, even for a vampire. He would need rest and blood before he'd be up to par. And he hadn't had any blood in a week. As that thought passed through my mind, I suddenly felt cold.

Cold all over.

Bill would be hungry. Really, really hungry. Crazy hungry.

And here I was—fast food.

Would he know who I was? Would he realize it was me, in time to stop?

It hurt even worse to think that he might not care enough anymore—care enough about me—to stop. He might just keep sucking and sucking, until I was drained dry. After all, he'd had an affair with Lorena. He'd seen me kill her, right in front of his eyes. Granted, she'd betrayed and tortured him, and that should have doused his ardor, right there. But aren't relationships crazy anyway?

Even my grandmother would have said, "Oh, *shit*."

Okay. I had stay calm. I had to breathe shallow and slow to save air. And I had to rearrange our bodies, so I could be more comfortable. I was relieved this was the biggest trunk I'd ever seen, because that made such a maneuver possible. Bill was limp—well, he was dead, of course. So I could sort of shove him without worrying too much about the consequences. The trunk was cold, too, and I tried to unwrap Bill a little bit so I could share the blanket.

The trunk was also quite dark. I could write the car designer a letter, and let him know I could vouch for its light-tightness, if that was how you'd put it. If I got out

of here alive, that is. I felt the shape of the two bottles
of blood. Maybe Bill would be content with that?

Suddenly, I remembered an article I'd read in a news
magazine while I was waiting in the dentist's office. It
was about a woman who'd been taken hostage and
forced into the trunk of her own car, and she'd been
campaigning ever since to have inside latches installed
in trunks so any captive could release herself. I wondered if she'd influenced the people who made Lincolns.
I felt all around the trunk, at least the parts I could reach,
and I did feel a latch release, maybe; there was a place
where wires were sticking into the trunk. But whatever
handle they'd been attached to had been clipped off.

I tried pulling, I tried yanking to the left or right.
Damn it, this just wasn't right. I almost went nuts, there
in that trunk. The means of escape was in there with me,
and I couldn't make it work. My fingertips went over
and over the wires, but to no purpose.

The mechanism had been disabled.

I tried real hard to figure out how that could have
happened. I am ashamed to confess, I wondered if somehow Eric knew I'd be shut in the trunk, and this was his
way of saying, "That's what you get for preferring Bill."
But I just couldn't believe that. Eric sure had some big
blank moral blind spots, but I didn't think he'd do that
to me. After all, he hadn't reached his stated goal of
having me, which was the nicest way I could put it to
myself.

Since I had nothing else to do but think, which didn't
take up extra oxygen, as far as I knew, I considered the
car's previous owner. It occurred to me that Eric's friend
had pointed out a car that would be easy to steal; a car
belonging to someone who was sure to be out late at
night, someone who could afford a fine car, someone
whose trunk would hold the litter of cigarette papers,
powder, and Baggies.

Eric had liberated the Lincoln from a drug dealer, I was willing to bet. And that drug dealer had disabled the inner trunk release for reasons I didn't even want to think about too closely.

Oh, give me a break, I thought indignantly. (It was easy just then to forget the many breaks I'd had during the day.) Unless I got a final break, and got out of this trunk before Bill awoke, none of the others would exactly count.

It was a Sunday, and very close to Christmas, so the garage was silent. Maybe some people had gone home for the holidays, and the legislators had gone home to their constituency, and the other people were busy doing . . . Christmas, Sunday stuff. I heard one car leave while I lay there, and then I heard voices after a time; two people getting off the elevator. I screamed, and banged on the trunk lid, but the sound was swallowed up in the starting of a big engine. I quieted immediately, frightened of using more air than I could afford.

I'll tell you, time spent in the nearly pitch-black dark, in a confined space, waiting for something to happen— that's pretty awful time. I didn't have a watch on; I would have had to have one with those hands that light up, anyway. I never fell asleep, but I drifted into an odd state of suspension. This was mostly due to the cold, I expect. Even with the quilted jacket and the blanket, it was very cold in the trunk. Still, cold, unmoving, dark, silent. My mind drifted.

Then I was terrified.

Bill was moving. He stirred, made a pain noise. Then his body seemed to go tense. I knew he had smelled me.

"Bill," I said hoarsely, my lips almost too stiff with cold to move. "Bill, it's me, Sookie. Bill, are you okay? There's some bottled blood in here. Drink it *now*."

He struck.

In his hunger, he made no attempt to spare me anything, and it hurt like the six shades of hell.

"Bill, it's me," I said, starting to cry. "Bill, it's me. Don't do this, honey. Bill, it's Sookie. There's True-Blood in here."

But he didn't stop. I kept talking, and he kept sucking, and I was becoming even colder, and very weak. His arms were clamping me to him, and struggling was no use, it would only excite him more. His leg was slung over my legs.

"Bill," I whispered, thinking it was already maybe too late. With the little strength I had left, I pinched his ear with the fingers of my right hand. "Please listen, Bill."

"Ow," he said. His voice sounded rough; his throat was sore. He had stopped taking blood. Now another need was on him, one closely related to feeding. His hands pulled down my sweatpants, and after a lot of fumbling and rearranging and contorting, he entered me with no preparation at all. I screamed, and he clapped a hand over my mouth. I was crying, sobbing, and my nose was all stopped up, and I needed to breathe through my mouth. All restraint left me and I began fighting like a wildcat. I bit and scratched and kicked, not caring about the air supply, not caring that I would enrage him. I just had to have air.

After a few seconds, his hand fell away. And he stopped moving. I drew air in with a deep, shuddering gasp. I was crying in earnest, one sob after another.

"Sookie?" Bill said uncertainly. "Sookie?"

I couldn't answer.

"It's you," he said, his voice hoarse and wondering. "It's you. You were really there in that room?"

I tried to gather myself, but I felt very fuzzy and I was afraid I was going to faint. Finally, I was able to say, "Bill," in a whisper.

"It is you. Are you all right?"

"No," I said almost apologetically. After all, it was

Bill who'd been held prisoner and tortured.

"Did I . . ." He paused, and seemed to brace himself. "Have I taken more blood than I should?"

I couldn't answer. I laid my head on his arm. It seemed too much trouble to speak.

"I seem to be having sex with you in a closet," Bill said in a subdued voice. "Did you, ah, volunteer?"

I turned my head from side to side, then let it loll on his arm again.

"Oh, no," he whispered. "Oh, no." He pulled out of me and fumbled around a lot for the second time. He was putting me back to rights; himself, too, I guess. His hands patted our surroundings. "Car trunk," he muttered.

"I need air," I said, in a voice almost too soft to hear.

"Why didn't you say so?" Bill punched a hole in the trunk. He *was* stronger. Good for him.

Cold air rushed in and I sucked it deep. Beautiful, beautiful oxygen.

"Where are we?" he asked, after a moment.

"Parking garage," I gasped. "Apartment building. Jackson." I was so weak, I just wanted to let go and float away.

"Why?"

I tried to gather enough energy to answer him. "Alcide lives here," I managed to mutter, eventually.

"Alcide who? What are we supposed to do now?"

"Eric's . . . coming. Drink the bottled blood."

"Sookie? Are you all right?"

I couldn't answer. If I could have, I might have said, "Why do you care? You were going to leave me anyway." I might have said, "I forgive you," though that doesn't seem real likely. Maybe I would have just told him that I'd missed him, and that his secret was still safe with me; faithful unto death, that was Sookie Stackhouse.

I heard him open a bottle.

As I was drifting off in a boat down a current that seemed to be moving ever faster, I realized that Bill had never revealed my name. I knew they had tried to find it out, to kidnap me and bring me to be tortured in front of him for extra leverage. And he hadn't told.

The trunk opened with a noise of tearing metal.

Eric stood outlined by the fluorescent lights of the garage. They'd come on when it got dark. "What are you two doing in here?" he asked.

But the current carried me away before I could answer.

"SHE'S COMING AROUND," Eric observed. "Maybe that was enough blood." My head buzzed for a minute, went silent again.

"She really is," he was saying next, and my eyes flickered open to register three anxious male faces hovering above me: Eric's, Alcide's, and Bill's. Somehow, the sight made me want to laugh. So many men at home were scared of me, or didn't want to think about me, and here were the three men in the world who wanted to have sex with me, or who at least had thought about it seriously; all crowding around the bed. I giggled, actually giggled, for the first time in maybe ten years. "The Three Musketeers," I said.

"Is she hallucinating?" Eric asked.

"I think she's laughing at us," Alcide said. He didn't sound unhappy about that. He put an empty TrueBlood bottle on the vanity table behind him. There was a large pitcher beside it, and a glass.

Bill's cool fingers laced with mine. "Sookie," he said, in that quiet voice that always sent shivers down my spine. I tried to focus on his face. He was sitting on the bed to my right.

He looked better. The deepest cuts were scars on his face, and the bruises were fading.

"They said, was I coming back for the crucifixion?" I told him.

"Who said that to you?" He bent over me, his face intent, dark eyes wide.

"Guards at the gate."

"The guards at the gates of the mansion asked you if you were coming back for a crucifixion tonight? This night?"

"Yes."

"Whose?"

"Don't know."

"I would have expected you to say, 'Where am I? What happened to me?' " Eric said. "Not ask whose crucifixion would be taking place—perhaps is taking place," he corrected himself, glancing at the clock by the bed.

"Maybe they meant mine?" Bill looked a little stunned by the idea. "Maybe they decided to kill me tonight?"

"Or perhaps they caught the fanatic who tried to stake Betty Joe?" Eric suggested. "He would be a prime candidate for crucifixion."

I thought it over, as much as I was able to reason through the weariness that kept threatening to overwhelm me. "Not the picture I got," I whispered. My neck was very, very sore.

"You were able to read something from the Weres?" Eric asked.

I nodded. "I think they meant Bubba," I whispered, and everyone in the room froze.

"That cretin," Eric said savagely, after he'd had time to process that. "They caught him?"

"Think so." That was the impression I'd gotten.

"We'll have to retrieve him," Bill said. "If he's still alive."

It was very brave for Bill to say he would go back in that compound. I would never have said that, if I'd been him.

The silence that had fallen was distinctly uneasy.

"Eric?" Bill's dark eyebrows arched; he was waiting for a comment.

Eric looked royally angry. "I guess you are right. We have the responsibility of him. I can't believe his home state is willing to execute him! Where is their loyalty?"

"And you?" Bill's voice was considerably cooler as he asked Alcide.

Alcide's warmth filled the room. So did the confused tangle of his thoughts. He'd spent part of last night with Debbie, all right.

"I don't see how I can," Alcide said desperately. "My business, my father's, depends on my being able to come here often. And if I'm on the outs with Russell and his crew, that would be almost impossible. It's going to be difficult enough when they realize Sookie must be the one who stole their prisoner."

"And killed Lorena," I added.

Another pregnant silence.

Eric began to grin. "You offed Lorena?" He had a good grasp of the vernacular, for a very old vampire.

It was hard to interpret Bill's expression. "Sookie staked her," he said. "It was a fair kill."

"She killed Lorena in a fight?" Eric's grin grew even broader. He was as proud as if he'd heard his firstborn reciting Shakespeare.

"Very *short* fight," I said, not wanting to take any credit that was not due me. If you could term it credit.

"Sookie killed a vampire," Alcide said, as if that raised me in his evaluation, too. The two vampires in the room scowled.

Alcide poured and handed me a big glass of water. I

drank it, slowly and painfully. I felt appreciably better after a minute or two.

"Back to the original subject," Eric said, giving me another meaningful look to show me he had more to say about the killing of Lorena. "If Sookie has not been pegged as having helped Bill escape, she is the best choice to get us back on the grounds without setting off alarms. They might not be expecting her, but they won't turn her away, either, I'm sure. Especially if she says she has a message for Russell from the queen of Louisiana, or if she says she has something she wants to return to Russell . . ." He shrugged, as if to say surely we could make up a good story.

I didn't want to go back in there. I thought of poor Bubba, and tried to worry about his fate—which he might have already met—but I was just too weak to worry about it.

"Flag of truce?" I suggested. I cleared my throat. "Do the vampires have such a thing?"

Eric looked thoughtful. "Of course, then I'd have to explain who I am," he said.

Happiness had made Alcide a lot easier to read. He was thinking about how soon he could call Debbie.

I opened my mouth, reconsidered, shut it, opened it again. What the hell. "Know who pushed me in the trunk and slammed it shut?" I asked Alcide. His green eyes locked onto me. His face became still, contained, as if he was afraid emotion would leak out. He turned and left the room, pulling the door shut behind him. For the first time, I registered that I was back in the guest bedroom in his apartment.

"So, who did the deed, Sookie?" Eric asked.

"His ex-girlfriend. Not so ex, after last night."

"Why would she do that?" Bill asked.

There was another significant silence. "Sookie was

represented as Alcide's new girlfriend to gain entrée to the club," Eric said delicately.

"Oh," Bill said. "Why did you need to go to the club?"

"You must have gotten hit on the head a few times, Bill," Eric said coldly. "She was trying to 'hear' where they had taken you."

This was getting too close to things Bill and I had to talk about alone.

"It's dumb to go back in there," I said. "What about a phone call?"

They both stared at me like I was turning into a frog.

"Well, what a good idea," Eric said.

THE PHONE, AS it turned out, was just listed under Russell Edgington's name; not "Mansion of Doom," or "Vampires R Us." I worked on getting my story straight as I downed the contents of a big opaque plastic mug. I hated the taste of the synthetic blood Bill insisted I drink, so he'd mixed it with apple juice, and I was trying not to look as I gulped it down.

They'd made me drink it straight when they'd gotten up to Alcide's apartment that evening; and I didn't ask them how. At least I knew why the clothes I'd borrowed from Bernard were really horrible now. I looked like I'd had my throat cut, instead of mangled by Bill's painful bite. It was still very sore, but it was better.

Of course I had been picked to make the call. I never met a man yet, above the age of sixteen, who liked to talk on the phone.

"Betty Joe Pickard, please," I said to the male voice that answered the phone.

"She's busy," he said promptly.

"I need to talk to her right now."

"She's otherwise engaged. May I take your number?"

"This is the woman who saved her life last night." No point beating around the bush. "I need to talk to her, right now. Tout de suite."

"I'll see."

There was a long pause. I could hear people walking by the phone from time to time, and I heard a lot of cheering that sounded as if it was coming from a distance. I didn't want to think about that too much. Eric, Bill, and Alcide—who had finally stomped back into the room when Bill had asked him if we could borrow his phone—were standing there making all kinds of faces at me, and I just shrugged back.

Finally, there was the click, click, click of heels on tile.

"I'm grateful, but you can't bank on this forever," Betty Jo Pickard said briskly. "We arranged for your healing, you had a place to stay to recuperate. We didn't erase your memory," she added, as if that was a little detail that had escaped her until just this moment. "What have you called to ask?"

"You have a vampire there, an Elvis impersonator?"

"So?" Suddenly she sounded very wary. "We caught an intruder within our walls last night, yes."

"This morning, after I left your place, I was stopped again," I said. We had figured this would sound convincing because I sounded so hoarse and weak.

There was a long silence while she thought through the implications. "You have a habit of being in the wrong place," she said, as if she were remotely sorry for me.

"They are getting me to call you now," I said carefully. "I am supposed to tell you that the vampire you have there, he's the real thing."

She laughed a little. "Oh, but . . ." she began. Then she fell silent. "You're shitting me, right?" Mamie Eisenhower would never have said *that*, I was willing to swear.

"Absolutely not. There was a vamp working in the morgue that night," I croaked. Betty Jo made a sound that came out between a gasp and a choke. "Don't call him by his real name. Call him 'Bubba.' And for goodness' sake, don't hurt him."

"But we've already . . . hold on!"

She ran. I could hear the urgent sound die away.

I sighed, and waited. After a few seconds, I was completely nuts with the two guys standing around looking down at me. I was strong enough to sit up, I figured.

Bill gently held me up, while Eric propped pillows behind my back. I was glad to see one of them had had the presence of mind to spread the yellow blanket over the bed so I wouldn't stain the bedspread. All this while, I'd held the phone clamped to my ear, and when it squawked, I was actually startled.

"We got him down in time," Betty Joe said brightly.

"The call came in time," I told Eric. He closed his eyes and seemed to be offering up a prayer. I wondered to whom Eric prayed. I waited for further instructions.

"Tell them," he said, "to just let him go, and he will take himself home. Tell them that we apologize for letting him stray."

I relayed that message from my "abductors."

Betty Jo was quick to dismiss the directions. "Would you ask if he could stay and sing to us a little? He's in pretty good shape," she said.

So I relayed *that*. Eric rolled his eyes. "She can ask him, but if he says no, she must take it to heart and not ask him anymore," he said. "It just upsets him, if he's not in the mood. And sometimes when he does sing, it brings back memories, and he gets, ah, obstreperous."

"All right," she said, after I'd explained. "We'll do our best. If he doesn't want to sing, we'll let him go right away." From the sound of it, she turned to someone by her. "He can sing, if he'll consent," she said, and the someone said, "Yippee!" Two big nights in a row for the crowd at the king of Mississippi's mansion, I guess.

Betty Joe said into the telephone, "I hope you get out of your difficulties. I don't know how whoever's got you got lucky enough to have the care of the greatest star in the world. Would he consider negotiating?"

She didn't know yet about the troubles that entailed. "Bubba" had an unfortunate predilection for cat blood, and he was addlepated, and he could only follow the simplest directions; though every now and then, he exhibited a streak of shrewdness. He followed directions quite literally.

"She wants permission to keep him," I told Eric. I was tired of being the go-between. But Betty Joe couldn't meet with Eric, or she'd know he was the supposed friend of Alcide's who'd helped me get to the mansion the night before.

This was all too complicated for me.

"Yes?" Eric said into the telephone. Suddenly he had an English accent. Mr. Master of Disguise. Soon he was saying things like, "He's a sacred trust," and, "You don't know what you're biting off," into the phone. (If I'd had any sense of humor that night, I would have thought the last statement was pretty funny.) After a little more conversation, he hung up, with a pleased air.

I was thinking how strange it was that Betty Joe hadn't indicated that anything else was amiss at the compound. She hadn't accused Bubba of taking their prisoner, and she hadn't commented on finding the body of Lorena. Not that she'd necessarily mention these things in a phone conversation with a human stranger; and, for that matter, not that there'd be much to find; vampires disintegrate pretty quickly. But the silver chains would still be in the pool, and maybe enough sludge to identify

as the corpse of a vampire. Of course, why would anyone look under the pool cover? But surely someone had
noticed their star prisoner was gone?

Maybe they were assuming Bubba had freed Bill
while he was roaming the compound. We'd told him not
to say anything, and he would follow that directive to
the letter.

Maybe I was off the hook. Maybe Lorena would be
completely dissolved by the time they started to clean
the pool in the spring.

The topic of corpses reminded me of the body we'd
found stuffed in the closet of this apartment. Someone
sure knew where we were, and someone sure didn't like
us. Leaving the body there was an attempt to tie us to
the crime of murder, which, actually, I had committed.
I just hadn't done that particular murder. I wondered if
the body of Jerry Falcon had been discovered yet. The
chance seemed remote. I opened my mouth to ask Alcide
if it had been on the news, and then I closed it again. I
lacked the energy to frame the sentence.

My life was spinning out of control. In the space of
two days I'd hidden one corpse and created another one.
And all because I'd fallen in love with a vampire. I gave
Bill an unloving glance. I was so absorbed in my
thoughts, I hardly heard the telephone. Alcide, who had
gone into the kitchen, must have answered it on the first
ring.

Alcide appeared in the door of the bedroom. "Move,"
he said, "you all have to move next door into the empty
apartment. Quick, quick!"

Bill scooped me up, blanket and all. We were out the
door and Eric was breaking the lock on the apartment
next to Alcide's before you could say "Jack Daniels." I
heard the slow grumble of the elevator arriving on the
fifth floor as Bill closed the door behind us.

We stood stock-still in the empty cold living room of

the barren apartment. The vampires were listening intently to what was going on next door. I began to shiver in Bill's arms.

To tell the truth, it felt great to be held by him, no matter how angry I had been at him, no matter how many issues we had to settle. To tell the truth, I had a dismayingly wonderful sense of homecoming. To tell the truth, no matter how battered my body was—and battered at his hands, or rather, his fangs—that body could hardly wait to meet up with his body again, buck naked, despite the terrible incident in the trunk. I sighed. I was disappointed in myself. I would have to stand up for my psyche, because my body was ready to betray me, big time. It seemed to be blacking out Bill's mindless attack.

Bill laid me on the floor in the smaller guest bedroom of this apartment as carefully as if I'd cost him a million dollars, and he swaddled me securely in the blanket. He and Eric listened at the wall, which was shared with Alcide's bedroom.

"What a bitch," Eric murmured. Oh. Debbie was back.

I closed my eyes. Eric made a little noise of surprise and I opened them again. He was looking at me, and there was that disconcerting amusement in his face again.

"Debbie stopped by his sister's house last night to grill her about you. Alcide's sister likes you very much," Eric said in a tiny whisper. "This angers the shapeshifter Debbie. She is insulting his sister in front of him."

Bill's face showed he was not so thrilled.

Suddenly every line in Bill's body became tense, as if someone had jammed Bill's finger in an electric socket. Eric's jaw dropped and he looked at me with an unreadable expression.

There was the unmistakable sound of a slap—even I could hear it—from the next room.

"Leave us for a moment," Bill said to Eric. I didn't like the sound of his voice.

I closed my eyes. I didn't think I was up to whatever would come next. I didn't want to argue with Bill, or upbraid him for his unfaithfulness. I didn't want to listen to explanations and excuses.

I heard the whisper of movement as Bill knelt beside me on the carpet. Bill stretched out beside me, turned on his side, and laid his arm across me.

"He just told this woman how good you are in bed," Bill murmured gently.

I came up from my prone position so fast that it tore my healing neck and gave me a twinge in my nearly healed side.

I clapped my hand to my neck and gritted my teeth so I wouldn't moan. When I could talk, I could only say, "He what? He *what*?" I was almost incoherent with anger. Bill gave me a piercing look, put his finger over his lips to remind me to be quiet.

"I *never* did," I whispered furiously. "But even if I had, you know what? It would serve you right, you betraying son of a bitch." I caught his eyes with mine and stared right into them. Okay, we were going to do this now.

"You're right," he murmured. "Lie down, Sookie. You are hurting."

"Of course I'm hurting," I whispered, and burst into tears. "And to have the others tell me, to hear that you were just going to pension me off and go live with her without even having the courage to talk to me about it yourself! Bill, how could you be capable of such a thing! I was idiot enough to think you really loved me!" With a savagery I could scarcely believe was coming from inside me, I tossed off the blanket and threw myself on him, my fingers scrabbling for his throat.

And to hell with the pain.

My hands could not circle his neck, but I dug in as hard as I could and I felt a red rage carry me away. I wanted to kill him.

If Bill had fought back, I could have kept it up, but the longer I squeezed, the more the fine rage ebbed away, leaving me cold and empty. I was straddling Bill, and he was prone on the floor, lying passively with his hands at his sides. My hands eased off of his neck and I used them to cover my face.

"I hope that hurt like hell," I said, my voice choking but clear enough.

"Yes," he said. "It hurt like hell."

Bill pulled me down to the floor by him, covered us both with the blanket. He gently pushed my head into the notch of his neck and shoulder.

We lay there in silence for what seemed like a long time, though maybe it was only minutes. My body nestled into his out of habit and out of a deep need; though I didn't know if the need was for Bill specifically, or the intimacy I'd only shared with him. I hated him. I loved him.

"Sookie," he said, against my hair, "I'm—"

"Hush," I said. "Hush." I huddled closer against him. I relaxed. It was like taking off an Ace bandage, one that had been wrapped too tight.

"You're wearing someone else's clothes," he whispered, after a minute or two.

"Yes, a vampire named Bernard. He gave me clothes to wear after my dress got ruined at the bar."

"At Josephine's?"

"Yes."

"How did your dress get ruined?"

"I got staked."

Everything about him went still. "Where? Did it hurt?" He folded down the blanket. "Show me."

"Of course it hurt," I said deliberately. "It hurt like

hell." I lifted the hem of the sweatshirt carefully.

His fingers stroked the shiny skin. I would not heal like Bill. It might take a night or two more for him to become as smooth and perfect as he had been, but he would look just as before, despite a week of torture. I would have a scar the rest of my life, vampire blood or no vampire blood. The scar might not be as severe, and it was certainly forming at a phenomenal rate, but it was undeniably red and ugly, the flesh underneath it still tender, the whole area sore.

"Who did this to you?"

"A man. A fanatic. It's a long story."

"Is he dead?"

"Yeah. Betty Joe Pickard killed him with two big blows of her fist. It kind of reminded me of a story I read in elementary school, about Paul Bunyan."

"I don't know that story." His dark eyes caught mine. I shrugged.

"As long as he's dead now." Bill had a good grip on that idea.

"Lots of people are dead now. All because of your program."

There was a long moment of silence.

Bill cast a glance at the door Eric had tactfully closed behind him. Of course, he was probably listening right outside, and like all vampires, Eric had excellent hearing. "It's safe?"

"Yes."

Bill's mouth was right by my ear. It tickled when he whispered, "Did they search my house?"

"I don't know. Maybe the vamps from Mississippi went in. I never had a chance to get over there after Eric and Pam and Chow came to tell me you'd been snatched."

"And they told you . . . ?"

"That you were planning on leaving me. Yes. They told me."

"I already got paid back for that piece of madness," Bill said.

"You might have been paid back enough to suit *you*," I said, "but I don't know if you've been paid back enough to suit *me*."

There was a long silence in the cold, empty room. It was quiet out in the living room, too. I hoped Eric had worked out what we were going to do next, and I hoped it involved going home. No matter what happened between Bill and me, I needed to be home in Bon Temps. I needed to go back to my job and my friends and I needed to see my brother. He might not be much, but he was what I had.

I wondered what was happening in the next apartment.

"When the queen came to me and said she'd heard I was working on a program that had never been attempted before, I was flattered," Bill told me. "The money she offered was very good, and she would have been within her rights not to offer any, since I am her subject."

I could feel my mouth twisting at hearing yet another reminder of how different Bill's world was from mine. "Who do you think told her?" I asked.

"I don't know. I don't really want to," Bill said. His voice sounded offhand, even gentle, but I knew better.

"You know I had been working on it for some time," Bill said, when he figured I wasn't going to say anything.

"Why?"

"Why?" He sounded oddly disconcerted. "Well, because it seemed like a good idea to me. Having a list of all America's vampires, and at least some of the rest of the world's? That was a valuable project, and actually, it was kind of fun to compile. And once I started doing research, I thought of including pictures. And aliases. And histories. It just grew."

"So you've been, um, compiling a—like a directory? Of vampires?"

"Exactly." Bill's glowing face lit up even brighter. "I just started one night, thinking how many other vampires I'd come across in my travels over the past century, and I started making a list, and then I started adding a drawing I'd done or a photograph I'd taken."

"So vampires do photograph? I mean, they show up in pictures?"

"Sure. We never liked to have our picture made, when photography became a common thing in America, because a picture was proof we'd been in a particular place at a particular time, and if we showed up looking exactly the same twenty years later, well, it was obvious what we were. But since we have admitted our existence, there is no point clinging to the old ways."

"I'll bet some vampires still do."

"Of course. There are some who still hide in the shadows and sleep in crypts every night."

(This from a guy who slept in the soil of the cemetery from time to time.)

"And other vampires helped you with this?"

"Yes," he said, sounding surprised. "Yes, a few did. Some enjoyed the exercise of memory . . . some used it as a reason to search for old acquaintances, travel to old haunts. I am sure that I don't have all the vampires in America, especially the recent immigrants, but I think I have probably eighty percent of them."

"Okay, so why is the queen so anxious to have this program? Why would the other vampires want it, once they learned about it? They could assemble all the same information, right?"

"Yes," he said. "But it would be far easier to take it

from me. And as for why it's so desirable to have this program . . . wouldn't you like to have a booklet that listed all the other telepaths in the United States?"

"Oh, sure," I said. "I could get lots of tips on how to handle my problem, or maybe how to use it better."

"So, wouldn't it be good to have a directory of vampires in the United States, what they're good at, where their gifts lie?"

"But surely some vampires really wouldn't want to be in such a book," I said. "You've told me that some vamps don't want to come out, that they want to stay in the darkness and hunt secretly."

"Exactly."

"Those vamps are in there, too?"

Bill nodded.

"Do you want to get yourself staked?"

"I never realized how tempting this project would be to anyone else. I never thought of how much power it would give to the one who owned it, until others began trying to steal it."

Bill looked glum.

The sound of shouting in the apartment next door drew our attention.

Alcide and Debbie were at it again. They were really bad for each other. But some mutual attraction kept them ricocheting back to each other. Maybe, away from Alcide, Debbie was a nice person.

Nah, I couldn't bring myself to believe that. But maybe she was at least tolerable when Alcide's affections weren't an issue.

Of course they should separate. They should never be in the same room again.

And I had to take this to heart.

Look at me. Mangled, drained, staked, battered. Lying in a cold apartment in a strange city with a vampire who had betrayed me.

A big decision was standing right in front of my face, waiting to be recognized and enacted.

I shoved Bill away, and wobbled to my feet. I pulled on my stolen jacket. With his silence heavy at my back, I opened the door to the living room. Eric was listening with some amusement to the battle going on in the next apartment.

"Take me home," I said.

"Of course," he said. "Now?"

"Yes. Alcide can drop my things by when he goes back to Baton Rouge."

"Is the Lincoln drivable?"

"Oh, yes." I pulled the keys out of my pocket. "Here."

We walked out of the empty apartment and took the elevator down to the garage.

Bill didn't follow.

# *Chapter Thirteen*

ERIC CAUGHT UP with me as I was climbing into the Lincoln.

"I had to give Bill a few instructions about cleaning up the mess he caused," he said, though I didn't ask.

Eric was used to driving sports cars, and he had a few issues with the Lincoln.

"Had it occurred to you," he said, after we'd rolled out of the city's center, "that you tend to walk away when things between you and Bill become rocky? Not that I mind, necessarily, since I would be glad for you two to sever your association. But if this is the pattern you follow in your romantic attachments, I want to know now."

I thought of several things to say, discarded the first few, which would have blistered my grandmother's ears, and drew a deep breath.

"Firstly, Eric, what happens between Bill and me is just none of your damn business." I let that sink in for a few seconds. "Second, my relationship with Bill is the only one I've ever had, so I've never had any idea what I'm going to do even from day to day, much less establishing a policy." I paused to work on phrasing my next idea. "Third, I'm through with you all. I'm tired of seeing all this sick stuff. I'm tired of having to be brave, and having to do things that scare me, and having to hang out with the bizarre and the supernatural. I am just a regular person, and I just want to date regular people. Or at least people who are *breathing*."

Eric waited to see if I'd finished. I cast a quick glance over at him, and the streetlights illuminated his strong profile with its knife-edge nose. At least he wasn't laughing at me. He wasn't even smiling.

He glanced at me briefly before turning his attention back to the road. "I'm listening to what you say. I can tell you mean it. I've had your blood: I know your feelings."

A mile of darkness went by. I was pleased Eric was taking me seriously. Sometimes he didn't; and sometimes he didn't seem to care what he said to me.

"You are spoiled for humans," Eric said. His slight foreign accent was more apparent.

"Maybe I am. Though I don't see that as much of a loss, since I didn't have any luck with guys before." Hard to date, when you know exactly what your date is thinking. So much of the time, knowing a man's exact thoughts can erase desire and even liking. "But I'd be happier with no one than I am now."

I'd been considering the old Ann Landers rule of thumb: Would I be better off with him, or without him? My grandmother and Jason and I had read Ann Landers every day when Jason and I had been growing up. We'd discussed all Ann's responses to reader questions. A lot of the advice she'd ladled out had been intended to help women deal with guys like Jason, so he certainly brought perspective to the conversations.

Right at this moment, I was pretty darn sure I was

better off without Bill. He'd used me and abused me, betrayed me and drained me.

He'd also defended me, avenged me, worshiped me with his body, and provided hours of uncritical companionship, a very major blessing.

Well, I just didn't have my scales handy. What I had was a heart full of hurt and a way to go home. We flew through the black night, wrapped in our own thoughts. Traffic was light, but this was an interstate, so of course there were cars around us from time to time.

I had no idea what Eric was thinking about, a wonderful feeling. He might be debating pulling over to the shoulder and breaking my neck, or he might be wondering what tonight's take at Fangtasia would add up to. I wanted him to talk to me. I wished he would tell me about his life before he became a vampire, but that's a real touchy subject with lots of vamps, and I wasn't about to bring it up tonight of all nights.

About an hour out of Bon Temps, we took an exit ramp. We were a little low on gas, and I needed to use the ladies' room. Eric had already begun to fill the tank as I eased my sore body carefully out of the car. He had dismissed my offer to pump the gas with a courteous, "No, thank you." One other car was filling up, and the woman, a peroxide blond about my age, hung up the nozzle as I got out of the Lincoln.

At one in the morning, the gas station/convenience store was almost empty besides the young woman, who was heavily made up and wrapped in a quilted coat. I spied a battered Toyota pickup parked by the side of the filling station, in the only shadow on the lot. Inside the pickup, two men were sitting, involved in a heated conversation.

"It's too cold to be sitting outside in a pickup," the dark-rooted blond said, as we went through the glass doors together. She gave an elaborate shiver.

"You'd think so," I commented. I was halfway down the aisle by the back of the store, when the clerk, behind a high counter on a raised platform, turned away from his little television to take the blond's money.

The door to the bathroom was hard to shut behind me, since the wooden sill had swollen during some past leakage. In fact, it probably didn't shut all the way behind me, since I was in something of a hurry. But the stall door shut and locked, and it was clean enough. In no hurry to get back in the car with the silent Eric, I took my time after using the facilities. I peered in the mirror over the sink, expecting I'd look like holy hell and not being contradicted by what I saw reflected there.

The mangled bite mark on my neck looked really disgusting, as though a dog had had hold of me. As I cleaned the wound with soap and wet paper towels, I wondered if having ingested vampire blood would give me a specific quantity of extra strength and healing, and then be exhausted, or if it was good for a certain amount of time like a time-release capsule, or what the deal was. After I'd had Bill's blood, I'd felt great for a couple of months.

I didn't have a comb or brush or anything, and I looked like something the cat dragged in. Trying to tame my hair with my fingers just made a bad thing worse. I washed my face and neck, and stepped back into the glare of the store. I hardly registered that once again the door didn't shut behind me, instead lodged quietly on the swollen sill. I emerged behind the last long aisle of groceries, crowded with CornNuts and Lays Chips and Moon Pies and Scotch Snuf and Prince Albert in a can . . .

And two armed robbers up by the clerk's platform inside the door.

*Holy Moses, why don't they just give these poor clerks shirts with big targets printed on them?* That was my first thought, detached, as if I were watching a movie with a convenience store robbery. Then I snapped into the here and now, tuned in by the very real strain on the clerk's face. He was awfully young—a reedy, blotched teenager. And he was facing the two big guys with guns. His hands were in the air, and he was mad as hell. I would have expected blubbering for his life, or incoherence, but this boy was furious.

It was the fourth time he'd been robbed, I read fresh from his brain. And the third time at gunpoint. He was wishing he could grab the shotgun under the seat in his truck behind the store and blast these sumbitches to hell.

And no one acknowledged that I was there. They didn't seem to know.

Not that I was complaining, okay?

I glanced behind me, to verify that the door to the bathroom had stuck open again, so its sound would not betray me. The best thing for me to do would be to creep out the back door to this place, if I could find it, and run around the building to get Eric to call the police.

Wait a minute. Now that I was thinking of Eric, where was he? Why hadn't he come in to pay for the gas?

If it was possible to have a foreboding any more ominous than the one I already had, that fit the bill. If Eric hadn't come in yet, Eric wasn't coming. Maybe he'd decided to leave. Leave me.

Here.

Alone.

*Just like Bill left you*, my mind supplied helpfully. Well, thanks a hell of a lot, Mind.

Or maybe they'd shot him. If he'd taken a head wound . . . and there was no healing a heart that had taken a direct hit with a big-caliber bullet.

There was no point whatsoever in standing there worrying.

This was a typical convenience store. You came in

the front door, and the clerk was behind a long counter to your right, up on a platform. The cold drinks were in the refrigerator case that took up the left wall. You were facing three long aisles running the width of the store, plus various special displays and stacks of insulated mugs and charcoal briquettes and birdseed. I was all the way at the back of the store and I could see the clerk (easily) and the crooks (just barely) over the top of the groceries. I had to get out of the store, preferably unseen. I spotted a splintered wooden door, marked "Employees Only" farther along the back wall. It was actually beyond the counter behind which the clerk stood. There was a gap between the end of the counter and the wall, and from the end of my aisle to the beginning of that counter, I'd be exposed.

Nothing would be gained by waiting.

I dropped to my hands and knees and began crawling. I moved slowly, so I could listen, too.

"You seen a blond come in here, about this tall?" the burlier of the two robbers was saying, and all of a sudden I felt faint.

Which blond? Me, or Eric? Or the peroxide blond? Of course, I couldn't see the height indication. Were they looking for a male vampire or a female telepath? Or . . . after all, I wasn't the only woman in the world who could get into trouble, I reminded myself.

"Blond woman come in here five minutes ago, bought some cigarettes," the boy said sullenly. Good for you, fella!

"Naw, that one done drove off. We want the one who was with the vampire."

Yep, that would be me.

"I didn't see no other woman," the boy said. I glanced up a little and saw the reflection off a mirror mounted up in the corner of the store. It was a security mirror so the clerk could detect shoplifters. I thought, *He can see me crouching here. He knows I'm here.*

God bless him. He was doing his best for me. I had to do my best for him. At the same time, if we could avoid getting shot, that would be a very good thing. And where the hell was Eric?

Blessing my borrowed sweatpants and slippers for being soft and silent, I crept deliberately toward the stained wooden "Employees Only" door. I wondered if it creaked. The two robbers were still talking to the clerk, but I blocked out their voices so I could concentrate on reaching the door.

I'd been scared before, plenty of times, but this was right up there with the scariest events of my life. My dad had hunted, and Jason and his buddies hunted, and I'd watched a massacre in Dallas. I knew what bullets could do. Now that I'd reached the end of the aisle, I'd come to the end of my cover.

I peered around the display counter's end. I had to cross about four feet of open floor to reach the partial shelter of the long counter that ran in front of the cash register. I would be lower and well hidden from the robbers' perspective, once I crossed that empty space.

"Car pulling in," the clerk said, and the two robbers automatically looked out the plate glass window to see. If I hadn't known what he was doing telepathically, I might have hesitated too long. I scuttled across the exposed linoleum faster than I would have believed possible.

"I don't see no car," said the less bulky man.

The clerk said, "I thought I heard the bell ring, the one that goes when a car drives across it."

I reached up and turned the knob on the door. It opened quietly.

"It rings sometimes when there ain't nobody there," the boy continued, and I realized he was trying to make

noise and hold their attention so I could get out the door.
God bless him, all over again.

I pushed the door a little wider, and duck-walked
through. I was in a narrow passage. There was another
door at the end of it, a door that presumably led to the
area behind the convenience store. In the door was a set
of keys. They wisely kept the back door locked. From
one of a row of nails by the back door hung a heavy
camo jacket. I poked my hand down in the pocket on
the right and came up with the boy's keys. That was just
a lucky guess. It happens. Clutching them to prevent
their jingling, I opened the back door and stepped outside.

There was nothing out here but a battered pickup and
a reeking Dumpster. The lighting was poor, but at least
there was some light. The blacktop was cracked. Since
it was winter, the weeds that had sprouted up from those
cracks were dry and bleached. I heard a little sound to
my left and drew in a shaky breath after I'd jumped
about a foot. The sound was caused by a huge old rac-
coon, and he ambled off into the small patch of woods
behind the store.

I exhaled just as shakily as I'd drawn the air in. I
made myself focus on the bunch of keys. Unfortunately,
there were about twenty. This boy had more keys than
squirrels had acorns. No one on God's green earth could
possibly use this many keys. I flicked through them desperately, and finally selected one that had GM stamped
on a black rubber cover. I unlocked the door and reached
into the musty interior, which smelled strongly of cigarettes and dogs. Yes, the shotgun was under the seat. I
broke it open. It was loaded. Thank God Jason believed
in self-defense. He'd showed me how to load and fire
his new Benelli.

Despite my new protection, I was so scared, I wasn't
sure I could get around to the front of the store. But I

had to scout out the situation, and find out what had happened to Eric. I eased down the side of the building where the old Toyota truck was parked. Nothing was in the back, except a little spot that picked up a stray fraction of light. The shotgun cradled in one arm, I reached down to run a finger over it.

Fresh blood. I felt old and cold. I stood with my head bowed for a long moment, and then I braced myself.

I looked in the driver's window to find the cab was unlocked. Well, happy days. I opened the door quietly, glanced in. There was a sizeable open box on the front seat, and when I checked its contents, my heart sank so low, I thought it'd come out the bottom of my shoes. On the outside, the box was stamped "Contents: Two." Now it contained one silver mesh net, the kind sold in "mercenary" magazines, the kind always advertised as "vampire proof."

That was like calling a shark cage a sure deterrent from shark bites.

Where was Eric? I glanced over the immediate vicinity, but I saw no other trace. I could hear traffic whooshing by on the interstate, but the silence hung over this bleak parking lot.

My eyes lit on a pocketknife on the dash. Yahoo! Carefully placing the shotgun on the front seat, I scooped up the knife, opened it, and held it ready to sink into the tire. Then I thought twice. A wholehearted tire-slashing was proof someone had been out here while the robbers were inside. That might not be a good thing. I contented myself with poking a single hole in the tire. It was just a smallish hole that might have come from anything, I told myself. If they did drive off, they'd have to stop somewhere down the road. Then I pocketed the knife—I was certainly quite the thief lately—and returned to the shadows around the building. This hadn't taken as long as you might think, but still it had been several minutes since I'd assessed the situation in the convenience store.

The Lincoln was still parked by the pumps. The gas port was closed, so I knew Eric had finished refueling before something had happened to him. I sidled around the corner of the building, hugging its lines. I found good cover at the front, in the angle formed by the ice machine and the front wall of the store. I risked standing up enough to peek over the top of the machine.

The robbers had come up into the higher area where the clerk stood, and they were beating on him.

Hey, now. That had to stop. They were beating him because they wanted to know where I was hiding, was my guess; and I couldn't let someone else get beaten up on my behalf.

"Sookie," said a voice right behind me.

The next instant a hand clapped across my mouth just as I was about to scream.

"Sorry," Eric whispered. "I should have thought of a better way to let you know I was here."

"Eric," I said, when I could speak. He could tell I was calmer, and he moved his hand. "We gotta save him."

"Why?"

Sometimes vampires just astound me. Well, people, too, but tonight it was a vampire.

"Because he's getting beaten for our sakes, and they're probably gonna kill him, and it'll be our fault!"

"They're robbing the store," Eric said, as if I were particularly dim. "They had a new vampire net, and they thought they'd try it out on me. They don't know it yet, but it didn't work. But they're just opportunistic scum."

"They're looking for *us*," I said furiously.

"Tell me," he whispered, and I did.

"Give me the shotgun," he said.

I kept a good grip on it. "You know how to use one of these things?"

"Probably as well as you." But he looked at it dubiously.

"That's where you're wrong," I told him. Rather than have a prolonged argument while my new hero was getting internal injuries, I ran in a crouch around the ice machine, the propane gas rack, and through the front door into the store. The little bell over the door rang like crazy, and though with all the shouting they didn't seem to hear it, they sure paid attention when I fired a blast through the ceiling over their heads. Tiles, dust, and insulation rained down.

It almost knocked me flat—but not quite. I leveled the gun right on them. They were frozen. It was like playing Swing the Statue when I was little. But not quite. The poor pimply clerk had a bloody face, and I was sure his nose was broken, and some of his teeth knocked loose.

I felt a fine rage break out behind my eyes. "Let the young man go," I said clearly.

"You gonna shoot us, little lady?"

"You bet your ass I am," I said.

"And if she misses, I will get you," said Eric's voice, above and behind me. A big vampire makes great backup.

"The vampire got loose, Sonny." The speaker was a thinnish man with filthy hands and greasy boots.

"I see that," said Sonny, the heavier one. He was darker, too. The smaller man's head was covered with that no-color hair, the kind people call "brown" because they have to call it something.

The young clerk pulled himself up out of his pain and fear and came around the counter as fast as he could move. Mixed with the blood on his face was a lot of white powder from me shooting into the ceiling. He looked a sight.

"I see you found my shotgun," he said as he passed by me, carefully not getting between the bad guys and me. He pulled a cell phone out of his pocket, and I heard the tiny beeps as he pressed numbers. His growly voice was soon in staccato conversation with the police.

"Before the police get here, Sookie, we need to find out who sent these two imbeciles," Eric said. If I'd been them, I'd have been mighty scared at the tone of his voice, and they seemed to be aware of what an angry vampire could do. For the first time Eric stepped abreast of me and then a little bit ahead, and I could see his face. Burns crisscrossed it like angry strings of poison ivy welts. He was lucky only his face had been bare, but I doubt he was feeling very lucky.

"Come down here," Eric said, and he caught the eyes of Sonny.

Sonny immediately walked down from the clerk's platform and around the counter while his companion was gaping.

"Stay," said Eric. The no-color man squeezed his eyes shut so he couldn't glimpse Eric, but he opened them just a crack when he heard Eric take a step closer, and that was enough. If you don't have any extra abilities yourself, you just can't look a vampire in the eyes. If they want to, they'll get you.

"Who sent you here?" Eric asked softly.

"One of the Hounds of Hell," Sonny said, with no inflection in his voice.

Eric looked startled. "A member of the motorcycle gang," I explained carefully, mindful that we had a civilian audience who was listening with great curiosity. I was getting a great amplification of the answers through their brains.

"What did they tell you to do?"

"They told us to wait along the interstate. There are more fellas waiting at other gas stations."

They'd called about forty thugs altogether. They'd outlaid a lot of cash.

"What were you supposed to watch for?"

"A big dark guy and a tall blond guy. With a blond woman, real young, with nice tits."

Eric's hand moved too fast for me to track. I was only sure he'd moved when I saw the blood running down Sonny's face.

"You are speaking of my future lover. Be more respectful. Why were you looking for us?"

"We were supposed to catch you. Take you back to Jackson."

"Why?"

"The gang suspected you mighta had something to do with Jerry Falcon's disappearance. They wanted to ask you some questions about it. They had someone watching some apartment building, seen you two coming out in a Lincoln, had you followed part of the way. The dark guy wasn't with you, but the woman was the right one, so we started tracking you."

"Do the vampires of Jackson know anything about this plan?"

"No, the gang figured it was their problem. But they also got a lot of other problems, a prisoner escape and so on, and lots of people out sick. So what with one thing and another, they recruited a bunch of us to help."

"What are these men?" Eric asked me.

I closed my eyes and thought carefully. "Nothing," I said. "They're nothing." They weren't shifters, or Weres, or anything. They were hardly human beings, in my opinion, but nobody died and made me God.

"We need to get out of here," Eric said. I agreed heartily. The last thing I wanted to do was spend the night at the police station, and for Eric, that was an impossibility. There wasn't an approved vampire jail cell any closer than Shreveport. Heck, the police station in Bon Temps had just gotten wheelchair accessible.

Eric looked into Sonny's eyes. "We weren't here," he said. "This lady and myself."

"Just the boy," Sonny agreed.

Again, the other robber tried to keep his eyes tight shut, but Eric blew in his face, and just as a dog would, the man opened his eyes and tried to wiggle back. Eric had him in a second, and repeated his procedure.

Then he turned to the clerk and handed him the shotgun. "Yours, I believe," Eric said.

"Thanks," the boy said, his eyes firmly on the barrel of the gun. He aimed at the robbers. "I know you weren't here," he growled, keeping his gaze ahead of him. "And I ain't saying nothing to the police."

Eric put forty dollars on the counter. "For the gas," he explained. "Sookie, let's make tracks."

"A Lincoln with a big hole in the trunk does stand out," the boy called after us.

"He's right." I was buckling up and Eric was accelerating as we heard sirens, pretty close.

"I should have taken the truck," Eric said. He seemed pleased with our adventure, now that it was over.

"How's your face?"

"It's getting better."

The welts were not nearly as noticeable.

"What happened?" I asked, hoping this was not a very touchy subject.

He cast me a sideways glance. Now that we were back on the interstate, we had slowed down to the speed limit, so it wouldn't seem to any of the many police cars converging on the convenience store that we were fleeing.

"While you were tending to your human needs in the

bathroom," he said, "I finished putting gas in the tank. I had hung up the pump and was almost at the door when those two got out of the truck and just tossed a net over me. It is very humiliating, that they were able to do that, two fools with a silver net."

"Your mind must have been somewhere else."

"Yes," he said shortly. "It was."

"So then what happened?" I asked, when it seemed he was going to stop there.

"The heavier one hit me with the butt of his gun, and it took me a small time to recover," Eric said.

"I saw the blood."

He touched a place on the back of his head. "Yes, I bled. After getting used to the pain, I snagged a corner of the net on the bumper of their truck and managed to roll out of it. They were inept in that, as well as robbery. If they had tied the net shut with silver chains, the result might have been different."

"So you got free?"

"The head blow was more of a problem than I thought at first," Eric said stiffly. "I ran along the back of the store to the water spigot on the other side. Then I heard someone coming out of the back. When I was recovered, I followed the sounds and found you." After a long moment's silence, Eric asked me what had happened in the store.

"They got me confused with the other woman who went in the store at the same time I went to the ladies' room," I explained. "They didn't seem to be sure I was in the store, and the clerk was telling them that there had been only one woman, and she'd gone. I could tell he had a shotgun in his truck—you know, I heard it in his head—and I went and got it, and I disabled their truck, and I was looking for you because I figured something had happened to you."

"So you planned to save me and the clerk, together?"

"Well . . . yeah." I couldn't understand the odd tone of his voice. "I didn't feel like I had a whole lot of choices there."

The welts were just pink lines now.

The silence still didn't seem relaxed. We were about forty minutes from home now. I started to let it drop. I didn't.

"You don't seem too happy about something," I said, a definite edge to my voice. My own temper was fraying around the edges. I *knew* I was heading in the wrong direction conversationally; I *knew* I should just be content with silence, however brooding and pregnant.

Eric took the exit for Bon Temps and turned south.

Sometimes, instead of going down the road less taken, you just charge right down the beaten path.

"Would there be something *wrong* with me rescuing the two of you?" We were driving through Bon Temps now. Eric turned east after the buildings along Main gradually thinned and vanished. We passed Merlotte's, still open. We turned south again, on a small parish road. Then we were bumping down my driveway.

Eric pulled over and killed the engine. "Yes," he said. "There is something wrong with that. And why the hell don't you get your driveway fixed?"

The string of tension that had stretched between us popped. I was out of the car in a New York minute, and he was, too. We faced each other across the roof of the Lincoln, though not much of me showed. I charged around it until I was right in front of him.

"Because I can't afford it, that's why! I don't have any money! And you all keep asking me to take time off from my job to do stuff for you! I can't! I can't do it anymore!" I shrieked. "I quit!"

There was a long moment of silence while Eric regarded me. My chest was heaving underneath my stolen jacket. Something felt funny, something was bothering me about the appearance of my house, but I was too het up to examine my worry.

"Bill . . ." Eric began cautiously, and it set me off like a rocket.

"He's spending all his money on the freaking Belle-fleurs," I said, my tone this time low and venomous, but no less sincere. "He never thinks about giving me money. And how could I take it? It would make me a kept woman, and I'm not his whore, I'm his . . . I used to be his girlfriend."

I took a deep, shuddering breath, dismally aware that I was going to cry. It would be better to get mad again. I tried. "Where do you get off, telling them that I'm your . . . your lover? Where'd that come from?"

"What happened to the money you earned in Dallas?" Eric asked, taking me completely by surprise.

"I paid my property taxes with it."

"Did you ever think that if you told me where Bill's hiding his computer program, I would give you anything you asked for? Did you not realize that Russell would have paid you handsomely?"

I sucked in my breath, so offended, I hardly knew where to begin.

"I see you didn't think of those things."

"Oh, yeah, I'm just an angel." Actually, none of those things had occurred to me, and I was almost defensive they hadn't. I was shaking with fury, and all my good sense went out the window. I would feel the presence of other brains at work, and the fact that someone was in my place enraged me farther. The rational part of my mind crumpled under the weight of my anger.

"Someone's waiting in my house, Eric." I swung around and stomped over to my porch, finding the key

I'd hidden under the rocker my grandmother had loved. Ignoring everything my brain was trying to tell me, ignoring the beginning of a bellow from Eric, I opened the front door and got hit with a ton of bricks.

# *Chapter Fourteen*

"WE GOT HER," said a voice I didn't recognize. I had been yanked to my feet, and I was swaying between two men who were holding me up.

"What about the vamp?"

"I shot him twice, but he's in the woods. He got away."

"That's bad news. Work fast."

I could sense that there were many men in the room with me, and I opened my eyes. They'd turned on the lights. They were in my house. They were in my home. As much as the blow to my jaw, that made me sick. Somehow, I'd assumed my visitors would be Sam or Arlene or Jason.

There were five strangers in my living room, if I was thinking clearly enough to count. But before I could form another idea, one of the men—and now I realized he was wearing a familiar leather vest—punched me in the stomach.

I didn't have enough breath to scream.

The two men holding me pulled me back upright.

"Where is he?"

"Who?" I really couldn't remember, at this point, what particular missing person he wanted me to locate. But, of course, he hit me again. I had a dreadful minute when I needed to gag but hadn't the air to do it. I was strangling and suffocating.

Finally, I drew in a long breath. It was noisy and painful and just heaven.

My Were interrogator, who had light hair shaved close to his scalp and a nasty little goatee, slapped me, hard, open-handed. My head rocked on my neck like a car on faulty shock absorbers. "Where's the vampire, bitch?" the Were said. He drew his fist back.

I couldn't take any more of this. I decided to speed things up. I pulled my legs up, and while the two at my sides kept desperate grips on my arms, I kicked the Were in front of me with both feet. If I hadn't had on bedroom slippers, it probably would have been more effective. I'm never wearing safety boots when I need them. But Nasty Goatee did stagger back, and then he came for me with my death in his eyes.

By then my legs had swung back to the floor, but I made them keep going backward, and threw my two captors completely off balance. They staggered, tried to recover, but their frantic footing was in vain. Down we all went, the Were along with us.

This might not be better, but it was an improvement over waiting to get hit.

I'd landed on my face, since my arms and hands weren't under my control. One guy did let go as we fell, and when I got that hand underneath me for leverage, I yanked away from the other man.

I'd gotten halfway to my feet when the Were, quicker than the humans, managed to grab my hair. He dealt a slap to my face while he wound my hair around his hand for a better grip. The other hired hands closed in, either to help the two on the floor to rise, or just to see me get battered.

A real fight is over in a few minutes because people wear out quick. It had been a very long day, and the fact was, I was ready to give up against these over-whelming odds. But I had a little pride and I went for the guy closest to me, a potbellied pig of a man with greasy dark hair. I dug my fingers into his face, trying to cause any damage I could, while I could.

The Were kneed me in the belly and I screamed, and the pig-man began to yell for the others to get me off of him, and the front door crashed open as Eric came in, blood covering his chest and right leg. Bill was right behind him.

They lost all control.

I saw firsthand what a vampire could do.

After a second, I realized my help would not be needed, and I decided the Goddess of Really Tough Gals would have to excuse me while I closed my eyes.

In two minutes, all the men in my living room were dead.

"Sookie? sookie?" eric's voice was hoarse. "Do we need to take her to the hospital?" he asked Bill.

I felt cool fingers on my wrist, touching my neck. I almost explained that for once I was conscious, but it was just too hard. The floor seemed like a good place to be.

"Her pulse is strong," Bill reported. "I'm going to turn her over."

"She's alive?"

"Yes."

Eric's voice, suddenly closer, said, "Is the blood hers?"

"Yes, some of it."

He drew a deep, shuddering breath. "Hers is different."

"Yes," Bill said coldly. "But surely you are full by now."

"It's been a long time since I had real blood in quantity," Eric said, just exactly like my brother, Jason, would have remarked it had been a long time since he'd had blackberry cobbler.

Bill slid his hands underneath me. "For me, too. We'll need to put them all out in the yard," he said casually, "and clean up Sookie's house."

"Of course."

Bill began rolling me over, and I began crying. I couldn't help it. As strong as I wanted to be, all I could think of was my body. If you've ever been really beaten, you'll know what I mean. When you've been really beaten, you realize that you are just an envelope of skin, an easily penetrated envelope that holds together a lot of fluids and some rigid structures, which in their turn can simply be broken and invaded. I thought I'd been badly hurt in Dallas a few weeks before, but this felt worse. I knew that didn't mean it was worse; there was a lot of soft tissue damage. In Dallas, my cheekbone had been fractured and my knee twisted. I thought maybe the knee had been compromised all over again, and I thought maybe one of the slaps had rebroken the cheekbone. I opened my eyes, blinked, and opened them again. My vision cleared after a few seconds.

"Can you speak?" Eric said, after a long, long moment.

I tried, but my mouth was so dry, nothing came out.

"She needs a drink." Bill went to the kitchen, having to take a less than direct route, since there were a lot of obstructions in the way.

Eric's hands stroked back my hair. He'd been shot, I remembered, and I wanted to ask him how he felt, but

I couldn't. He was sitting on his butt beside me, leaning on the cushions of my couch. There was blood on his face, and he looked pinker than I'd ever seen him, ruddy with health. When Bill returned with my water—he'd even added a straw—I looked at his face. Bill looked almost sunburned.

Bill held me up carefully and put the straw to my lips. I drank, and it was the best thing I'd ever tasted.

"You killed them all," I said in a creaky voice.

Eric nodded.

I thought of the circle of brutish faces that had surrounded me. I thought of the Were slapping me in the face.

"Good," I said. Eric looked a little amused, just for a second. Bill didn't look anything in particular.

"How many?"

Eric looked around vaguely, and Bill pointed a finger silently as he toted them up.

"Seven?" Bill said doubtfully. "Two in the yard and five in the house?"

"I was thinking eight," Eric murmured.

"Why did they come after you like that?"

"Jerry Falcon."

"Oh," said Bill, a different note in his voice. "Oh, yes. I've encountered him. In the torture room. He is first on my list."

"Well, you can cross him off," Eric said. "Alcide and Sookie disposed of his body in the woods yesterday."

"Did this Alcide kill him?" Bill looked down at me, reconsidered. "Or Sookie?"

"He says no. They found the corpse in the closet of Alcide's apartment, and they hatched a plan to hide his remains." Eric sounded like that had been kind of cute of us.

"My Sookie hid a corpse?"

"I don't think you can be too sure about that possessive pronoun."

"Where did you learn that term, Northman?"

"I took 'English as a Second Language' at a community college in the seventies."

Bill said, "She is mine."

I wondered if my hands would move. They would. I raised both of them, making an unmistakable one-fingered gesture.

Eric laughed, and Bill said, "Sookie!" in shocked admonishment.

"I think that Sookie is telling us she belongs to herself," Eric said softly. "In the meantime, to finish our conversation, whoever stuffed the corpse in the closet meant to saddle Alcide with the blame, since Jerry Falcon had made a blatant pass at Sookie in the bar the night before, and Alcide had taken umbrage."

"So all this plot might be directed at Alcide instead of us?"

"Hard to say. Evidently, from what the armed robbers at the gas station told us, what's remaining of the gang called in all the thugs they knew and stationed them along the interstate to intercept us on the way back. If they'd just called ahead, they wouldn't now be in jail for armed robbery. And I'm certainly sure that's where they are."

"So how'd these guys get here? How'd they know where Sookie lived, who she really was?"

"She used her own name at Club Dead. They didn't know the name of Bill's human girlfriend. You were faithful."

"I hadn't been faithful in other ways," Bill said bleakly. "I thought it was the least I could do for her."

And this was the guy whom I'd shot the bird. On the other hand, this was the guy who was talking like I wasn't in the room. And most importantly, this was the guy who'd had another "darling," for whom he'd planned to leave me flat.

"So the Weres may not know she was your girlfriend; they only know she was staying in the apartment with Alcide when Jerry disappeared. They know Jerry may have come by the apartment. This Alcide says that the packmaster in Jackson told Alcide to leave and not return for a while, but that he believed Alcide had not killed Jerry."

"This Alcide . . . he seemed to have a troubled relationship with his girlfriend."

"She is engaged to someone else. She believes he is attached to Sookie."

"And is he? He has the gall to tell this virago Debbie that Sookie is good in bed."

"He wanted to make her jealous. He has not slept with Sookie."

"But he likes her." Bill made it sound like a capital crime.

"Doesn't everyone?"

I said, with great effort, "You just killed a bunch of guys who didn't seem to like me at all." I was tired of them talking about me right above my head, as illuminating as it was. I was hurting real bad, and my living room was full of dead men. I was ready for both those situations to be remedied.

"Bill, how'd you get here?" I asked in a raspy whisper.

"My car. I negotiated a deal with Russell, since I didn't want to be looking over my shoulder for the rest of my existence. Russell was in a tantrum when I called him. Not only had I disappeared and Lorena vanished, but his hired Weres had disobeyed him and thus jeopardized business dealings Russell has with this Alcide and his father."

"Who was Russell angriest with?" Eric asked.

"Lorena, for letting me escape."

They had a good laugh over that one before Bill continued his story. Those vamps. A laugh a minute.

"Russell agreed to return my car and leave me alone if I would tell him how I'd escaped, so he could plug the hole I'd wiggled out of. And he asked me to put in a bid for him to share in the vampire directory."

If Russell had just done that in the first place, it would have saved everyone a lot of grief. On the other hand, Lorena would still be alive. So would the thugs who'd beaten me, and perhaps so would Jerry Falcon, whose death was still a mystery.

"So," Bill continued, "I sped down the highway, on the way to tell you two that the Weres and their hired hands were pursuing you, and that they had gone ahead to lie in wait. They had discovered, via the computer, that Alcide's girlfriend Sookie Stackhouse lived in Bon Temps."

"These computers are dangerous things," Eric said. His voice sounded weary, and I remembered the blood on his clothes. Eric had been shot twice, because he'd been with me.

"Her face is swelling," Bill said. His voice was both gentle and angry.

"Eric okay?" I asked wearily, figuring I could skip a few words if I got the idea across.

"I will heal," he said, from a great distance. "Especially since having all that good . . ."

And then I fell asleep, or passed out, or some blend of the two.

Sunshine. it had been so long since I'd seen sunshine; I'd almost forgotten how good it looked.

I was in my own bed, and I was in my soft blue brushed-nylon nightgown, and I was wrapped up like a mummy. I really, really had to get up and get to the bathroom. Once I moved enough to establish how awful walking was going to be, only my bladder compelled me to get out of that bed.

I took tiny steps across the floor, which suddenly seemed as wide and empty as the desert. I covered it inch by painful inch. My toenails were still painted bronze, to match my nails. I had a lot of time to look at my toes as I made my journey.

Thank God I had indoor plumbing. If I'd had to make it into the yard to an outhouse, as my grandmother had as a child, I would've given up.

When I had completed my journey and pulled on a fleecy blue robe, I inched my way down the hall to the living room to examine the floor. I noticed along the way that the sun outside was brilliant and the sky was the deep rich blue of heaven. It was forty-two, said the thermometer Jason had given me on my birthday. He'd mounted it for me on the window frame, so I could just peek out to read it.

The living room looked real good. I wasn't sure how long the vampire cleaning crew had been at work the night before, but there were no body parts visible. The wood of the floor was gleaming, and the furniture looked spanky clean. The old throw rug was missing, but I didn't care. It had been no wonderful heirloom anyway, just a sort of pretty rug Gran had picked up at a flea market for thirty-five dollars. Why did I remember that? It didn't matter at all. And my grandmother was dead.

I felt the sudden danger of weeping, and I pushed it away. I wasn't going to fall back into a trough of self-pity. My reaction to Bill's unfaithfulness seemed faint and far away now; I was a colder woman, or maybe my protective hide had just grown thicker. I no longer felt angry with him, to my surprise. He'd been tortured by the woman—well, the vampire—he'd thought loved him. And she'd tortured him for financial gain—that was the worst.

To my startled horror, suddenly I relived the moment when the stake had gone in under her ribs, and I was feeling the movement of the wood as it plowed through her body.

I made it back to the hall bathroom just in time.

Okay, I'd killed someone.

I'd once hurt someone who was trying to kill me, but that had never bothered me: oh, the odd dream or two. But the horror of staking the vampire Lorena felt worse. She would've killed me a lot quicker, and I was sure it would have been no problem whatsoever for Lorena. She probably would've laughed her ass off.

Maybe that was what had gotten to me so much. After I'd sunk the stake in, I was sure I'd had a moment, a second, a flash of time in which I'd thought, *So there, bitch*. And it had been pure pleasure.


A COUPLE OF hours later, I'd discovered it was the early afternoon, and it was Monday. I called my brother on his cell phone, and he came by with my mail. When I opened my door, he stood for a long minute, looking me up and down.

"If he did that to you, I'm heading over there with a torch and a sharpened broom handle," he said.

"No, he didn't."

"What happened to the ones who did?"

"You better not think about it too much."

"At least he does some things right."

"I'm not gonna see him anymore."

"Uh-huh. I've heard that before."

He had a point. "For a while," I said firmly.

"Sam said you'd gone off with Alcide Herveaux."

"Sam shouldn't have told you."

"Hell, I'm your brother. I need to know who you're going around with."

"It was business," I said, trying a little smile on for size.

"You going into surveying?"

"You know Alcide?"

"Who doesn't, at least by name? Those Herveauxes, they're well known. Tough guys. Good to work for. Rich."

"He's a nice guy."

"He coming around anymore? I'd like to meet him. I don't want to be on a road crew working for the parish my whole life."

That was news to me. "Next time I see him, I'll call you. I don't know if he'll be stopping by anytime soon, but if he does, you'll know about it."

"Good." Jason glanced around. "What happened to the rug?"

I noticed a spot of blood on the couch, about where Eric had leaned. I sat down so my legs were covering it. "The rug? I spilled some tomato sauce on it. I was eating spaghetti out here while I watched TV."

"So you took it to get it cleaned?"

I didn't know how to answer. I didn't know if that was what the vampires had done with the rug, or if it'd had to be torched. "Yes," I said, with some hesitation. "But they may not be able to get the stain out, they said."

"New gravel looks good."

I stared at him in gape-mouthed surprise. "What?"

He looked at me as if I were a fool. "The new gravel. On the driveway. They did a good job, getting it level. Not a single pothole."

Completely forgetting the bloodstain, I heaved myself

up from the couch with some difficulty and peered out the front window, this time really looking.

Not only was the driveway done, but also there was a new parking area in front of the house. It was outlined with landscaping timbers. The gravel was the very expensive kind, the kind that's supposed to interlock so it doesn't roll out of the desired area. I put my hand over my mouth as I calculated how much it had cost. "It's done like that all the way to the road?" I asked Jason, my voice hardly audible.

"Yeah, I saw the Burgess and Sons crew out here when I drove by earlier," he said slowly. "Didn't you fix it up to have it done?"

I shook my head.

"Damn, they did it by mistake?" Quick to rage, Jason flushed. "I'll call that Randy Burgess and ream his ass. Don't you pay the bill! Here's the note that was stuck to the front door." Jason pulled a rolled receipt from his front pocket. "Sorry, I was going to hand that to you before I noticed your face."

I unrolled the yellow sheet and read the note scribbled across it. "Sookie—Mr. Northman said not to knock on your door, so I'm sticking this to it. You may need this in case something is wrong. Just call us. Randy."

"It's paid for," I said, and Jason calmed a little.

"The boyfriend? The ex?"

I remembered screaming at Eric about my driveway. "No," I said. "Someone else." I caught myself wishing the man who'd been so thoughtful had been Bill.

"You sure are getting around these days," Jason said. He didn't sound as judgmental as I expected, but then Jason was shrewd enough to know he could hardly throw many stones.

I said flatly, "No, I'm not."

He eyed me for a long moment. I met his gaze.

"Okay," he said slowly. "Then someone owes you, big time."

"That would be closer to the truth," I said, and wondered in turn if I myself was being truthful. "Thanks for getting my mail for me, Big Bro. I need to crawl back in bed."

"No problem. You want to go to the doctor?"

I shook my head. I couldn't face the waiting room.

"Then you let me know if you need me to get you some groceries."

"Thanks," I said again, with more pleasure. "You're a good brother." To our mutual surprise, I stood on tiptoe and gave him a kiss on the cheek. He awkwardly put his arm around me, and I made myself keep the smile on my face, rather than wincing from the pain.

"Get back in bed, Sis," he said, shutting the door behind him carefully. I noticed he stood on the porch for a full minute, surveying all that premium gravel. Then he shook his head and got back into his pickup, always clean and gleaming, the pink and aqua flames startling against the black paint that covered the rest of the truck.

I watched a little television. I tried to eat, but my face hurt too much. I felt lucky when I discovered some yogurt in the refrigerator.

A big pickup pulled up to the front of the house about three o'clock. Alcide got out with my suitcase. He knocked softly.

He might be happier if I didn't answer, but I figured I wasn't in the business of making Alcide Herveaux happy, and I opened the door.

"Oh, Jesus Christ," he said, not irreverently, as he took me in.

"Come in," I said, through jaws that were getting so sore I could barely part them. I knew I'd said I'll call Jason if Alcide came by; but Alcide and I needed to talk.

He came in and stood looking at me. Finally, he put the suitcase back in my room, fixed me a big glass of iced tea with a straw in it, and put it on the table by the couch. My eyes filled with tears. Not everyone would have realized that a hot drink made my swollen face hurt.

"Tell me what happened, chere," he said, sitting on the couch beside me. "Here, put your feet up while you do." He helped me swivel sideways and lay my legs over his lap. I had plenty of pillows propped behind me, and I did feel comfortable, or as comfortable as I was going to feel for a couple of days.

I told him everything.

"So, you think they'll come after me in Shreveport?" he asked. He didn't seem to be blaming me for bringing all this on his head, which frankly I'd half expected.

I shook my head helplessly. "I just don't know. I wish we knew what had really happened. That might get them off our backs."

"Weres are nothing if not loyal," Alcide said.

I took his hand. "I know that."

Alcide's green eyes regarded me steadily.

"Debbie asked me to kill you," he said.

For a moment I felt cold down to my bones. "What did you tell her back?" I asked, through stiff lips.

"I told her she could go fuck herself, excuse my language."

"And how do you feel now?"

"Numb. Isn't that stupid? I'm pulling her out of me by the roots, though. I told you I would. I had to do it. It's like being addicted to crack. She's awful."

I thought of Lorena. "Sometimes," I said, and even to my own ears I sounded sad, "the bitch wins." Lorena was far from dead between Bill and me. Speaking of Debbie raised yet another unpleasant memory. "Hey, you told her we had been to bed together, when you two were fighting!"

He looked profoundly embarrassed, his olive skin flushing. "I'm ashamed of that. I knew she'd been having a good time with her fiancé; she bragged about it. I sort of used your name in vain when I was really mad. I apologize."

I could understand that, even though I didn't like it. I raised my eyebrows to indicate that wasn't quite enough.

"Okay, that was really low. A double apology and a promise to never do it again."

I nodded. I would accept that.

"I hated to hustle you all out of the apartment like that, but I didn't want her to see the three of you, in view of conclusions she might have drawn. Debbie can get really mad, and I thought if she saw you in conjunction with the vampires, she might hear a rumor that Russell was missing a prisoner and put two and two together. She might even be mad enough to call Russell."

"So much for loyalty among Weres."

"She's a shifter, not a Were," Alcide said instantly, and a suspicion of mine was confirmed. I was beginning to believe that Alcide, despite his stated conviction that he was determined to kept the Were gene to himself, would never be happy with anyone but another Were. I sighed: I tried to keep it a nice, quiet sigh. I might be wrong, after all.

"Debbie aside," I said, waving my hand to show how completely Debbie was out of our conversational picture, "*someone* killed Jerry Falcon and put him in your closet. That's caused me—and you—a lot more trouble that the original mission, which was searching for Bill. Who would do something like that? It would have to be someone really malicious."

"Or someone really stupid," Alcide said fairly.

"I know Bill didn't do it, because he was a prisoner. And I'd swear Eric was telling the truth when he said he didn't do it." I hesitated, hating to bring a name back up. "But what about Debbie? She's . . ." I stopped myself from saying "a real bitch," because only Alcide should call her that. "She was angry with you for having a date," I said mildly. "Maybe she would put Jerry Falcon in your closet to cause you trouble?"

"Debbie's mean and she can cause trouble, but she's never killed anyone," Alcide said. "She doesn't have the, the . . . grit for it, the sand. The will to kill."

Okay. Just call me Sandy.

Alcide must have read my dismay on my face. "Hey, I'm a Were," he said, shrugging. "I'd do it if I had to. Especially at the right time of the moon."

"So maybe a fellow pack member did him in, for reasons we don't know, and decided to lay the blame on you?" Another possible scenario.

"That doesn't feel right. Another Were would have— well, the body would've looked different." Alcide said, trying to spare my finer feelings. He meant the body would have been ripped to shreds. "And I think I would've smelled another Were on him. Not that I got that close."

We just didn't have any other ideas, though if I'd tape-recorded that conversation and played it back, I would have thought of another possible culprit easily enough.

Alcide said he had to get back to Shreveport, and I lifted my legs for him to rise. He got up, but went down on one knee by the head of the couch to tell me good-bye. I said the polite things, how nice it had been of him to give me a place to stay, how much I'd enjoyed meeting his sister, how much fun it had been to hide a body with him. No, I didn't really say that, but it crossed my mind, as I was being Gran's courteous product.

"I'm glad I met you," he said. He was closer to me than I'd thought, and he gave me a peck on the lips in farewell. But after the peck, which was okay, he returned for a longer good-bye. His lips felt so warm; and after a second, his tongue felt even warmer. His head turned slightly to get a better angle, and then he went at it again. His right hand hovered above me, trying to find a place to settle that wouldn't hurt me. Finally he covered my left hand with his. Oh boy, this was good. But only my mouth and my lower pelvis were happy. The rest of me hurt. His hand slid, in a questioning sort of way, up to my breast, and I gave a sharp gasp.

"Oh, God, I hurt you!" he said. His lips looked very full and red after the long kiss, and his eyes were brilliant.

I felt obliged to apologize. "I'm just so sore," I said.

"What did they do to you?" he asked. "Not just a few slaps across the face?"

He had imagined my swollen face was my most serious problem.

"I wish that had been it," I said, trying to smile.

He truly looked stricken. "And here I am, making a pass at you."

"Well, I didn't push you away," I said mildly. (I was too sore to push.) "And I didn't say, 'No, sir, how dare you force your attentions on me!' "

Alcide looked somewhat startled. "I'll come back by soon," he promised. "If you need anything, you call me." He fished a card out of his pocket and laid it on the table by the couch. "This has got my work number on it, and I'm writing my cell number on the back, and my home number. Give me yours." Obediently, I recited the numbers to him, and he wrote them down in, no kidding, a little black book. I didn't have the energy to make a joke.

When he was gone, the house felt extra empty. He was so big and so energetic—so alive—he filled large spaces with his personality and presence.

It was a day for me to sigh.

Having talked to Jason at Merlotte's, Arlene came by at half past five. She surveyed me, looked as if she were suppressing a lot of comments she really wanted to make, and heated me up some Campbell's. I let it cool before I ate it very carefully and slowly, and felt the better for it. She put the dishes in the dishwasher, and asked me if I needed any other help. I thought of her children waiting for her at home, and I said I was just fine. It did me good to see Arlene, and to know she was struggling with herself about speaking out of turn made me feel even better.

Physically, I was feeling more and more stiff. I made myself get up and walk a little (though it looked more like a hobble), but as my bruises became fully developed and the house grew colder, I began to feel much worse. This was when living alone really got to you, when you felt bad or sick and there was no one there.

You might feel a little sorry for yourself, too, if you weren't careful.

To my surprise, the first vampire to arrive after dark was Pam. Tonight she was wearing a trailing black gown, so she was scheduled to work at Fangtasia. Ordinarily, Pam shunned black; she was a pastels kind of female. She yanked at the chiffon sleeves impatiently.

"Eric says you may need a female to help you," she said impatiently. "Though why I am supposed to be your lady's maid, I don't know. Do you really need help, or is he just trying to curry favor with you? I like you well enough, but after all, I am vampire, and you are human."

That Pam, what a sweetie.

"You could sit and visit with me for a minute," I suggested, at a loss as to how to proceed. Actually, it would be nice to have help getting into and out of the bathtub, but I knew Pam would be offended to be asked to perform such a personal task. After all, she was vampire, I was human. . . .

Pam settled into the armchair facing the couch. "Eric says you can fire a shotgun," she said, more conversationally. "Would you teach me?"

"I'd be real glad to, when I'm better."

"Did you really stake Lorena?"

The shotgun lessons were more important than the death of Lorena, it seemed.

"Yes. She would've killed me."

"How'd you do it?"

"I had the stake that had been used on me."

Then Pam had to hear about that, and ask me how it felt, since I was the only person she knew who'd survived being staked, and then she asked me exactly how I'd killed Lorena, and there we were, back at my least favorite topic.

"I don't want to talk about it," I admitted.

"Why not?" Pam was curious. "You say she was trying to kill you."

"She was."

"And after she had done that, she would have tortured Bill more, until he broke, and you would have been dead, and it all would have been for nothing."

Pam had a point, a good one, and I tried to think about it as a practical step to have taken, rather than a desperate reflex.

"Bill and Eric will be here soon," Pam said, looking at her watch.

"I wish you had told me that earlier," I said, struggling to my feet.

"Got to brush your teeth and hair?" Pam was cheerfully sarcastic. "That's why Eric thought you might need my help."

"I think I can manage my own grooming, if you wouldn't mind heating up some blood in the microwave—of course, for yourself as well. I'm sorry, I wasn't being polite."

Pam gave me a skeptical look, but trotted off to the kitchen without further comment. I listened for a minute to make sure she knew how to operate a microwave, and I heard reassuringly unhesitating beeps as she punched in the numbers and hit Start.

Slowly and painfully, I washed off in the sink, brushed my hair and teeth, and put on some silky pink pajamas and a matching robe and slippers. I wished I had the energy to dress, but I just couldn't face underwear and socks and shoes.

There was no point putting on makeup over the bruises. There was no way I could cover them. In fact, I wondered why I'd gotten up from the couch to put myself through this much pain. I looked in the mirror and told myself I was an idiot to make any preparation for their arrival. I was just plain primping. Given my overall misery (mental and physical), my behavior was ridiculous. I was sorry I had felt the impulse, and even sorrier Pam had witnessed it.

But the first male caller I had was Bubba.

He was all decked out. The vampires of Jackson had enjoyed Bubba's company, it was apparent. Bubba was wearing a red jumpsuit with rhinestones on it (I wasn't too surprised one of the boy toys at the mansion had had one) complete with wide belt and half boots. Bubba looked good.

He didn't seem pleased, though. He seemed apologetic. "Miss Sookie, I'm sorry I lost you last night," he said right away. He brushed past Pam, who looked surprised. "I see something awful happened to you last night, and I wasn't there to stop it like Eric told me to be. I was having a good time in Jackson, those guys there really know how to throw themselves a party."

I had an idea, a blindingly simple idea. If I'd been in a comic strip, it would have shown itself as a lightning bolt over my head. "You've been watching me every night," I said, as gently as I could, trying hard to keep all excitement out of my voice. "Right?"

"Yes'm, ever since Mr. Eric told me to." He was standing straighter, his head full of carefully combed hair gelled into the familiar style. The guys at Russell's mansion had really worked hard on him.

"So you were out there the night we came back from the club? The first night?"

"You bet, Miss Sookie."

"Did you see anyone else outside the apartment?"

"I sure did." He looked proud.

Oh, boy. "Was this a guy in gang leathers?"

He looked surprised. "Yes'm, it was that guy hurt you in the bar. I seen him when the doorman threw him out back. Some of his buddies came around back there, and they were talking about what had happened. So I knew he'd offended you. Mr. Eric said not to come up to you or him in public, so I didn't. But I followed you back to the apartment, in that truck. Bet you didn't even know I was in the back."

"No, I sure didn't know you were in the back of the pickup. That was real smart. Now tell me, when you saw the Were later, what was he doing?"

"He had picked the lock on the apartment door by the time I snuck up behind him. I just barely caught that sucker in time."

"What did you do with him?" I smiled at Bubba.

"I broke his neck and stuffed him in the closet," Bubba said proudly. "I didn't have time to take the body anywhere, and I figured you and Mr. Eric could figure out what to do about it."

I had to look away. So simple. So direct. Solving that

mystery had just taken asking the right person the right question.

Why hadn't we thought of it? You couldn't give Bubba orders and expect him to adapt them to circumstances. Quite possibly, he had saved my life by killing Jerry Falcon, since my bedroom was the first one the Were would have come to. I had been so tired when I finally got to bed, I might not have woken until it was too late.

Pam had been looking back and forth between us with a question on her face. I held up a hand to indicate I'd explain later, and I made myself smile at Bubba and tell him he'd done the right thing. "Eric will be so pleased," I said. And telling Alcide would be an interesting experience.

Bubba's whole face relaxed. He smiled, that upper lip curling just a little. "I'm glad to hear you say so," he said. "You got any blood? I'm mighty thirsty."

"Sure," I said. Pam was thoughtful enough to fetch the blood, and Bubba took a big swig.

"Not as good as a cat's," he observed. "But mighty fine just the same. Thank you, thank you very much."

# Chapter Fifteen

**W**HAT A COZY evening it was turning out to be— yours truly and four vampires, after Bill and Eric arrived separately but almost simultaneously. Just me and my buds, hanging at the house.

Bill insisted on braiding my hair for me, just so he could show his familiarity with my house and habits by going in the bathroom and getting my box of hair doodads. Then he put me on the ottoman in front of him as he sat behind me to brush and fix my hair. I have always found this a very soothing process, and it aroused memories of another evening Bill and I had begun just about the same way, with a fabulous finale. Of course, Bill was well aware he was pushing those memories to the fore.

Eric observed this with the air of one taking notes, and Pam sneered openly. I could not for the life of me understand why they all had to be here at the same time, and why they all didn't get sick of one another—and me—and go away. After a few minutes of having a comparative crowd in my house, I longed to be alone once more. Why had I thought I was lonely?

Bubba left fairly quickly, anxious to do some hunting. I didn't want to think too closely about that. When he'd left, I was able to tell the other vampires about what had really happened to Jerry Falcon.

Eric didn't seem too upset that his directions to Bubba had caused the death of Jerry Falcon, and I'd already admitted to myself that I couldn't be too wrought up about it, either. If it came down to him, or me, well, I liked me better. Bill was indifferent to Jerry's fate, and Pam thought the whole thing was funny.

"That he followed you to Jackson, when his instructions were just for here, for one night . . . that he kept following his instructions, no matter what! It's not very vampiric, but he's certainly a good soldier."

"It would have been much better if he'd told Sookie what he'd done and why he'd done it," Eric observed.

"Yes, a note would have been nice," I said sarcastically. "Anything would have been better than opening that closet and finding the body stuffed in there."

Pam hooted with laughter. I'd really found the way to tickle her funny bone. Wonderful.

"I can just see your face," she said. "You and the Were had to hide the body? That's priceless."

"I wish I'd known all this when Alcide was here today," I said. I'd closed my eyes when the full effect of the hair brushing had soothed me. But the sudden silence was delightful. At last, I was getting to amuse my own self a little bit.

Eric said, "Alcide Herveaux came here?"

"Yeah, he brought my bag. He stayed to help me out, seeing as how I'm banged up."

When I opened my eyes, because Bill had quit brushing, I caught Pam's eyes. She winked at me. I gave her a tiny smile.

"I unpacked your bag for you, Sookie," Pam said

smoothly. "Where did you get that beautiful velvet shawl-thing?"

I pressed my lips together firmly. "Well, my first evening wrap got ruined at Club—I mean, at Josephine's. Alcide very kindly went shopping and bought it to surprise me . . . he said he felt responsible for the first one getting burned." I was delighted I'd carried it up to the apartment from its place on the front seat of the Lincoln. I didn't remember doing that.

"He has excellent taste, for a Were," Pam conceded. "If I borrow your red dress, can I borrow the shawl, too?"

I hadn't known Pam and I were on clothes-swapping terms. She was definitely up to mischief. "Sure," I said.

Shortly after that, Pam said she was leaving. "I think I'll run home through the woods," she said. "I feel like experiencing the night."

"You'll run all the way back to Shreveport?" I said, astonished.

"It won't be the first time," she said. "Oh, by the way, Bill, the queen called Fangtasia this evening to find out why you are late with her little job. She had been unable to reach you at your home for several nights, she said."

Bill resumed brushing my hair. "I will call her back later," he said. "From my place. She'll be glad to hear that I've completed it."

"You nearly lost everything," Eric said, his sudden outburst startling everyone in the room.

Pam slipped out the front door after she'd looked from Eric to Bill. That kind of scared me.

"Yes, I'm well aware of that," Bill said. His voice, always cool and sweet, was absolutely frigid. Eric, on the other hand, tended toward the fiery.

"You were a fool to take up with that she-demon again," Eric said.

"Hey, guys, I'm sitting right here," I said.

They both glared at me. They seemed determined to finish this quarrel, and I figured I would leave them to go at it. Once they were outside. I hadn't thanked Eric for the driveway yet, and I wanted to, but tonight was maybe not the time.

"Okay," I said. "I'd hoped to avoid this, but . . . Bill, I rescind your invitation into my house." Bill began walking backward to the door, a helpless look on his face, and my brush still in his hand. Eric grinned at him triumphantly. "Eric," I said, and his smile faded. "I rescind your invitation into my house." And backward he went, out my door and off my porch. The door slammed shut behind (or maybe in front of?) them.

I sat on the ottoman, feeling relief beyond words at the sudden silence. And all of a sudden, I realized that the computer program so desired by the queen of Louisiana, the computer program that had cost lives and the ruin of my relationship with Bill, was in my house . . . which not Eric, or Bill, or even the queen, could enter without my say-so.

I hadn't laughed so hard in weeks.

# *About the Author*

Charlaine Harris has produced two mystery series in addition to her Sookie Stackhouse books. She lives in southern Arkansas with her husband, three children, two dogs, two ferrets, and a duck. An avid reader, mild cinemaphile, and occasional weightlifter, her favorite activity is cheering her children on in various sports while sitting on uncomfortable bleachers. Her website is www.charlaineharris.com.

The fourth novel in the
"extraordinarily riveting, erotic and exotic"*
*SOUTHERN VAMPIRE* series

# DEAD TO THE WORLD
## BY
## CHARLAINE HARRIS

### A *NEW YORK TIMES* BESTSELLER

"Harris weaves storytelling magic in a tale of
vampires and small town Louisiana."
—*Lynn Hightower

**THE SOOKIE STACKHOUSE STORIES ARE:**

"POWERFUL."
—*BOSTON GLOBE*

"EXTRAORDINARY."
—*LIBRARY JOURNAL*

"FIRST RATE."
—*WASHINGTON POST BOOK WORLD*

# CHARLAINE HARRIS

The author who brought you the *New York Times*
bestselling Southern Vampire series is in to
something more mysterious...

# The Lily Bard Mystery Series

Shakespeare, Arkansas, is home to endless backroads,
colorful residents, and the occassional murder.
It is also home to Lily Bard, the local karate
expert/cleaning woman who has a knack for
finding skeletons in closets.

## Shakespeare's Trollope
0-425-19699-2

And coming soon:
## Shakespeare's Counselor
0-425-20114-7

Available wherever books are sold or at
www.penguin.com

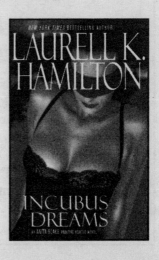